A PERSON
IS A PRAYER

A PERSON
IS A PRAYER

AMMAR KALIA

Oldcastle Books

First published in 2024 by Oldcastle Books,
Harpenden, Herts, UK

oldcastlebooks.co.uk
@OldcastleBooks

A CIP catalogue record for this book is available from the British Library.

This is a work of fiction. Names, characters, places, and incidents either are the
product of the author's imagination or are used fictitiously, and any
resemblance to actual persons, living or dead, businesses, companies,
events or locales is entirely coincidental.

ISBN
978-0-85730-585-5 (Hardback)
978-0-85730-589-3 (Trade Paperback)
978-0-85730-586-2 (eBook)

2 4 6 8 10 9 7 5 3 1

Typeset 13.2pt Adobe Garamond Pro
by Avocet Typeset, Bideford, Devon, EX39 2BP
Printed and bound by TJ Books, Padstow, Cornwall

MIX
Paper from
responsible sources
FSC
www.fsc.org   FSC® C013056

'A person is a prayer through his or her longing.'
Jon Fosse

For my grandfather,
who thought this book was about him

BEDI FAMILY TREE

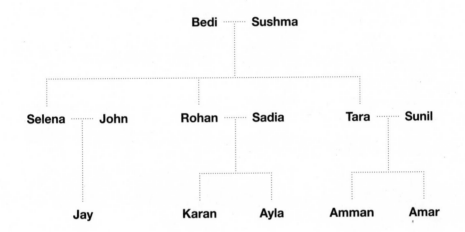

Part I

19 March 1955

'Life happens in the margins'

1

'Not now,' he spluttered. The breath whipped from his lungs leaving him hollow. It was happening again.

He stopped walking, hunched over and covered his quivering mouth. He was starting to sweat profusely, threatening to seep through his only suit. He saw himself looking like one of the clerical workers on the sunrise trains who had crescent moons of damp cupping their flopping breasts. But he would have to worry about his appearance another time.

He placed his palm on the damp wall of a shack as two passing boys in greying vests glared at him. He tried to breathe but could only wheeze out a rattling sound. They were so skinny they were probably worried he'd eat them. He was careful not to lean too hard in case the whole facade caved in.

This place seemed nothing more than the sun, dust and an eternal hum of competing voices. He made sure the boys couldn't see him touch his pocket to check that his wad of rupees was still there, along with the worn paper of his train ticket. As long as he had his cash, he would be alright, he reassured himself. His breathing loosened. Money always bestowed a protective aura – it was so much more efficient than the empty promises of prayer.

He decided to start moving again; it couldn't be too much further. There were no pavements around him, just stacks of assorted rubble people hopped over while avoiding the meandering chaos of the rickshaws. It also stank of shit, thanks to the open gutters sloshing along the side of the road. Every time he passed a waiting, solemn cow in the street he had to avoid dipping his polished brogues into the filth. He didn't belong in a place like this.

Maybe his heart was thumping and his lungs were squirming because this was supposed to be his homecoming, a return to the country of his people. But there was no fanfare waiting, only lingering looks. He felt like shouting. Didn't they know it was rude to stare?

In India, Bedi was a tourist, not a prodigal son. He had been born in a different country, into a different shade of skin from the locals and a different sense of loyalty to their rulers. It was all because his father took up the offer of moving to another colony to work on the railroads, the offer of a better life. He was worried these Indians could smell the subservience on him and he hoped the family he was coming to see wouldn't be so perceptive. He was on his way to meet and impress their daughter – some village girl he would be expected to spend the rest of his life providing for. Some deal.

It was his father's idea. Ever since his mother had died and Bedi had started shooting out of bed to gulp the cool night air – to calm this pair of lungs he was sure was growing too fast inside his chest – his dad had begun to notice him again.

As kids, he and his three brothers only experienced their dad as a soothing absence or a terrifying presence. He was often on week-long trips to Mombasa, sloshing petrol into his cap to cool his bald head as the inferno of the engine enveloped him. While he was away, the boys would become the men of the house, hurrying to the bank to withdraw their father's weekly salary, purchasing groceries for their mother –

with added luxuries – and feeling like they were giving back some of the care she so freely gave them. When their father returned, it was always a different story. Now, they stood to attention by the dinner table, ready to deliver salt or sabzi as he kept his eyes fixed on the table and ate with fastidious care. They were equally ready to receive a kick on the backside or a slap along the legs if they were too slow or spilled the goods on their way. At 25, Bedi still struggled to eat before someone told him he could do so. He felt his stomach rumble with anticipation.

He didn't have a watch so he didn't know what time it was, but it felt like he was late. That feeling like the world was moving too fast and he was going too slowly, like the seconds were clicking offbeat, gently reminding him that he should be running. He could have taken a rickshaw from the station but Mrs Bhatia, that plump know-it-all who had set this whole thing up, had assured him it was only a short walk. He made her tell him the route twice, taking into account his terrible sense of direction, and she made sure to click her tongue as he noted down each turn, exasperated at this need for guidance. Did other men just always know where they were going?

At least his breathing was getting better. He made an effort to try and place himself back within his body and to exorcise whatever spirit kept kicking him out. He felt the sun warming the brim of his hat, he noted how his left knee crunched if he extended his leg too far and he took a big breath in, ballooning his chest outwards to suck up what felt like a teaspoon of the road's gravel. He coughed reflexively and spat a wet slick of the grit back, spraying his shoes in the process.

'Penchod,' he muttered.

He heard a giggle and turned to notice those same two dark boys following him around the corner. He shooed them with a flick of his wrist and a kick of his leg that made his knee crack, again. They trotted off, unbothered and bored.

Had he once been as carefree as they were? He couldn't remember. All he could recall as he pushed the jangling bones of his body along the roadside was always being on the move. Always walking.

Like that eternal walk to school. Two miles every day to be told by his teachers that he was of less worth than the bricks in the walls that surrounded him. That hurt – not as much as when they threw those books at his head while he was daydreaming. He might not care much for the knowledge the books contained, but he felt he must have something he could offer the world, eventually. Even if it wasn't his brain.

He still hadn't figured out what that something was. In fact, he felt like life was just spent waiting for something to happen. And perhaps that something was bad – in both cases. Maybe those two boys felt the same? He looked back to see if they were still tailing him, but they must have disappeared into the throngs of waiting men, overstuffed carts and animals. They were probably just dazed and hungry, like he always was when he was their age: five, six, seven, eight.

He remembered waking up then with a gnawing at the pit of his stomach and feeling that no matter what leftover scraps his mother fed him, he was never satisfied. It was like waking without sleep and being catapulted into an adrenalised haze, running on the need for more but not knowing where to find it.

There was one promising avenue: looking through the bins on the way to school. Any bits of unrotten banana, unchewed sugar cane or unmouldy bread would soon find their way into his fist, under his nose and then eventually – after consultation with his friends – into his mouth. It all served to carry his grazed knees and dry soles to the hard chair in which he could then spend the next four hours being hungry again.

One morning, he came upon an unexpected prize: a pristine, unopened packet of biscuits. He couldn't believe his luck – his stomach practically leapt at the sight – and he gingerly swiped them from the other foul remains, before anyone saw or could find the chance to tell him off for it.

He was with his friend Raj – he was always with his friend Raj, before he died at 14 of tuberculosis – and he offered to share the bounty. 'I don't like the look of those,' he remembered him saying. 'You'll get into all sorts of trouble if you eat that, Bedi.'

Still, he had already torn back the paper package and was feeling the soft lozenge between his fingers, popping it into his waiting mouth before his brain realised what his hands were doing. He offered another to Raj but he simply shook his head and gave a quizzical smile that said, 'You're on your own now.'

They kept on walking – past the market stalls, shopfronts and makeshift houses, off into the large fields that surrounded the tiny school building. Raj's smile started to play in Bedi's mind as he realised that there was something meaty about the biscuits. Still, he continued eating them – he couldn't waste the packet now – and with each bite he felt their grain between his teeth, a warm grease running through the pressed shape.

His mouth had become worryingly dry and filled with chewy bits of biscuit debris. He tilted his head back to try and swallow, mildly panicking that he might choke otherwise. It went down, slowly, and he was reassured by the warmth of the morning sun on his face, steaming. He felt a little heavier, like he was carrying the weight of the air that was softly imprinting on his skin. It's just one foot in front of the other, he told himself.

Those feet began dragging and Raj, who was always keen to avoid a beating for being late, was pulling ahead. 'Come on, Bedi,' he urged, offering his hand to pull him forwards. Bedi wanted to take it but he found himself slowing as something started to come up. A cold sweat beaded on his forehead and a rush of saliva pushed its way from the back of his mouth to his lips. He tried to calm himself by thinking of when the sudden rain would fall with such force that it seemed the whole world was crashing down. Like the sky wanted to get close and touch him.

The next minute he wretched a slick pool of bile – a green and brown impression – churning the dusty road into mud.

He needed to get a hold of himself, Bedi thought as he carried on now, a man walking. Why was he bringing up a memory that made him want to gag? At least once he was sick it was over, unlike this spasming of his lungs that seemed like it would never go away. He had his mother's comfort back then too, her soft voice telling him it would be ok – a counter to his dad's bark that soon told him he had been eating biscuits made for animals. 'If you want to be a dog so much, you should start living outside,' he remembered him laughing.

Like all men, Bedi missed his mother. He missed her voice and he missed her dependence, her need for love. He wished now that he could have shown her more, told her how much he would miss her when she was no longer here. Of course, somehow, he assumed she would live forever. The quiet ones always survive, he used to think; his father with his swagger and shout, he would be long gone, but his mother would grow old with him. Finally, they would be together.

Yet, once she died, his dad decided his eldest son needed to be married off immediately. His mother would have probably liked to keep him home permanently but now her ashes were scattered, his father had given Bedi until 25 to find an acceptable wife. He responded by spending almost all of his late teens and early twenties drinking, chasing the wrong girls and trying his hand at gambling his pay packets away. That time had soon run out. Now, he needed to be married off, otherwise his other seven siblings would start to look like a bad deal, like there was something wrong with the Bedi family name. His father would retire soon and Bedi's new wife would need to help take care of the family. Bedi's hands became slick with sweat at the thought; he swiftly wiped them on his trousers.

At least he was starting to recognise where he was now. He was where he should be – a central square with four walled compounds surrounding a water fountain. Behind the fountain he spotted the thin, leaning trunk of a sandalwood tree. Its sharp leaves were fanning out to mottle with shade the men sat smoking beneath it. He could detect a hint of its earthy musk in the air. He took a slow breath and felt his heart thrum with anticipation. His body was hiccuping back into a sense of stability.

'Sushma, Sushma, Sushma,' he whispered to himself, like an incantation. The name of the girl he had come all this way to meet.

He had only seen a picture of her but he had been thinking about it ever since Mrs Bhatia posted it to him. She must have been in her finest sari, since its folds lent a silken softness to the otherwise heavy contrasts of the black and white image. Her eyes were turned away from the camera's lens and her skin looked so blurred and delicate that he felt like reaching out to touch it. But there was also something in her gaze that said she wasn't particularly interested in what he wanted. She looked past him, as if to something better just over his shoulder, and it made him want to get her attention – for once, to be seen. Her head was perfectly straight; she had the air of a schoolgirl's obedience and the kindness of a mother in the gentle bow of her lips. She was someone who would stare straight into the sun without blinking.

He was fast approaching her home now, where she apparently lived with her parents and two brothers: the Sinhas. He hoped no one was peering out of the window as he shuffled closer to their whitewashed wall to straighten his tie, smooth the damp creases of his shirt front and rub the leather tops of his shoes against the itching wool of his Oxford bags. Their trouser legs were so wide he could have fit himself in at least twice, but he was assured that these were the latest fashion back in England. He had carried them across continents and dragged them through this dusty town to make a good first impression. And it was needed, not least to justify the week he had spent on the boat crossing over here, on top of turning down that one buck-toothed girl his father had pushed on him, and the other painfully shy one who turned out to be his second cousin.

He couldn't let on that he was the son of a train driver, that he was just a motherless child playing in this plump man's body, that he had never known how to show love, but only to receive it from the one person who was no longer here to give it.

Part I

Bedi felt that as a man, pain came in many new and exciting forms. It seemed like there was a big stone now where his heart used to be, one that knocked around his chest and pummelled his organs, making them bleed as they jostled for space. Or there was his tickle-tackle, usually standing to attention and always ready for action at the least useful moments. Now it just slept like a soft worm between his legs. He wished he too could be so untroubled by life.

This was no time for concentrating his thinking between his legs. That might come later, he smirked to himself.

His chest fluttered at the anticipation and he pounded it with his fist, making his hat brim tilt forward. He stepped through the wooden gate in the wall and took his time walking along a surprisingly manicured pathway, bordered by a tall guard of ferns. The house was bigger than he had expected for the salary of a mere teacher, wide-fronted and holding a sturdy two floors without a crack or flake of old paint in sight. These must be fastidious people. He made sure his trousers were properly buttoned up.

He must be better now, he reminded himself.

He took the warm, curved iron of the knocker into his hand and gave two firm raps on the door.

He heard only stillness. He waited.

2

'We thought you were trying to break in, looking through the windows like that,' Pintu laughed.

The middle brother, always a shit, Bedi thought. His own brothers ran the gamut of the painfully shy youngest to an enterprising second-eldest and an outright terror in the middle. He was likely just viewed as an unworthy leader and it was an opinion that was starting to make sense, since he couldn't even seem to get through a front door without making a bad impression.

Sushma's family had spent all morning preparing for their guest, making sure the floors were cleaned, the glasses were dry and that the food was simmering to a salivating intensity. They wanted their only daughter married off to the right man and that meant making the right first impression. She had been upstairs readying herself too, applying a thin line of kohl to bring out the darkness of her eyes, just as her mother had shown her, and neatly folding the pleats of her sari so that it would cascade straight to the floor without a kink disrupting the simple line of her figure. She pinned her hair back and wet the stray baby hairs that always sat on the edge of her forehead to frame her face cleanly. There were no mirrors in this house, so she had to make do with her reflection in spoons, windows, or – best of all – the glass doors of the cabinet downstairs.

Part I

That's where she was, practising her smile and trying to make herself seem politely interested and interestingly aloof, without showing the wonky front teeth she was so embarrassed by, when she noticed a man's image overlapping her reflection. She jumped back and let out a strained yelp. The image grew bigger for a second, then disappeared. Her brother Pintu charged in.

'Another mouse?' He was somehow already armed with his cricket bat, ready to dispatch one of the rodents that kept scurrying across their polished floors. He seemed to enjoy bludgeoning them and then picking up their string-like tails to toss them out for the stray cats and dogs to savour. Their mother would be left to scrub the smears of blood from the tiles and to berate him for his act of violence. Still, he would do it again, since there were never any consequences for his actions. It made Sushma grit her teeth at the thought.

She shook her head and pointed at the window. A flicker of fear kicked in his gut on seeing how wide and white his sister's eyes were. He wasn't sure what would greet him on the other side, but when he gingerly stepped forward to look, there was nothing there except for a pear-shaped man in an ill-fitting beige suit, pacing outside the front door. He was wearing the baggiest pair of trousers Pintu had ever seen. This was either some pervert eyeing up his sister, or it was the boy who was supposed to be coming later to meet her. He could have been a pervert too, for all Pintu knew.

He decided to sling his cricket bat over his shoulder as he flung open the door – a show of strength.

'Um, yes, hello – sorry – I am Mr Bedi,' he paused, clearly startled. Pintu was unsure why this man was speaking in a shaky English accent. 'I am here to see Sushma. From Mrs Bhatia.'

So it was the boy, but was he a simpleton or something?

Pintu thought. He could barely string a sentence together. He gave him a big, toothy grin and decided to have some fun.

'I don't know any Mrs Bhatia. Why are you here? What do you want with my sister?' He wanted Bedi to say it out loud.

'Well, I am visiting – stopping by – you see.' Pintu could see Bedi sweating underneath the slant of his hat. 'To see your sister for our marriage – our possible marriage, I mean.' Bedi almost shouted that last part, he was so quick to rectify his assumption. Pintu couldn't help it, he started snickering.

'What are you doing letting all this hot air in?' It was Pintu's mother – he smelled the sandalwood oil in her hair before he heard her approach and swiftly caught his laughter in his throat.

'Stand up straight, young man.' She placed a firm hand on Pintu's lower back. 'And put that bat away, for God's sake. I assume this isn't one of your cricketing friends?' She took a breath and looked into the visitor's eyes. 'You must be Mr Bedi, yes?'

He nodded solemnly. 'You're early but that is no problem, this is the house of a teacher, so there is nothing worse than being late!' She let out a practised giggle to follow her usual refrain. Not better late than never; in this household, if you were late you had better not come at all.

'So I thought you were spying on her or something.' Pintu was still goading him now in the front room as Bedi took off his hat to reveal a damp and worryingly thin head of hair. 'But you're here for something else entirely, aren't you?'

Bedi's cheeks burned hot with shame. He was only trying to see if anyone was in; if this was indeed the right house or if he had followed his carefully annotated directions incorrectly, owing to his various fits of breathlessness, coughing and

PART I

gagging. When he realised that it was the girl in the window – his girl – well, perhaps his girl, he just wanted to get a better look, to see if she matched the picture Mrs Bhatia had sent. He recognised that it was the same sari from the photograph and that she still had the same flowing thick hair neatly tied into a bun. She had her back turned to him and was doing some kind of clowning at her reflection, smiling and then dropping her cheeks into a mannered pout. He was transfixed by the rhythm, trying to catch a proper glimpse of her face or the lingering trace of that gaze she had first given the camera. He needed to know which part of her was real, or if it was all an act.

He certainly should have rehearsed his own act more, Bedi thought, faced with this petulant teenager's insistent questioning. He decided not to respond but rather to quietly seethe instead, smoothing the pencil line of his moustache with his thumb and forefinger. The boy must have been only 16 but he was so sure of himself; he carried his beanstalk frame with the plodding arrogance of someone born to a family of a far higher caste. And what was with that cricket bat? He needed to be disciplined into having some respect for his elders, but his father was likely too lenient with him, Bedi thought. It would have been unusual, since every teacher Bedi had known as a child was a sadist – there was no kindness in their desires to control and punish children.

Where was the old man anyway? Bedi softly sighed and pondered why he had been left with the child to shift uncomfortably in a hard-backed chair while the adults busied themselves in other rooms. It was the father he would need to impress most. He crossed his legs and then uncrossed them, swiftly remembering his own father's comment that sitting like that made him 'look like a pansy'.

'And what is your name, young man?' Bedi gave the boy his haughtiest managerial tone, leaning towards him ever so slightly. They may as well make small talk if they were going to be stuck here together.

'I'm Pintu,' he snapped back, without meeting his gaze, instead only focusing on picking the dry skin from the edge of his gnawed thumbnail. 'What's your name? Your full one,' he mumbled with his hand dropping from his mouth into his lap.

'Well, we call him chotu, don't we?' It was the mother, cutting Bedi off before he could answer and serenely sweeping in with a metal tray weighed down by a teapot, cups and a leaning stack of small plates. Pintu's cheeks reddened ever so slightly.

'Ah, we call my youngest brother the same – little one – but you're not the youngest are you, chotu?' It was Bedi's turn now to rile him. He needed to make sure he wasn't smiling.

'Well, no, I have a younger brother, Raj.' The name made Bedi jump. Not its existence, it was common enough, but the fact that he had just been thinking of his friend on the way over here. Like he had willed him into being again. He made a mental note to write to Raj's parents once he was home; it had been far too long.

'He came along much later,' the mother interjected as she laid out five plates around their small table. 'We thought we had our only chotu but I always wanted more children. Life can be full of many miracles.' She trailed off wistfully.

Bedi couldn't remember his mother talking like this when she was alive – giving any glimpse of her hopes and desires. Nor did he ever think she had looked so young and beautiful. He noticed the curve of Mrs Sinha's cheekbones, the kindness in the slight downward slant of her eyes, the careful grasp of her long fingers. He had no idea what to expect of the girl now, whenever she might emerge. He hoped in the meantime that her mother would pour some tea and get the snacks out – he hadn't eaten for hours and his mouth was starting to smack from its dryness. He should stop staring at her, too.

He turned his head to the walls. There were books and pamphlets everywhere in this house – stacked between photo frames on the shelves, piled in hazardous towers in each corner of the light-filled front room, and even stuffed under one of the table legs to keep it level with the ground. Bedi assumed they were the father's and, perhaps for the first time, he regretted not reading more at school. Was he supposed to go toe-to-toe with this intellectual for his daughter's hand? He could feel his breathing quicken at the thought.

As Bedi's heart thrummed, Mr Sinha padded into the silent room. He was stooped forward like the curl of a question mark, with his left hand extended and eternally gesturing to punctuate his words. His shuffling movements were so arrhythmic, they seemed on the verge of tipping him to the floor. He was wearing his favourite slippers, the ones that had poked out at the front to accommodate his lengthy big toes and were scooped at the heel from years of use. He was in a simple white kurta, sleeveless grey sweater and brown corduroys, since he always dressed for comfort and practicality, rather than the approval of the onlooker. His wife and daughter had spent their lives begging him to at least wear matching items, but it was surely too late to change now.

He adored silence – there was so much to hear in it – and he had always thought the sign of a strong relationship was the ability to sit together quietly, to simply be in each other's company, rather than to fill it with the noise of what one thought the other wanted to hear. He had been waiting outside the doorway for a few moments, taking in the quiet ever since his wife had recounted the miraculous birth of little Raj. He remembered all of the miscarried children they had lost before him and it was like their nameless, unformed bodies were held in that silence – listed without speech to whoever might have been listening.

'Sir, Mr Sinha, a pleasure.' Bedi leapt out of his chair and broke that peaceful beauty almost immediately.

'Call me Chand, please,' he replied and met the boy's outstretched palm to be crushed by his eager handshake. 'I see you were all lost in thought here,' he continued, wincing. 'You can get the measure of a man without having to say anything at all.'

Bedi was disarmed. How long had the old man been silently waiting and listening to their awkward conversation? Had he been judging the tone he was using with his eldest son? And what was all that about knowing about a man without him saying anything? Did he know him by his smell instead? Did he smell foul? His thoughts were spiralling, not least because he was sure he might have also broken one of his fingers in response to that limp handshake.

'Of course, quite,' was all he could think to respond before pulling up some of the material at the knees of his trousers and gingerly sitting back down.

'Bedi, is it?' The boy hadn't even introduced himself yet so Chand thought it best to take on that responsibility for him.

'Yes, sir, Chand.'

Chand wished he would stop calling him 'sir' – he didn't even have his students call him that. It was always Chand, since he believed the best learning environment was one where the students and their teachers were equals. That was the only way to build respect and from respect the foundations of knowledge could be built. 'Respect was invented to cover the empty place where love should be,' he remembered Tolstoy writing in *Anna Karenina*. All these decades on from reading it, he was still trying to figure out what he meant. Perhaps that respect is public and love is private, he thought, although he believed there was always some love latent in respect.

'Well, how was your journey? You must be starving, please have some tea and I believe we have jalebis too – Pintu, beta, go fetch them from the kitchen, please.'

Bedi's own father had never called him 'beta', nor had he ever asked him please, come to think of it. Politeness was like gristle in his mouth, to be spat out, never swallowed.

'Thank you, please.' Bedi picked up a swirl of fluorescent orange from the platter and placed it on to his saucer, next to his steaming cup of chai. He made sure not to dunk the jalebi in, as he would have done at home, but rather to take a measured sip and then a small bite, letting the almost bitter sweetness dissolve on to his tongue. He would certainly be falling asleep on the train back to the city after this, he thought.

'My journey went very well, thank you. I am used to the trains, of course, but it was a novelty to be on the water, taking in that sea air and now arriving back in my mother country. It has been far too long...' He trailed off as Sushma finally walked into the room.

She was beautiful, he realised definitively. She moved like she had purpose – time to get where she needed to be but she wouldn't waste it. It was like she was gliding beneath that sari, making the room's afternoon light follow her as she knelt at her father's feet and poured herself tea. He placed a hand softly on her head, careful not to push a strand of arranged hair out of place.

'My daughter, Sushma. My beauty,' Chand announced. 'I hear you may have already met?' he added, mischievously. His wife glanced over at him and rolled her eyes to silently say, 'Leave the poor boy alone, he's had an earful already.'

Bedi immediately began sweating. He had blown it already, hadn't he? He looked too much, spoke too much, and probably smelled too much too. He may as well just politely finish his tea and then be on his way. His second cousin would have to do.

He let out an effeminate chuckle in response and folded his legs. 'Sorry, that, yes. I wasn't sure if this was the right abode, you see. A silly mistake, my apologies.'

Abode – such formality – Chand thought the Nairobi education system might have bestowed a more consistent vocabulary on its young men and women. Still, the boy was probably just nervous. Sushma, meanwhile, was transfixed by these parachute trousers. What was the point of her dressing up and trying to impress, to do a good job representing her family and justifying this man's long trip, if he was going to arrive early, sweaty and dressed like a clown?

'Of course, of course. Not a problem.' It was like Chand could feel the gears of his daughter's sharp mind turning. 'So, tell us about your life. I understand from Mrs Bhatia that you are the son of a train driver, that you are a railyard marshal and that you have seven brothers and sisters? Quite the household.' He felt like he was preparing one of his students for an oral exam while the boy looked on at him blankly, waiting to respond.

'Yes, it is a large family but we manage. I take my commitment to my parents and siblings seriously and I have worked hard to become a deputy marshal. I am well on my way to being promoted to head yard marshal soon, with a large salary increase.' Bedi felt the need to lay out his earning potential quickly – something he hoped Chand would be impressed by. 'Perhaps within the year.'

'Hmm,' Chand gave him the courtesy of feigned appreciation with a slow nod. But he knew the facts and figures from Mrs Bhatia already. The boy had solid ambition but not too much that it would take over his life; equally, he would earn well but not so much that he would only become concerned with money. No, he had invited him here because he wanted to know who he was beneath the facts and the figures. What gave him his purpose? What was the abiding character that would cut through his status in the world?

He decided to take a different tack. 'My condolences on the death of your dear mother, also.' He knew it had only been a few years since the woman had died and that grief would expose Bedi to the raw facts of himself. 'It is never easy for one to lose their mother, it leaves a lasting mark,' he added, for sympathy.

Bedi was startled by the mention of his mother, since he always tried to avoid the fact of her death in conversation. But then he saw Sushma look up at him for the first time and they both intuitively locked eyes. She sensed there might be more to him than his awkward appearance and mannered speech.

For Bedi, it was like he fell into her. He fell into the dark brown – almost black – of her gaze. The rest of the room, and all of the worries it brought, dropped away. It was just them now, and it felt like it always had been. There was a certainty in her stare, like she saw him, even though he knew it would be enough to just be looked at. He got the sense he would be spending much of his life simply looking for her too, if he was lucky.

'Thank you,' he heard his mouth say while his eyes looked for another, less important place to rest upon. 'She was a wonderful mother, raising so many of us. If I can share just some of the love she showed me, I would be very happy.' He took a breath. 'I hope she would be proud of me now, of the man I am and would like to be. I would like to make her proud, you see.'

He hadn't meant to speak so freely but Sushma's naked gaze encouraged him. It was like he saw the loving vulnerability of his mother there, as well as everything she thought he could be, and he needed to meet it with honesty. He wanted to be himself now but he wasn't sure how.

Sushma felt herself softly blush at the yearning of his response. 'Well said, beta,' Chand reassured him, nodding slowly at the table.

Bedi's heart calmed, knowing he was at least held in this man's kindness for now. He felt the urge to respond in kind, or to answer his original question, but he couldn't come up with the words. He waited in the stuffy, indoor air for a sense of movement.

Chand was glad to hear that there was more to the boy than just posturing attempts to impress him with his credentials. He was glad, too, that he could sit in the silence he had created. He wondered what his daughter made of his awkward vulnerability – it had been her idea to get married, after all, to 'lessen the burden' on her parents now that Raj would need schooling too. He had told her she could stay and live with them for as long as she wanted, that she should only marry when she was ready, but his wife had been quietly encouraging.

She knew they couldn't afford another dependant for much longer.

When Chand had married, he hadn't even been given the luxury of seeing his wife until he lifted the chunni over her head in the temple. They were too young to make any decisions more lasting than the next day's breakfast dish but there they found themselves tethered for life. His wife eagerly rose to the challenge and she showed him that life was so much more manageable when it was lived with another, that its twists and turns were a flow to succumb to, not a tide to fight, and that it was possible to support each other without smothering one's own independence. He was lucky. It was an experience that taught Chand how love didn't have to come from thin air, that it could instead be built slowly from companionship, intimacy and respect. Perhaps that was what Tolstoy meant when he wrote those words – that respect should not exist without love, otherwise it is only an empty place, a shallow covering.

He caught his wife's eye again – he could tell she wanted him to keep questioning the boy, to do his due diligence, rather than allow their daughter to marry on the basis of an hour's silence. Chand tilted his head to the side and playfully raised his eyebrows to say, 'If you want him to answer questions, please go ahead and ask.' The two of them really didn't need to speak anymore – they had a lifetime's worth of looks to draw upon instead.

'Tell me, what books do you enjoy?' she asked, making Chand smile.

It was inevitable, Bedi thought. He had a good run but now this was where it would all fall apart. He may as well be honest, it seemed to help when he had spoken about his mother.

'I don't read very much, I'm afraid.' He could see Pintu smirking out of the corner of his eye. He wasn't too sure that boy could even read himself. He concentrated on the mother instead and the entreating smile she gave him to continue. 'I would like to read more but I was never very good in school, you see. Better with my hands.'

Sushma glanced up from her cup at him again. She had worried he would turn out to be a simpleton and this might be proof. Maybe she had rushed into this whole marriage thing? she thought, feeling her heart beat harder. She wanted to get herself into the world, since she felt like there must be more to life than this house, her parents and their eccentricities, but she wouldn't be allowed to do it alone. She would have to find a man to facilitate her exit from the family home and preferably he would be a kind one – someone who would let her get on with her life without imposing too much of his. If the only world he knew was his mother's, he would want to keep her where she was, in her place.

Her own mother knew differently. She thought that her daughter, above all, wanted to be wanted. She recognised so much of herself in her child, in the fact that she felt a deep urge to be desired for who she was, on her own terms, and to be someone who smiled with all of her teeth, not a closed mouth. Sushma wanted to be someone who could make her own mistakes. She could tell that she wanted to say something now – to correct Bedi and to assert herself more in the meeting. But she knew better than to open her mouth and to give a bad impression of her entire family. The girls only spoke when asked to in these situations. She would be a silent sponge instead, absorbing impressions. She would hate that.

PART I

'But I think intelligence can come from other places, from living in the world, not only from reading about it.' Bedi was still going, carrying on to fill the space expected of him. He hoped he wasn't offending the Sinhas and their literary way of life, but he felt like saying: what was the point of spending your life with your nose in a book, trying to escape reality, when you could be actually living? Wasn't life for doing and being, for taking chances and getting things wrong as much as right, rather than being paralysed by thought? Nothing came from dreams except restlessness, his father had told him, you had to work instead with the hand life had dealt you. Why hope for more? You would only be disappointed.

Instead, he meekly continued: 'I see you have many, many books here – I am ashamed to say I probably can't name any of them. I'm sure I would if I had a teacher as good as you, sir. Chand, I mean.'

'Oh, many of these are Mrs Sinha's, dear boy, a fantastic mind. Sushma too,' Chand replied. The honesty of the boy's ignorance somehow made him happy. It was the naivety he spotted in his schoolchildren, a gap that could be easily filled with the right approach. 'Perhaps she could teach you a thing or two about the world of books and the meaning they can lend to a life.'

'I, I would like that very much.' He stole another glance at Sushma and he could see she was smiling, briefly flashing the whites of her teeth. He wasn't sure if it was a smirk of sympathy or derision, so he felt it best to continue talking.

'I suppose, what I meant is that I never enjoyed reading because my life already felt too busy to be able to stop and imagine a fantasy instead.'

'Perhaps you were never given the chance to try?' Mrs Sinha replied.

'Yes, possibly. There were always responsibilities.' He paused, leaving Mrs Sinha unsure whether he had finished. She blinked at him. 'I wasn't sure how I could stick to them while also doing something that felt – I'm not sure – selfish?' he continued, falteringly.

'Ah, well, there is nothing selfish about bettering yourself, my boy.' Chand stepped in, pausing to slurp his tea through his front teeth. 'The world can become clearer through learning – it is why I have devoted my life to it. And I believe my family feels the same.' He looked to them for approval and both children nodded their heads. He would like to ask Raj the same question but he was being looked after next door, and he could barely speak yet.

Bedi felt he was still missing something. It was irritating him, poking at a knot he hadn't felt tangle inside himself before. He wanted to be heard. 'That is lovely to see, but maybe not all of us can be better, or be bettered by anything as simple as the lines in a book? Maybe we can forget ourselves when we escape into a story – but how do we get back to reality afterwards?'

'Well, perhaps your reality isn't something all of us want,' Chand snapped. 'Life isn't all about work you know – at least not work that involves being on the hot, stinking rails all day.'

Silence. Bedi looked at his knees and Chand felt his pulse beating in his neck. Why was this boy so insistently questioning him? What did he know of the world? he thought. What narrowness of life his parents must have shown him. He clearly expected nothing more from his existence than to eat, work, sleep and die. He daren't look at his wife and her surely reprimanding stare. He decided to break the tension – more softly this time.

'What I mean is that forgetting ourselves is sometimes exactly what we need. To leave that other person behind and to become something new – even if it isn't "better", at least you are trying to grow, like the plant that fights to find the light. Since living is to be in the flow of life. You are being.'

Bedi felt like Chand was trying to strangle him with the back-and-forth confusion of his words. This was all too much talk.

'Being sounds like a fight indeed,' Bedi forced out a chuckle. He needed air, lightness.

'That it is. But life happens, don't you worry about it. It is just a question of whether you want to be here for it or if you want to simply go through the motions.' Chand was on a roll now, he could feel it in his bones. Like when a question from one of his students prompted a new thought and he found himself teasing it from the tapestry, tugging at the thread until the whole thing unravelled.

'The reality is always here – life happens in the margins of the book while you read it – but what do you want from it? I read simply to understand more of the world; by taking me out of myself it helps me to feel more aware, more alive.'

Sushma had been growing quietly impatient at her father's verbosity. She knew he was taking this as a 'teaching moment' and she was learning nothing about her potential husband in the process. She didn't care about his philosophies of realities or 'margins' – they made little sense to her. In fact, she only felt sorry for Bedi being backed into a corner. Once he got going, her father could talk the tongue out of his own mouth. Her pulse quickened.

'That's enough, papa,' she said gently, placing a hand on his knee. 'We can discuss this another time.'

'Ah of course, quite right you are, beti. Always. There is a life's worth of discovery to be had for the two of you.' Chand caught himself and took another sip of tea. He was back to reality now. He probably shouldn't have pushed the boy but he was about to take his only daughter from him. He had to make sure that he had a backbone. He would need one if he wanted to spend the rest of his life with her – otherwise she would certainly wipe the floor with him.

Pintu let out a long yawn and shifted in his seat. Sushma gave him a sharp look, signalling him to quieten down. She knew he would much rather still be out playing cricket today and that he was probably so bored he was beyond caring about this Bedi anymore. But she wanted to know more about him. Beneath that bumbling acquired English accent and ridiculous suit, there was a person hiding – someone with hopes and fears and worries to impart. Watching him seemed to have brought her further out of herself; perhaps he was just as excited about living in the world as she was.

She wanted to be someone who had somewhere to go, a place to be, rather than finding herself forever where she had grown up. She had seen the world through her parents' books, but she was growing tired of yearning for romance, luscious landscapes and the thrill of another body in black and white words. She wanted to be in the story. In fact, she wanted to write it, to give shape to something new, something taken from her own mind and experiences. She had been spending the past few months transforming her diary into the fantasies of an entirely new life and it had made the days pass by so much quicker. Maybe she would write about today too, she thought.

'Well, I think we've had quite enough talk for one day,' Chand said, as he got up from his chair and placed his cup gingerly on the table. 'I think it's all gone rather well, don't you? We'll make a fine man out of you yet, Bedi.' He went to shake the boy's hand again, hoping he wouldn't crush it this time.

'Of course, the most important thing is what my Sushma thinks and I fear I have taken up far too much of her time with my rambling. Perhaps the two of you would like a moment to talk alone?' He knew he would have wanted this luxury when it had been his turn to marry.

'Do please take a walk in the garden.' Chand paused, catching his wife's eye. He wanted to be considerate but she cautioned him that equally he shouldn't make the boy think he was too lenient. 'We can always keep an eye on you from the window, ha!'

Bedi reddened, again, but he couldn't believe his luck. He was expecting more questions on his finances, on his plans for the future and how he was expected to provide for his wife. Perhaps Mrs Bhatia had sold him already on that front. Whatever had happened, he was thankful to be given the chance. He may have pulled this off and he hadn't realised until now just how much he wanted to. This didn't feel like a game of ego or appearances anymore. He could sense there was much more to Sushma than he had imagined – no one he knew had ever told their father to stop talking in front of company, for starters – and at the very least he wanted to thank her for her kindness. For just letting him be in her space, in her home.

He had no idea what she was thinking. He cracked her a wide smile and caught those dark, deep brown eyes again.

'Shall we?'

3

'What are these trousers, then?' Sushma blurted out, surprising herself.

'Oh, well, they are Oxford bags.' He rubbed his eyes like a tired child. 'They are fashionable in England, I assure you.'

She tried not to laugh. 'Indeed, they are just rather large.'

She looked back to the house and saw her mother Asha peering out of the kitchen window, keeping an eye on proceedings, as promised. She had told her that morning to be direct when she had the chance, to ask everything she wanted, as this would be her only moment.

She took a deep breath. 'Do you like drinking?'

'Not particularly, no. My father doesn't either.'

She was asking the first questions that found their way into her mouth, pushing him. 'What about gambling?'

'Not at all.'

'Do you like your food?' She tried not to look at his belly. 'I mean, do you cook?'

'Not necessarily – cooking, I mean – I do enjoy food. Like the next man. It sustains me. My mother used to do all of the cooking and now my sisters do, but they aren't as learned as she was in the kitchen.' Sushma bristled at the thought of having to be chained to the stove for the rest of her life.

'Have you been with many other women?'

PART I

He smiled at the corners of his mouth. 'No, of course not.'

She wasn't sure why he was smiling. She felt riled, like he was lying. 'Do you feel sad about your mother?'

'What?' He pretended he hadn't heard. Good, she thought, now he was frustrated too.

They padded along the pathway bordering the garden in silence.

'My mother is a hot topic of conversation today it seems,' Bedi finally muttered.

She shouldn't have spoken so out of turn, she thought, as they stepped into the tree-lined patch of grass her father liked to call his 'orchard'. It was her favourite time of year: spring was bleeding into summer and the violet splashes of crocuses dotted the vibrant green of the ground. Soon it would be too hot to venture outside – the grass would be burned a crisp brown and the air would be thick with humidity – but until then she could spend her afternoons sitting on the reading bench her father had built, wondering about the stories she might write, about the possible shapes of the future she hoped for – like an artist planning the form of his canvas.

'I hope I didn't seem too rude in telling my father to stop speaking. He can just get carried away sometimes, like he only wants to hear himself,' Sushma said, breaking the difficult silence she had created.

'That is alright. I hope I also didn't cause any offence with my ignorance about book-learning,' Bedi replied. 'I wasn't sure what I was saying.' He paused, stealing a glance at her as they kept walking side by side. 'Yours is a good father, though.'

She thought he would say more but he didn't. Typical, she said to herself. She would have to do everything.

'Why do you say he is a good father?' she asked. She wanted

to know if Bedi had come round to his strange worldview, or if he was unconvinced.

'Very different from mine.'

'How so?'

He looked uncomfortable. Like he was suffering from a bad bout of indigestion. 'Oh, well, he is just stern. Strict, I suppose. Hard to understand.'

'You don't seem like that,' Sushma replied. His cheeks flushed. 'I mean, we can understand each other, no?' She smiled, trying to make him feel more at ease. 'I suppose parents try their best, when they can.'

'Yes, absolutely. I know I will too, when it is my turn. I want my children to have so much more than I have had. Like this garden for instance – it's so peaceful here. I don't think I've ever spent such time outside without working or rushing to get somewhere.'

She wasn't surprised. 'It's beautiful isn't it – my favourite place,' she added.

They both trailed off, listening to a bird's melismatic whistle. This was proving to be tough work, Sushma thought, keeping up a facade of politeness while trying to work out who this man really was. She took a sharp breath in and looked up at him. He was scratching the tip of his nose.

'What do you see in me?'

'Oh, well, a fine young lady, of course.' He was mumbling his words.

'No, what do you *see* in me? Why me?'

'Well, it is…' He paused for so long she thought he had forgotten about her. He stopped walking and rubbed a shoe on the back of his trouser leg. Then he got going again. 'It was your photograph, first. Your beauty, of course, but there was just something else there – I'm not sure how to explain it.' He stopped again. 'Perhaps that seems silly now.'

'It is silly to see so much from just a picture. You don't even know me.' He dropped his head like a sullen child. That was maybe too harsh, she realised. 'But I'm glad it communicated so much. I just hope I'm not your choice because you want someone to silently follow you through life. I want to be in it too.'

'No, no – I…' He was bumbling again. She folded her arms. 'Well, I suppose I hadn't thought about it. Until now,' he continued. 'But I don't want you to silently follow me either. You should have your own life too. I wish my mother had had more of one.' He rubbed his other shoe against the other trouser leg. 'What do you see in me?'

'You seem like a nice man.' She was going to continue but her mind suddenly emptied. Surely there was more to him than that but the longer she tried to think of the reasons why he was acceptable to her, the longer the silence, and the more she felt like maybe he only liked her because she gave him the chance to do right by his departed mother. She didn't want to be someone's stand-in – the replacement for an absence. She let the silence of her whirring thoughts carry.

He probably wanted her to at least say he was handsome but she wasn't sure yet – so many of these men looked the same to her and it was only in the ways they acted that she began to find herself being quietly drawn to them. Not that she had much experience, since her father usually kept her away from their passing glances and strained greetings.

She realised that this was the first potential husband who had made it to their house and past the scrutiny of her parents. This was now the longest Sushma had spent speaking to a man that wasn't her father.

'Have you seen much of the world outside of Nairobi?' she asked.

'Not particularly. Not apart from the train routes and coming here, of course.'

Perhaps this was the longest Bedi had spent speaking to a woman, too, Sushma thought. That would explain a lot.

'You don't want to see more?'

'Well, I am not sure I would need to. None of my family ever has and they have gotten along just fine.' He was looking ahead, blankly. 'Do you?'

She felt her stomach sink. This perhaps wasn't the man who would get her out of this place and to somewhere new and exciting. She might have to make that journey alone, she thought, even if she wouldn't be allowed to.

'Of course, I want to,' she said, somewhat more petulantly than she had intended. 'Sometimes I feel as if I am – I don't know – suffocating here, like I need to get out so I can breathe.'

He nodded, like she had touched a nerve with the word 'suffocate'. He waited, inhaling several times as if he were about to speak and then stopping just short of making a sound.

'You have plenty of space out here to breathe.' He even gestured to the gnarled tree trunk they were standing next to, as if its oxygen would sustain her. He was making excuses, she thought.

'That is not quite what I meant. It's different.' She paused. 'I want to get *out*.'

'But, but doesn't that worry you?'

His voice shook, like he was scared. She hadn't expected him to be scared, just foolish. 'What worries me is staying. I'm not scared about experiencing the world.' She paused and thought she detected the hint of a tremble in his arm. 'I'm not my father, you know. I like books but I don't need them to make sense of things.'

'Leaving what you know, though, doesn't that scare you? I mean, perhaps I have experienced more of how difficult life can be than you have.'

She scoffed. She was sure his life was full of quaint conveniences. What did he really know of her life? He didn't know how trapped she was, how she sometimes wished she was born into another body in another place, somewhere she didn't have to live in her father's shadow or according to her mother's hopes. Where she was free to make mistakes, to be her own person.

'I just mean that since my mother has been gone, things seem more uncertain. If the thing – the person – you know and who knows you best can be taken away, who is to say that even worse might not happen to you in a place that is unfamiliar, where you are not known?'

'I'm not sure I understand, sorry.' The mother again – she was thrown. She felt bad for assuming his life had been so easy. They paused in front of the burnt orange glow of a marigold plant, directing their eyes at its bright cluster rather than looking at each other.

'It's fine. I suppose I am saying that once the worst thing has happened to you, you want to keep things as they are, you want to stay in control. Since, what would stop something even worse from happening again, something I cannot even begin to imagine?' He paused. 'Perhaps if I stay put, do what I am meant to do – what my father tells me to do – I will be spared and I can carry on with my life, simply.'

She looked up at him and felt a lump in her throat at how brutal death was on those left behind. She swallowed hard.

His fear must have been rubbing off on her and she didn't like it. She felt like all the ideas she so confidently had before were being shaken and she was angry at him for questioning her, for not just leaving her alone. She began walking again, turning towards the house.

'It will be ok,' she found herself saying, unconvincingly.

He gave her a smile and something loosened.

'I don't mean to think or worry about these things, I just do sometimes,' he said, quietly.

'Perhaps you are right – that doing it alone is scary,' she replied. 'But that doesn't mean we shouldn't try? That you shouldn't be happy?'

'I am happy,' he said, unconvincingly. He turned the question back to her quickly. 'Are you?'

'Maybe. I want to be happy, of course.' She could feel her stomach fizzing gently. 'But I suppose I don't know yet. I won't know until I've tried.' She found herself smiling back at him. 'Did your mother want you to stay where you are, though? To live meekly? Or did she want you to be your own person?' She felt her own mother's gentle insistence guiding her.

'She always said I needed to be more brave.' He stopped and they listened to a whispering breeze shake through the leaves. 'She said I had to do more with my life than she had, that I should make sure my brothers and sisters were safe and that we always stuck together.'

They listened again.

'Hmm, you may be right,' he continued, finally. 'I'm not sure I actually know either – if I'm happy.' He let out a nervous giggle and she laughed back, surprised. The air felt a little lighter now they had let slip that neither of them knew what they were doing.

'Maybe we can find out then?' she said, catching her breath. 'That we could be happy and that some things are meant to be shared – or that they are easier that way?'

'Yes, I would like that.'

They kept walking, passing under the gentle boughs of her mother's apple tree. Its leaves were readying themselves for a bloom and the eventual bitterness of their hard fruit.

She sensed that they were running out of time. Her mother was still looking through the window, probably itching for Bedi to leave so that she could have the full report. Sushma wasn't sure what that might contain yet, but she knew she still had more she would like to find out. Bedi had surprised her and she felt she had much to think about – but the reckoning could come later. Best to keep on with the questions for now.

'If we were to do this then – to be together – what would happen?' she asked, tentatively.

'We would have to live with my family back in Nairobi, but you would like it there, I promise.' He looked longingly at her. 'Plenty of greenery and sunshine and reading to be done. You will love my sisters too.' It was as if he hadn't been listening to her at all and had parroted out a rehearsed answer.

'What about after that? What about for the rest of our lives?' she pushed.

'Well, children, of course. Two, or maybe three? I don't think seven is practical, do you?' He let a small, forced laugh escape.

Her cheeks and forehead began to prickle. 'But what about the rest of it? I mean, would we keep doing as you are doing and follow in your father's footsteps, or do you have other hopes? What do you want from our life? Don't you want more?'

He was thinking hard, she could tell now, since he had stopped walking and was staring blankly into the distance. 'I'd want us to find out, I suppose. Maybe we start with seeing what makes us happy, like you said, and then go from there? We can try – something new.'

She was about to ask him another question but she stopped. Finally, he had given her an answer she had been waiting for, some freedom from the well-worn paths of their parents. Her persistence was working – he must have been listening to her after all.

'How about you?' he asked, looking her straight in the eye and letting the back of his hand just brush past her knuckles. 'What do you want from us?' She felt a flicker in her abdomen.

'I'm not sure, I suppose. I would need to think about it.' She was being coy and she wasn't sure why. She wanted to say that she didn't want to be someone else's person, but there would be time for that later, without the risk of really scaring him off when he was just starting to make progress. She heard her mother's voice, telling her to give this moment a chance.

'We might have to get you to stop wearing those "Oxford bags", though. I don't care what the English fashion is.'

He let out a whoop and she heard a nearby bird flutter off its branch at the sound. It was like she could feel the vibrations his thumping heart was making in the air between them. She felt pleased with herself.

'Will you come back into the house in the meantime?' She smiled at him.

Part II

2 February 1994

'The dying always have to reassure the living'

1

You're on your own, at least for now, he thinks. He carefully ties his shoelaces, his London Underground standard issue, steel-toed boots, boots to last a lifetime. God, it was a good idea to retire. For once he had done as his father had said and not worked a minute longer than his fiftieth birthday, even if he couldn't afford it. Now, his days were just spent pottering around the house – the one they had managed to buy after arriving in Bournemouth and staying in a filthy bedsit for nine months, after living with his brother and his mean wife in London for 17 years, after his only son was born. Now he felt kind of free actually. He wasn't really thinking of life at all, he was spending his time trying to erase the past, to eat as much as possible and to just ruin the future generally. He was also busy playing dumb, not engaging in his grown kids' lives anymore, nor using his energy to distance himself from caring; now, his care had finally dissolved into a distant hum, something apart and something manageable.

Everyone thinks that when he leaves the house each day, with no work to get to, that he spends his time at the pub – another man avoiding his responsibilities. But he is still deep in that responsibility, circling around it and kicking his way through. Every new step in this country is one he had never imagined. More often, he simply wants to catch himself in the murky building-glass reflections as he walks, and every time he fails to recognise himself. He used to be smart, always in a suit and tie that would hang off his six-foot frame, as if there was nothing his broad shoulders couldn't bear. Now he stoops in his itching black sweaters, his boots dragging along, thudding to remind him of each needless step, while his hair is long gone and his cartoonish pencil moustache grown out to a messy box around his slanted lips.

This is what it must be to look like a real man, he thinks. None of the arrogance of suits and leather and collared shirts. Being a man, instead, is the obliteration of detail. Only the form remains, the flesh relegated to the same status as its cheap housing: rough, uncared for, unadorned.

'Don't forget the semiya,' Sushma calls at him. She's making their absurdly pregnant daughter's favourite dessert tonight: rasmalai, that sweet, sickly sludge of milk and sugar. Her first pregnancy was brutal: a 36-hour labour, a baby boy that kicked so hard, he almost damaged her bladder and, to top it off, brought on a bout of diabetes. The years spent after the birth weren't that easy either: her boy, her firstborn Amman, suffered from fits of epilepsy caused by his new body overheating. How he screamed at her for his pain, like he was trying to spit the words out before they could be formed, like he was blaming her for being born. And Sushma replied to these squeals with food, days and days of it, knowing that everything would either be good or be forgotten with time, so the only thing left to do was to make sure the body was stable and strong. If the heart was unwilling, at least the legs could still carry the burden.

She would spend hours kneading the flour and the tepid water together, making the dough, breaking it into fist-sized balls and rolling them out into discs before slapping them on to the flat iron tava and toasting on the open flame. Then, getting the oil hot and angry in the pan, pushing the roughly cut onions in and frying them until they got translucent, spooning in the spices (haldi, jeera, garam masala, mirch) from their steel tins and letting them bubble to a skin-like brown, gently mixing in the half-boiled vegetables and then adding the water and tomato paste. Lid on for it to cook down and then turn to the simmering dal, which needs its tarka now, adding salt and more chillies, as well as checking on that rasmalai on the other burner, the milk boiling down with cardamom, sugar, a pinch of saffron, more sugar, raisins and semiya. A simple meal, nothing showy, but the kind of food Bedi would have seen maybe only once a year when he was a child in Nairobi and when his dad was having one of his good years. This was when his dad was working the railways and giving a heartfelt thanks to God – Brahma, whoever – for allowing him to leave his family for a while. Now his son eats like this every day if he likes (he does) and it's two generations on and a third to come – another labour, another birth, more family – and that's what we're here for, he thinks.

But to his wife he just grunts the usual wordless reply.

The air has a faint, sickly smell of diesel to it and the morning mist is being burned through by the hot-cold January sun. The pavement is cracked and coated in droplets of rubbery chewing gum. His white pants are riding up his ass and need fishing out. The ass swiftly relieved of its strain, he jangles his change in his pocket as he walks to Mr Shah's, just as he used to when he was newly arrived in this country and working as a bus conductor. He still knows all the routes – 111 to the Treaty Centre, H28 to Heston, 95 to Hanworth Library – but every time he steps back on to the deck now he feels a warm panic rising. From a railway yard marshal in Nairobi, earning more than his father ever did, to an uneducated conductor, cowering in his booth beneath the stairs, dreading having to ask the passengers for their fares, especially the ones who had just got on from The Warren, six pints down. His boots then were the only things that kept him from falling, or jumping – their weight as he plodded down the aisle marking out a counterpoint to his pounding heart, a grounding for this moving hell. And they are the only things he keeps from that life: his boots, unsentimental and trusting. He looks down at them now and a smile plays in the corners of his grey moustache. These are something that he can believe in: the power of lasting, man-made creation. He steps into some newly denuded gum, pulling his foot back from the paving. 'Penchod,' he mutters.

'Daughter had her baby yet, Bedi?' Mr Shah asks from behind his counter as he opens the door to his shop.

'No, you know how it is with these things – goes on forever and then suddenly there it is, new baby, new stress.'

'Oh yes, always a struggle with these kids now,' Shah says. 'When my boy had his second, his wife was in hospital for two weeks after – he couldn't look after his other by himself so they had to live with us.'

The newborn died in that fortnight – it was delivered at only 23 weeks – and Shah's son Alok moved in with his parents for good then. Alok's wife couldn't care for her other surviving child now, she would just look at him as he hobbled around the room, giggling, putting his tiny fist into his mouth and dribbling on to his Lego. They cremated the foetus and spread his ashes on to a rose bush in the parents' garden. They tried not to speak of it again.

'Yes, always difficult. But it's God's will.'

Part II

He buys a pack of Silk Cut and a lottery ticket. They talk more about how their friend Sanjay's wife had been diagnosed with breast cancer – stage 4 – about the horse race coming up later today and the bookies' choices, about Sushma's youngest daughter's engagement to a white engineer, but he isn't really listening. He already knows the answers: the kids could do what they wanted now, he only ever picked his horses based on the names he liked best and we'll all die of cancer at some point. No, he wants to get the right numbers down for the lottery draw, so he lights a cigarette while he nods along to Shah's monologue and thinks. Maybe this could be it: 5, 23, 35, 41, 56. Only chance, it feels purer this way.

'You should come by the house one day,' Shah says entreatingly. 'My wife will cook something nice – not as good as yours, of course. How is Sushma anyway?'

'Fine, the usual, still complaining with that asthma but all she talks about now is this new baby and the engagements.'

Bedi's youngest son, 23, and middle daughter, 30, had in the past two months both got engaged. He felt sorry for his son. He was too young for the chaos that was yet to come, but he had given up. He had the usual story: falling in love with a girl at university, a Muslim girl, her parents disapproving of their relationship and his sense of duty overriding any emotion, leaving him heartbroken and her with an arranged marriage on the cards. He had given up; he didn't elope, he didn't persuade her that things would be ok with just his parents on board and that hers would come around, he just decided to get married as quickly as possible to the first person he could bear to be with. And so the usual processes started up: calls to relatives, friends, religious men and talkative wives, meetings with parents and children at the house at Number 52 and, after all the qualifications were examined, the thicknesses of the hair gleaned and the whiteness of the teeth seen, it was agreed. A 22-year-old with a degree in computer science, gold hoops in her ears, a loud laugh and a tolerance for arguing, built from a life living with four other sisters. His daughter, meanwhile, he never understood. She, too, was loud and argumentative but also closed off and unpredictable. When she was a child, she was secretive and it scared him and made him more than a little envious to see how easily she could lie. When he looked at her now, he was shocked at how he could have made someone so white, so unconcerned with tradition or family, only caring about herself and her needs. It made sense then, he thought, that she was marrying a typical Englishman: uneducated, docile and shit-scared of him. When he asked for his permission to marry his daughter, he could see his hands shaking, sweat beading on his balding scalp, the blue veins pulsing through his translucent skin, and it made him queasy. But he never seemed to have the energy to argue with his children's choices anymore. It was different now. Where once he would only want to fight, to languish in their obedience, now he just wants to be left alone, to be respected from a distance, to ultimately be ignored.

He starts coughing, spluttering and gasping for breath as flecks of his spittle darken his beige shirt and the cracked concrete. He pounds his lungs into submission with the fist of his left hand and takes another drag of his cigarette deep into his chest, the smoke spurting back out through his nose. He can feel the phlegm rising, a thick ball lodges at his sternum, and he keeps coughing, eventually pushing it into his mouth. He can feel it coating his tongue like the fat he so loves to suck from the bone marrow of slow-cooked mutton. He moves it

Part II

around his palate a little more and then spits on to the tarmac with a deep, sighing satisfaction. It is dark green and foreign and makes him think how little he knows about the workings of this body he lives in.

The old Indian lady sitting beside him at the bus stop looks at him – through him – with disdain and covers her mouth and nose with her scarf. He looks back at her and smiles, cursing himself for the politeness he keeps having to muster in this place, even with his own people. His people, once. It's like he had left something of himself there – in India or in Kenya – something solid and something important, something he kept yearning to go back for but that he also couldn't bear to find. He filled its place instead and hardened around it. The memory of who he once was spiralled meaninglessly outwards and dissipated into anecdotes and fake recollections.

No matter now he thinks, the bus is here.

2

He kept dreaming about dogs. Dogs of all sizes – little fluffy ones bounding around his feet, big ones lurching forward – all of them coming at him. Coming to bite him. They were rabid and furious and their teeth were sharp; they would launch themselves at his face and when he put his forearm out just in time, they would sink their teeth deep into his flesh, sending short sparks of hot pain fizzing through his body. And there would always be people standing around and watching, people that he either knew or those he might see on the street (the mother with a pram, struggling to contain her children and her shopping, the man smoking in a long overcoat, the shop owner packing away his store front) and they would all ignore him. They would let him be mauled and fight until he finally kicked himself awake in the bed and then went to sit in the bathroom, feeling the cool tiles beneath his feet coaxing him back.

He had never liked dogs. Back home, in Nairobi, they existed for protection only; they were chained in the front garden, ready to gnaw at anything that came near. Once, his family's dog – a mud-brown Alsatian – managed to get into the house and as soon as it saw his father open the door into the room, it ran for him, jumping up to his belly ready to bite. He watched his dad kick the dog away, swatting at it like a housefly.

Part II

Here, there is a reverence for dogs he'd never seen before – they spent their lives inside eating off plates, sleeping on beds and being mourned like family members. He hated how people trusted them, how they couldn't see that they were just animals. They should be made to eat from the floor, they should fear their owners, they should not be touched.

There is a dog staring at him now on the bus, taunting him. He wants to kick it away but knows better – he shuffles his legs into the back of the seat in front of him instead. It keeps on looking up at him, its head tilted to one side as if ready to ask a question, but he ignores its sad entreaties and keeps on staring out the window instead. They are passing through the side streets of Hounslow, winding through the litter-strewn back lanes and terraced houses full of people standing and talking to each other as if waiting for something to happen.

It is a Friday and he is always amazed at how nobody in this city seems to work – they are always walking and talking and eating, never wanting for a purpose. Of course, he might look like one of these people too, so he makes sure to get quickly from place to place, so they can see he is a man of purpose, a man who rightfully deserves the freedom to attend to his own matters.

He shudders as he gets off the bus, the wind suddenly picking up and biting through his thin overcoat. He used to look forward to the rain and those crisp days back at home – the brief moments where the damp was sucked from the air and he felt he could breathe again.

It felt like it wouldn't stop raining the day his mum died, the clouds descending almost close enough to touch and heaving down sheets and sheets of rain. He could taste the metallic sense of it in the air while he was at work in the rail yard – it coated him on his walk home, pushing his shirt to stick to his hot skin. His brothers were gathered around his mother's bed when he finally got back and there she was, half-sitting up, her hair stuck to her forehead and pleading for them to leave her alone. He shooed them off and put his cheek to hers, feeling her fever burning.

It would pass, he thought. His mother had always been sickly and she had only just come through a bout of tuberculosis – a moment when he really thought he would lose her. He brought her a glass of water and slumped down into a chair to drink a beer and doze off, his brothers and sisters running around him. Of course, by the time his father had come back from wherever he'd been, she was dead.

It broke him, that did. Not just the death but how he didn't even know, he didn't even hear. She just went quietly. Is that how it really happens, he thought? He'd seen that boy crushed by a car when he was younger and he screamed so loud he could still feel the fillings in his mouth rattle thinking about it. It made him salivate. But she just went while he was slowly peeling the label off his beer bottle in the next room. She had nothing to say, nothing important to tell him before she went. She didn't say that she loved him, her firstborn, and he never got to tell her he loved her.

His father blamed him, of course. His negligence, his inattention to detail. At least he was there though, at least there was some witness to her being, to her not being alone. He was thinking about her more and more these days and he kept finding his mind drifting to the possibility of dying alone, in pain. I just want to go in my sleep, he thinks, next to my wife. I want to go quietly, too. It really broke him, her death and his not hearing.

PART II

Now, he needs to buy something. He steps through the slick faux marble floors of the Treaty Centre – the town's grotesque new shopping centre. He walks by the key cutters and Wilkinson's, past the shoe shop and into Woolworths. He buys a bag of salted pistachios, shucking them while he paces and pocketing the shells. He likes feeling their remnants in his pocket, along with smooth and worn shreds of paper, coins and receipts.

There are kids, white kids, running past him and shouting to each other like little thieves. Where are their parents, he thinks, little shits.

At least they'll watch their parents die too.

God, what a horrible thing to think, he thinks. Let them be free for now. Let them feel like they have the world, like life is just something to get through.

He often wonders what his own kids think of him as a dad. He knows they only love him because they have to, but he has to be hard on them, he has to try and protect them from that silent gnawing of ambition and expectation. Better to just accept your lot, hope for nothing and only expect for life to be difficult and, if you're lucky, too long. His dad had never told him anything about life, he just told him to find a wife by 25. Maybe she would take it from there? The rest seemed to be a blind fumbling for crumbs of attention and before you knew it you were only aching, bored, hungry and old.

He crushes another pistachio between his teeth, chewing on the rubbery salt to make his mouth water. He has visited Kwality Foods and filled their little plastic bags with okra, aubergine, chillies, garlic, ginger, lemons, oranges, coconut milk, dal, milk, potatoes and chevra. The handles of the bags are cutting into his fingers and he needs to take a break from shuffling through the overcrowded shopfronts, from being around the people asking for money. They get so close they almost touch him.

His old friend Raju is again wearing his beige overcoat which is too long for his arms. His cuffs are rolled high, showing the tatty checked pattern underneath that, somehow, still has turmeric stains on it. He has a habit of cracking his dark, discoloured knuckles while he is thinking. Thinking about his two sons, probably, neither of whom is married, neither of whom seems too concerned about his existence – thumb, forefinger, middle finger – and thinking about his shrinking bank account, the rising mortgages for his courier business and – ring finger, little finger – his mother's house squeezing his savings dry.

'Bedi, come sit with me,' Raju gestures to the hard plastic seat he is perched on, a hexagonal plinth in the middle of the main walkway. His right eye twitches as he speaks, a nervous punctuation. 'It's good to see you – how are things?'

'Same, same – I'm just out getting ingredients for dinner tonight, we have the children coming over.'

'Ah, yes, your eldest is pregnant again, no?'

Bedi hates this small talk – endless questioning, feigning interest in each other's lives when all these people really want is gossip, an idea that someone else's existence is progressing worse than their own, something they can tell others about to reassure themselves that their lives are secure, that they will never be seen as anything other than how they see themselves. He never wants these people in his life; their inability to be with themselves means that they have to live through their ideas of others. Raju isn't even clean – just look at the state of that jacket.

'Yes, due anytime now – we are very happy.'

'Of course, of course, wonderful news.' Raju's eyes are focused elsewhere, watching these little tracksuit kids chasing each other through the shopping centre and on to the street. Bedi looks at his watch: it is 2pm.

'These bloody Polish have no respect for this country,' Raju says.

Bedi nods quietly in response. He can feel another of Raju's rants coming on. 'Why aren't these children in school? Just running around here; if I ever caught my boys like that I'd give them a smack, I would be so ashamed. But we came to this country when no one wanted us. The English were happy taking over our homes, but they never thought we'd come to theirs, did they?'

Bedi nods again and starts gently rubbing his hand where the plastic bags have left an indent.

'So when we arrived,' Raju continues, 'we were just Pakis to them, they shouted at us to leave and to go home but we didn't know what that was anymore, did we? They'd spent our whole lives telling us that where we were was a dirty little place with nothing to offer apart from hard work and hard lives. No, in Britain the streets were paved with gold; that's where life should be lived! When I got here, I really thought there would be gold in the pavements, that there would be something other than this grey everywhere. But no, no gold, it was just so cold and everyone looked so sad.'

Bedi had heard this story so many times it had lost all meaning. He had lived through it himself, so why did these people always feel the need to remind him of it? Yes, he also was told that the streets were paved with gold here. And yes, when he arrived he had partly believed it. Knowing others were just as stupid and easily fooled as him didn't make it any easier to swallow. No wonder the British took India so easily, Bedi thinks, we must have been like those feather-headed tribespeople in America who sold their land for some beads. But we didn't even get that.

'They didn't want us here, and we soon realised that we didn't even want to be here, but where could we go now? Nowhere. So we just accepted our lives and we worked hard, we had to keep quiet and keep moving forwards and we made sure our children knew just how hard we were working so they didn't end up wasting it all. They had to make this a new home and maybe one day they would be able to go back. But look at these Polish – they have a home to go back to and no one asked them to come here; they just live here to work and to send money home or all they do is take benefits and drink their vodka and shout at their fat women. They pay no taxes and they let their children run around here where no one is allowed to shout at them the way we were shouted at. Look at them, they aren't even scared – there is no word like Paki for a Pole, is there?'

Raju trails off. Bedi wonders if he asking a genuine question. 'No, I don't think so,' he mutters by way of reply. Raju is right about their women being big, though. He never understood how they found them attractive; they had such broad shoulders and wide noses and their faces were so pink like a pig's, it made him shudder to think of them undressing.

'Didn't you find it funny that they used to call us Pakis, though, Raju?' he asks. 'Because I'm from Kenya and my father was Indian and you're from India too. These British were so stupid they didn't realise they were using a word for a country they invented, which none of us even belonged to. I used to just shrug it off.'

Shrug wasn't quite the word for it; it was more like a desperate effort not to react so they wouldn't take it upon themselves to do something worse, like spit or throw their bottle or start punching. Just pretend it is another word that makes no sense and that has nothing to do with you, like how they always say your name wrong or never give you a name at all and only use your surname instead: Bedi, Berry, Ben.

'Yes, yes, well there's no word for them, though, is there? They get to be loud and filthy and racist in peace because they're white too. The whites always stick together, just see how they will always let them into this country with open arms to take their benefits and work on their building sites and clean their houses, while we are their doctors and accountants, we have been living here for decades but no, there is no home here for us still. We should just eat our curry and go home.'

'You've been eating your dal in that jacket at least – I can see the stain on your sleeve.'

'Yes, well, I've been trying to get it out, but I am a busy man, I just eat when I can – I don't have the time of a retired man like you.'

Bedi is so self-righteous, Raju thinks, just because his wife is obedient and quiet, he could stop work early and now he spends all day pacing around town like he has somewhere to go, but really he just sits here talking to us and judging us. He could always hide behind his silence, and Raju never trusted a man who didn't have the confidence to speak his mind. No, Bedi is a coward. He would do nothing for his people; it was because of people like him that India had been taken by the British in the first place. People who simply never put up a fight, for anything.

Kelly, another long-retired acquaintance with little else to do, is hobbling over to the two of them now, wheeling his tartan shopping carrier behind him while his trousers begin to slowly sag further and further, inching perilously close to dropping off his hips and on to the floor. He lets out a long groan as he hitches them up just in time to sit down heavily, placing his carrier between his legs. He was a master tabla player once but his hands seem to have lost their dextrous power.

'Kelly, we haven't seen you here in a while. How are you?' Raju asks.

'Yes, fine, or, you know, my health isn't so good and I've been in hospital, which is making me lose weight, which is good, but now none of my clothes fit me so my wife told me to come out and buy some new ones, that the fresh air would do me some good, so here I have just been looking in a few shops you know, TK Maxx and the like, and I found a few things but everything is so expensive, you know, so I was going back to see if I could have some of my old clothes taken in and –'

Listening to Kelly speak is like hearing a meditation; it is one of Bedi's favourite things to do. The old man must be nearing 80, if not older, and his thoughts are like one meandering stream, his voice warbling through his speech, pausing in the middle of words like 'hospital' or 'expensive', always emphasising the wrong syllable so that it almost makes it impossible to follow what he is saying. You have to surrender yourself to the song of it, you know, to allow it to envelop you and allow him to have his say – whatever that is.

Looking at him is one of Bedi's least favourite things. Kelly has become this walking reminder of mortality, of the fact that no matter how strong you have been in persisting and wading through the shit of life, you will never be allowed to rest. That when you think you have finally found a safe place to quietly exist, your insides will start eating you, your body will explode in full revolt, destroying itself until you wear your own skin like it is a baggy shirt, pulling down at your bones that have housed you for so long. You can see it in his eyes, which have become yellow and milky and which are constantly watering as if he is crying while he speaks. His shaky hands mean he never shaves properly anymore either and so there are always stray white whiskers framing the corners of his mouth and sprouting underneath his chin. You can see his kindness still, in the way he punctuates his song with a toothless smile or a tilt of the head, but all of it just makes Bedi sad, reminding him of the human who once lived in this body and who is now dissolving away. Yellow eyes like the sun-bleached film of a photograph that has been sitting out on a windowsill for too long.

'– ah yes, how is your health?' Raju asks – typically cutting straight to the gossip, Bedi thinks. 'How long have the doctors said you have now?'

'You know they never tell you the truth, Raju, not like when we were children – or I was a child – when the doctor would always be announcing death like it was nothing, telling mothers of their dying children and children of their soon-to-be-dead parents like it was the weather forecast, you know. Here they only tell you that they can't say anything properly, that it could be months or years because everyone responds differently but they can't really say and then they smile at you like you are a dog or a simple child, you know, like the smile will make it all seem better or like the smile is the answer itself, the answer to the biggest question, but really they don't know themselves, they are waiting just like you are, except that when it happens to me it will be the end and to them it will be another piece of paper –'

He trails off here and closes his eyes briefly – maybe he really was meditating? Or he has fallen asleep. Raju clears his throat and that brings Kelly back into the room as he slowly opens his eyes again, his lids lifting heavily.

'I'm sorry to hear that, my friend. But, you know, doctors get these things wrong all the time – I'm sure you have plenty of time in you left!' He flashes his nicotine-stained teeth and wheezes out a small, false laugh. He gives Bedi a pleading look at the same time, as if entreating him to laugh at this man's unknowing too. But Bedi just places his hand on Kelly's shoulder and gives it a small squeeze instead, feeling the sinew and bones moving beneath as he looks up to give him a smile. The dying always have to reassure the living, he thinks.

'I was just telling Bedi about these Polish and how they go on as if they own this country, hiding the fact that most of them probably don't pay any taxes, working on building sites and cleaning for cash only. It's people like this that are using up this country, meaning good men like you, Kelly, can't get the treatment you need, instead leaving you here not knowing when you might, you know...'

Raju has almost pronounced this man's death; he really is so tactless, Bedi thinks. No wonder his family always seemed to hate him. Whenever he saw the group of them together his sons and wife would always keep a few steps away from him, as if he were a stranger or an undesirable. You could see how they just tolerated him in their stiff shoulders and their shuffling walk, while Raju bounded forward, his head held high, always oblivious. Bedi hoped his own family weren't like that around him. How must his family look walking down the street, he wonders. He hopes they are the type of family that looks contented, that seems like they have everything they need in life.

PART II

When Bedi was a boy, his father always made him and his brothers and sisters walk behind him; he was the man and he would lead. When it came to dinner, Bedi and his younger brother would stand to attention on either side of him, waiting for him to call out for another hot roti, which their mother would be cooking in the kitchen, or a glass of water or salt. He realised how his entire childhood had revolved around his father's satisfaction, how he couldn't do anything without his approval or ignorance. He had no idea how his mother had lived with this man for so long; how trapped she must have felt marrying so young and seeing his bitterness rise within him so quickly. She was always forgiving and assumed the best in everyone surrounding her, or that's how it seemed.

Another fixture of a weekday afternoon in the shopping centre, Shokat, walks over. He is eating one of those mini corn on the cobs slathered in mayonnaise as he approaches. Bits of it are smeared on to his chin and specks of golden half-chewed nuggets drop to the floor as he shuffles forward. Why can't he just sit down to eat like everyone else? Bedi thinks. He's like the rest of us, in no rush and with nowhere to go. As they move along to make space for him and he sits, he continues silently gnawing at the corn with a singular focus, only wiping the remnants from his face with a paper napkin and dropping the husk into his carrier bag when it is picked clean. He lets out a groan of satisfaction.

'Afternoon,' he rasps, clearing his throat. 'My back is still killing me. God, it feels like I'm falling apart.' He massages his lower spine as he speaks, stretching his chest out and puffing. 'When did we all get so old?'

Shokat must only be in his mid-forties. He carries with him the air of a lonely man, that slightly desperate need to be seen and an endless desire to be heard. He is also what Bedi considers overly groomed; his hair dyed pitch-black to mask the encroaching greys, his beard trimmed to form a thin frame around his sagging face, and gold jewellery everywhere – a thick roped chain on his hairy wrist, opal rings and dangling om necklaces. He buys all his clothes from Asda and he must have been shopping in the children's section lately because his baggy trousers and diamanté-studded t-shirts make him look like an attention-seeking teenager.

Bedi sort of likes him, though. He reminds him of the old days for some reason, perhaps because of the seemingly endless sense of duty he shows to his elders. He has lived alone with his mother his entire life and while his siblings find him a useful caretaker, they generally see him as a nuisance at best or an embarrassment at worst. There have always been rumours about his being a bit 'fishy' when it comes to his romantic appetites, especially since he has never been married and never even accepted any arranged meetings, but the gossip has stopped now; he is too old for children and so he is past any concern about his love life. If anything, Bedi feels sorry for the poor girl he might one day resort to. Instead, Shokat is devoted to his mother utterly and with her moods as the only punctuation to his monotonous days, he passes over his peers and only spends time with hers instead, endlessly checking in on relatives, delivering medication, making time to sit and talk.

He tells Bedi and the others about his bad back – one of many, many ailments – an ache he refuses to take any medication for, since he believes that no medications actually work and that problems can be healed with the mind. He also tells them about a series of unfortunate 'investments': a sky-blue BMW

M4 convertible; shares in a bottled water company with access to a Moldovan well of spring water, which had turned out to be neither a well nor in Moldova; a down payment on a friend's new weightlifting and, for some reason, car hi-fi business – the list continued. But he is also keeping his spirits up with a series of litigious prospects.

'You know I've sued the local council and the police – twice each – and every time, I've won,' he says triumphantly. 'That's four times I've taken these idiots to court and won, me on my own, no representation, no university education, just a library card, and they couldn't believe it.' Bedi nods, Raju yawns, Kelly is maybe asleep again. 'And now they want to take me to court again for not paying parking tickets when clearly they're fake. Maybe the only good thing about this country is that I can always have my say. I could take any of you to court if I liked and I would probably win, even with the white judges taking one look at me and just assuming I'm another uneducated Indian.'

'Aren't you tired of all the paperwork, though, all the arguing?' Bedi asks, mainly to stop him from listing the many ways he could take them all to court – and win.

'I can't let myself be tired, Bedi – this is my fight; I can't let them win. You know, if you let them beat you once, they'll think you're weak and then that's it, next thing you know they're taking advantage of you whenever and wherever they can. You have to stand up to be taken seriously.'

Fine for someone who has lived his whole life hiding in his mother's house rather than facing the real world, Bedi wants to say. But he nods quietly instead.

'Hear, hear,' Raju agrees, causing Shokat's chest to puff out an inch or two in the process. 'I wish my sons were more like you, Shokat, wanting to do something with their lives, striving for more rather than just being happy to climb the ladder, to keep their heads down and eventually forget their old dad. If only they were more considerate like you, so good in looking after your mother always and never complaining – I hope they do the same for me when I need it.'

This is the affirmation Shokat has needed; a smile plays at the corners of his mouth and then he sits up a little straighter, no longer fumbling with his bags and his back. It was all worth it, the duty and the care, for the respect – no matter how little nor how passing. But of course, when his mother dies it will be a disaster, Bedi thinks, no child should be that attached to their parent and no parent should let their child be that attached to them. Shokat had first lived for his father's approval, that quietly austere man Bedi knew from the corner shop he had run for decades. Relentlessly meticulous he was, forever counting and recounting his stock, making sure he was turning a profit, no matter how meagre. He did it all so his son wouldn't end up behind the shop counter for the rest of his life too, but then he just ended up behind a different kiosk – the train ticket counter – and when his father died, Shokat knew he was a disappointment. The least he could do, his dying father had told him, was to look after his mother when he was gone. And so that was now his purpose – he had become a son, father and partner to his mother, looking to her for love, looking after her with his care and never once looking outside for anything more.

So, when his mother dies, what else will there be for him to do? It will be too late for his life to begin again; he has already spent the most useful part of it in his petty jealousies and warped sense of duty. When his mother dies, he too will die – even if he decides to keep on living.

Poor sod, Bedi thinks. Or maybe he said it aloud at the same time too.

Raju is still lamenting his children's lack of interest in him and Bedi knows he will keep going until his wife comes to fetch him or the rest of them filter off. It is time to go, especially if Shokat has just heard him. He says his goodbyes to the three of them – shaking each of their hands – and as he speaks to Kelly he feels a quivering panic in his voice, as if something bad is going to happen to him soon, or that he might not see him again. He tells himself to stop thinking so much about death or the end of things, he will have time for that later.

He gathers up his tangle of plastic bags and heaves them through the sliding doors on to the high street again. The grocers are shouting their prices to anyone who passes by; calls for strawberries and peaches and apples getting caught in the winds between the people moving past each other. He sometimes likes how this city can make you disappear so easily, how in spite of all the noise and how many times you are shouted at and looked at, no one will ever really see you. As he walks, he can feel their eyes on him but he knows they are looking through him, that they don't care where he is going or why.

He is walking like an old man now, his back stooped and his feet dragging themselves forward; he is becoming a curled question mark and he isn't particularly sure what is keeping all the jangling parts of himself together anymore.

From here he can see a mass of tired, dejected bodies waiting at the bus stop, their belongings at their feet and their heads turned away from each other, all claiming different parts of the distance for their gaze. He hears a baritone rumble in the pit of his stomach and realises he hasn't eaten anything for hours apart from that bag of pistachios. Hopefully his wife has started cooking and he can have a taste when he gets home, but that won't be for a while yet.

'We have to remember that Christ's message is one of forgiveness, that no matter what He was made to endure, He would ultimately be forgiving, as that is the price He paid for our sins.' He can hear a sermon wafting from the open doors of the church, always the same story of guilt and shame, pain and then, somehow, forgiveness.

'If He could endure, so can we and so we must. We must take His pain and take solace in the fact that it was endured with a purpose of love.' All of these religious men talk in circles, he thinks. At least at the temple they sing to break up the pandit's ramblings. Here these poor people have to sit and endure like their saviour and try not to fall asleep.

He likes the sense of purpose and confidence that belief gives people. He wishes he could believe more but whenever he really thinks about God or gods he is left unconvinced. If our lives are part of some grand plan, why do they have to be so painful? Why should we always be tested? Is it not enough that we try to be good and that we should be trusted to carry on however we can? He doesn't find the idea of being watched over comforting. He thinks about his mother, again, and how she would always tell him that his life and that of his brothers and sisters was part of 'God's plan', that no matter how difficult things became, it was always in service to a greater purpose, something she had always implied would lead to a beautiful, forgiving happiness. And he wonders where she is now, if her prophecy had come true to lead her to some reincarnated joy, rich and contented where she didn't need to worry about anything other than her desires.

PART II

Like everyone else, he only looked to God when he was really in trouble. Then he would pray for forgiveness, making promises to be better and convincing himself to be more faithful so that he might be better protected next time. Like an excellent insurance plan. Of course, when the next time came, he was no more pious nor better prepared, but he would still close his eyes, clasp his hands together and start reasoning with the blackness behind his eyelids. He had tried to instil some kind of faith in his kids also, making sure they went to temple, did their pooja and kept their fasts, but that all dissolves in the minds of children — it soon became the same ritual he remembered from his childhood and that he was eager to forget when he was old enough to feel his own independence. So, it was only his wife who kept to the routine now, fasting each week, performing the pooja each afternoon, making sure he and their family were always blessed no matter what those blessings failed to bring.

'We must remember that our hearts are much like our memory,' the priest says to his sparse congregation. 'Our hearts have no shape nor limit to them and so they can store as much as we are willing to give. But if we do not tend to them, they will start to empty and forget. And the more we forget, the harder it is to remember and to therefore keep our hearts open. Without being open, we are not human at all.' Bedi preferred listening to Kelly speak, he thinks, at least his spiralling words had some kind of logic behind them.

The overheard sermon is making him think about his own memories and how the faces of his childhood have been fading more and more recently. He cannot picture his parents at all now, never mind hear their voices or imagine how they felt and smelled. Even the roads he walked down and the school he felt so imprisoned in as a child are all dreamlike, ready to evaporate as soon as he opens his eyes.

'How can we tend to our hearts?' he mutters aloud, startling the others beside him at the bus stop.

3

Sushma has been, again, cooking all day. She once told herself she would never become one of those women chained to a stove, but her family always needed feeding and God knows the best Bedi could do is burnt beans on toast. On the days they now come over, she is there, washing pans, endlessly chopping, sautéing, mixing spices, tasting, and letting those smells sink into her hair, her fingers and her clothes. It is relentless – the day-in-day-out-ness of standing in that galley, juggling utensils and fighting to keep the mess at bay, all to feed whoever is waiting in the other room, and then having to clear up and start all over again only a few hours later. She has taken to sitting on a little stool next to the fridge now while she is waiting for sauces to simmer down; her legs get too wobbly otherwise and she doesn't want to have to go into the front room where the TV and her husband invariably are, bringing those smells with her. So, she perches on the plastic wicker, enveloped in the steam and heat, and closes her eyes for just a moment, pretending she is somewhere else, a place she might long to go but now never would. Or, a stray piece of broken twine digs into her behind as she thinks about what order of ingredients need to come next and which pans need to be washed and reused.

Today she is thinking about her kids, which always makes her smile and then feel a gnawing worry at the pit of her stomach. It amazes her how different they all are and yet how

77

she is still their mother. Her youngest, Rohan, so sensitive and still so confused about the world, needing her guidance and reassurance before he makes any decisions; her middle child, Selena, so argumentative and confident, yet just as sensitive and secretly confused about herself; her eldest, Tara, her favourite – although she knows she isn't supposed to admit that – the child who reminds her the most of herself in her quiet, infinite patience, her tenderness and her gullibility. She worries about her the most; she hopes she can find a strong, kind man to keep her from being taken advantage of in life, as this was no place for softness. Of course, Tara already has a husband and a child and another on the way but Sushma still isn't sure if this man is strong or kind enough yet to look after his family. He is just so quiet and he doesn't even use his real name in public because people don't say it correctly. How could you have faith in someone who changes their own name for other people? But he certainly loves her, she can see that in the way he follows her around the room, places his hand softly on his son's head to stop him from knocking into other people, and how he still treats her – his mother-in-law – with respect, asking how she is and if she needs any help – although she can tell from the way he nervously holds his hands behind his back that he doesn't know the first thing about this domestic world she lives in.

It will be good to see them all again – these meals are really the only things she looks forward to now, the only way she marks the monotony of the passing weeks.

Bedi is fiddling with his keys outside the front door, putting all of his bags down as he fishes in his coat pocket for his keyring – which is attached via a metal chain to the belt buckle hoop on his corduroy trousers – and with his left foot he steadies the shopping to stop it from rolling into the overgrown front garden (he really needs to remember to cut the grass before it rains again, he thinks). He wants to open the door without his wife having to come over and do it for him; that is one small mercy he can afford her.

'I'm back,' he groans as he heaves the shopping in, making sure to let out a deep sigh as he places the bags in the kitchen. She immediately starts unpacking, barely looking at him while she places items in the drawers of the fridge, on the counter top, in cupboards or just smelling them and throwing them straight into the simmering pans on the stove. God, it smells so delicious, he thinks, the sweet caramel onions just burning the tip of his nose with the hit of fried garlic and chillies, and then the creamy dal tickling the back of his throat with its bubbling coconut milk and coriander. While her back is turned, putting the bread into the breadbin, he picks up the metal ladle and slurps some of the piping hot liquid.

'Hey!' she slaps him on the arm.

'Some of your best work, my darling, I could just eat it all now...'

'No, go and get cleaned up and changed – they'll all be arriving soon and I still have lots to do.'

He pats her bum and she tuts before turning back to the stove, shaking her head at the ladle as she takes it from the pan and rinses it in the sink. He walks up the stairs and into their small bedroom and begins to undress, sitting on the edge of the bed to take off his socks and then standing to roll down his trousers before lifting his shirt over his head. He plods into the bathroom to switch on the shower and feels a cold spray on his forearm. He takes a furtive look into the mirror and pulls at his slack cheeks, feeling along his jawline and beard that needs trimming and then he dares to look down at his ever-increasing pot belly, bursting forth from his grey, once-white vest. He daren't look down when he takes off his underpants – whatever was there he had long since grown tired of and wilfully neglected, apart from the occasional fumble under the sheets in the morning while his wife was downstairs busying herself with making the breakfast. Compared to her – still straight-backed and grateful with her thick, sweeping hair and smooth, rounded face – he feels almost deformed. He can't help but feel that Sushma stopped wanting him years ago.

'Ah, you forgot to bring the semiya!' she shouts up at him. He lets out a long, rumbling groan, loud enough for her to hear.

'Are you sure it's not in one of the bags?'

'No, I've unpacked everything. It's not here and I need it.'

He leaves the shower running, pulls on his underwear and trudges back down the stairs. She is quite right, there is no semiya as he tears through the remaining plastic sacks on the kitchen tiles – he has forgotten, probably distracted by Raju and Kelly and Shokat and their complaints.

'Sorry, can't you make something else? I must have forgotten it.'

'No, I said to Tara I would make it as a treat – it's her favourite, you know that.'

'Well, the shower is running now, let me at least get dressed and then I'll go back out for it – maybe Shah will have some.'

She pauses, clearly angry but allowing their decades of flimsy compromise to make her doubt her own frustration. 'It's ok, you get ready and we'll see, maybe I can find some here or I can run out before they arrive. You'll need to keep an eye on all of this if I do, though, ok?'

'Of course.' He gives her arm a little squeeze and a smile.

He hopes he doesn't have any remnants of pistachio between his teeth.

'You were probably talking to Raju and the others and forgot, eh? Those men have nothing to do – you'd think they were homeless the amount of time they waste sitting and complaining in that horrible shopping centre.'

He giggles as he walks back up the stairs. He is lucky to have her, he thinks, ever since he had met her parents that first time in their darkened, stuffy two-room house and announced that he wanted to bring her to Nairobi and raise a family there, really she had led the way. She was the one who raised his children, who made sure they were saving enough money to eventually buy this house and then enough to see their children engaged and married off. She had kept the house clean, kept food always on the table and all this while fighting for her breath, always reaching for that inhaler. She did so much there was barely anything left for him to take on. If anything, he was taking up space; if he died before she did, she would be just fine. If she went before him, he would have no idea where to begin. That's what love is, he thinks: wanting to die first.

By the time he towels off and tends to his stray beard hairs, it is already darkening outside, the grey gloom of the day passing into a purplish night. He can see the street lamps blinking on one by one, providing small footsteps of light along the road. There is that new Debenhams shirt he should wear tonight, giving some much-needed space for his stomach when he sits to eat, tucked into the same corduroys and finished off with his brown socks, which are starting to fray at the big toe of his left foot. He'd need to get that darned soon.

He pads down the stairs and peers into the empty kitchen. The hobs have been turned off and all the pots have their lids clamped on, while the pressure cooker is steaming away in the corner. It still smells delicious as he walks through the kitchen and around the corner to look into the living room, which is also empty. On the table by the TV is a note that has his wife's instantly recognisable, shaky handwriting: 'Gone to get semiya can you lay the table.'

Luckily the tablecloth is already out, replete with all manner of stains, and he smooths it with his hands as he lays out the mats, cramming them into the corners of the table to squeeze in all nine of them who will be eating. His knees crack as he bends to get the stacks of frilled plates and bowls out from the cupboard under the kitchen counter, arranging them neatly on to the mats, with forks and spoons at the sides and the glasses for water at the corners. Taking a step back, he smiles at his handiwork – setting a table is one of the few domestic chores he can actually finish – and then he goes back into the kitchen to steal another taste of that dal.

Maybe he will watch the beginning of the evening news, since the thundering clang of the opening music always soothes him. It reminds him of the days when they had first moved to the country and were all packed into his younger brother's house in Bournemouth, watching the news religiously each night. Even among all the chaos, he misses those days. There was something cosy about them all being in one place, about sticking together in the face of so much uncertainty. That was when he had felt they were all at the beginnings of their lives and that, really, things could and would only improve. The news was their word from God, their access to the foreign and seemingly inaccessible outside world they had moved into. If they could just stay informed, they would keep their tentative place in this new life they were trying to live. Now, of course, he watches the news with the same level of scepticism and disbelief as everyone else, using it as a reason to vent the day's frustrations to the blank, professional faces on the screen.

They are reeling off the day's headlines – growth in the economy after the recession, the Tories' grip on power weakening, the arrest of a serial killer's wife – when he hears the doorbell ring. The shrill buzz makes him jump – his wife must have forgotten her keys again.

'Hi, Dad.'

His son Rohan stands in the doorway and briefly looks him in the eyes before peering down at the doorstep. There is a cutting chill in the breeze that has just whipped into his chest as he holds the door open. He moves aside to let him in.

'You're early.'

'Sorry, I know, but class just finished and I didn't think I'd have time to get home first before getting here.'

He wonders if he had been this meek when he was his son's age. He had always thought of himself as a strong man, as someone who knew what he wanted and had ground his teeth down through persistence to get it, but seeing his son now, carefully untying his shoelaces and placing his shoes by the foot of the stairs, shaking off his coat and hanging it on the end of the bannister before heading softly into the kitchen, he is not so sure. He spent much of his son's childhood telling him to stand up straight, to look people in the eye when he spoke to them and to carry himself with confidence, but he is so tall and so stooped now, always looking down on everyone without ever once noticing them looking up.

'Where's Mum?' Rohan calls from the living room, while sitting at the sofa and laying out a copy of this week's *Chronicle* on his folded legs.

'She's gone out to get semiya for dinner for your sister, she'll be back soon. Where is Sadia?'

'She'll be coming after work, shouldn't be too long.'

He can't quite figure out what it is that he dislikes about Sadia, but it is something. She is loud and bossy with his son, but that isn't a problem as he would need someone to tell him what to do in his life once he and his mother weren't around. No, it is something to do with the way she carries herself, like she wants you to think she is just the same as you when she has in fact already long convinced herself that she is better. She wants to be above it all but she is yet to realise that the only thing that marks her out from the rest of them is her youth. Otherwise, she is just the same as anyone else – tired and confused.

He doesn't want to trust her but he realised years ago that he needs to allow his children their own mistakes. Just as there had been no watchful eye guiding his failures, he knows that even if he tried he would never be able to keep his own children from the many pitfalls that await them. And so he didn't even begin to try, instead he had mutely watched his son fall in love, finding himself in another's understanding, and then he stood aside as he had his heart broken and his hopes drained to their smallest fragments, ultimately settling for what he thought his life should be – dutiful, mundane and uninspiring. He would have liked to have asked him if he was happy, if he felt that he had made the right choices and if he was excited about his many futures to come. Perhaps he didn't need to be trying so hard to become an accountant, enrolling in these classes while he worked part-time; perhaps he could just keep on living at home instead and take his time to think about where he actually wanted to be. He would like to tell him that he didn't need to be worried about his approval, that he should just focus on his own life and be selfish while he still could – that now was the time for hope and excitement.

'Good, it will be good to see her,' he says instead.

Rohan is only pretending to read the paper. He is preoccupied thinking about how much he hates his skin. His forehead is aching with the beginnings of a painful spot forming right above his brow and all he can focus on is how it will soon break out into a hideous cyst, a purplish bubo marking him for at least the next fortnight with its repulsiveness. He has always had bad skin; from the moment he hit puberty as a greasy 12-year-old, there came the rashes of spots prickling the entirety of his epidermis, from the insides of his nostrils to his ear canal. He was a constantly throbbing, oozing entity. After two years of endurance and fastidious cleanliness with zero results he finally built the courage to ask his mother to take him to the doctor to see if there could be any chemical way to stop his body from conducting such a disgusting revolt. It turned out there almost was: a pill the size of a lozenge taken once a day, an experimental treatment that pulverised his liver and left him with the organ scarring of a five-pints-a-day drinker. But it also gave him a merciful five years with which he could try and scramble together an adolescence: warm cans of Foster's pilfered in the park, a drag of a cigarette on the swings of the abandoned moonlit playground, a fumble through a pair of buttoned jeans into the cotton folds of that unknown heaven. But then the familiar ache came back, searing the creases of his face with their reminder of his deep, inevitable inadequacy.

He is thinking how anyone could ever love him. With a long, awkward face like his, with a skin that takes every chance to try and tear away from itself, it is no wonder Misha had left him.

He mustn't think about her, though – he has moved on. Sadia is his future now, his arranged and preordained future, the one he would not escape. But they hadn't even fucked yet, so what if the sex was awful? What if she had hidden a lumpy, malformed body beneath her baggy jeans and blouses? What if she found his body – that overstretched combination of jangling bones and thinly spread fat – disgusting, didn't want to touch it, let alone allow part of it inside of her? He mustn't think of any of this, he thinks, things will work out ok. Won't they?

It is like he can still smell the synthetic, sweet tickle of Misha's perfume, and see how strands of her thick black hair would fall across her face and catch on to her eyelashes, moving as she blinked at him. Or the dark knuckles on her veiny hands, soft yet worked like the palms of a woman twice her age, pillowy when they touched but always firm in their resolve. Her teeth, too, somehow so brilliantly white in spite of all the cigarettes constantly rolled, pinched, sucked on.

I want you to want me.

'What?' Bedi asks from the entrance to the kitchen.

'Oh, nothing, sorry.' He must have muttered that last thought aloud. He turns back quickly to his paper instead, his face burning hot with its blush.

The bell rings. Again, it isn't Bedi's wife, just another child. He is beginning to get impatient; the food will be getting cold.

'Well, you don't look so happy to see me, Dad.'

'Sorry, it's just your mother, she left a while ago to the shops and isn't back yet. But she should be soon.'

Tara heaves her taut, pregnant belly into the hallway with her son galloping up behind, careening straight for Bedi's crotch. He tousles his greasy hair to gently shove him away and thanks God that the boy's father is now here too, grunting and guiding the child into the living room where he immediately begins tearing the paper away from his uncle's hands.

Bedi peers into the kitchen, he isn't sure what for, mainly just to be doing something, to keep himself busy and away from all the kids crowding into his living room, sitting on his chair, playing with his remote and his TV. His daughter is perched on that rickety wicker stool, just as his wife would, holding her belly and staring at the cooker.

'You look just like your mother there, you know,' he says, a little surprised at how the words have left his mouth before he can work out where they came from.

'What was she like when she was pregnant with me?'

'Oh, she was just so happy – all that time I just remember her always smiling and saying how grateful she was that we were going to have a child. She never complained.'

'I'm sure she did but you probably just didn't notice.' She pauses. Bedi isn't sure how to reply. Is she having a go at him? 'No one enjoys this, being pregnant,' she continues. 'Your body is changing all the time, running away from you until there is nothing left but a misshapen mess; a reminder that all you can do now is hold another being. Something so small it isn't even itself without you.'

He feels the need to defend himself now. To show that his version of the events is the truth – he was actually there, for God's sake. 'Well, I remember her happy, cooking, talking about the future and what things could be like. It was a good time we had then, maybe it was one of the best. But then, I don't know, maybe we like to remember things differently to what they were. It was such a long time ago now anyway. It feels like another life. Why do you ask?' He can feel himself getting frustrated. His cheeks are hot.

'I just realised I don't know much about you, the two of you I mean. Like, what it was like getting married without knowing each other, what it felt like moving to a new place where no one wanted you, having children, growing old together. Being people, you know, not just my parents.'

'Ah, we're not that old yet! And life just happens to you, you know that. You enjoy it when you can, you keep moving forwards, time passes and next thing you know your eldest child is having another child and when you see her you can't believe how big she has become. Me and your mother were lucky, you see, we found each other and we realised we could be better at being happier if we were together. But that's just what you have to do – find a wife or a husband, have your own children and then wait. The waiting is meant to be when you enjoy yourself.'

There is a pause. He is pleased with his philosophising, his life's experience just imparted to his eldest child. But she is still staring at the cooker. Is she even listening?

'But I look at you and sometimes I wonder, how did you happen?' he adds, to fill the gap.

A pause. He hopes she doesn't take his question literally.

'But what I mean is, how do you know you are happy?' Tara asks, searching his face for an answer.

It is the bell again.

He sighs and turns back down the hallway to the front door, where he can see the silhouette of his other daughter through the frosted glass. A merciful interruption. She looks like she is vibrating.

'Sorry, Dad, I really need to pee!'

She shoves past and runs upstairs without even taking off her fur-hooded jacket and boots, leaving John to shuffle in behind and make her excuses.

PART II

'Good to see you, Bedi, how are you?'

John sticks out a cold, clammy palm that Bedi gently takes and then swiftly pushes down, moving it away from himself. He hates the formality. And John still won't look him properly in the eye, even though he and Selena are now going to be married and have Bedi's approval. What a strange little man. Also, he notices his hair thinning at the crown; that is never a good sign – another bald man in the family. But he knows better than to interfere – just like he had thought only moments ago – so he grunts the usual 'fine' and ushers him into the living room where the others are now all sat, jumbled on the cracking faux leather sofas.

His grandson is bouncing in his TV chair, hammering at the remote and trying to get to the Teletext pages. Bedi wants to snatch it from his hand and tip him out on to the floor, but he quietly pulls an uncomfortable seat from the dining room and sits down on it instead, looking back at this chaos of people who have invaded his house.

His daughters are sat together, hands on Tara's belly, whispering to each other and giggling just like when they were naughty children, while his son is sat in between the other men, their legs comically squeezed together, desperately trying not to touch. They are pointing at Rohan's paper, taking turns to shake their heads and then all tutting in unison, glancing up to the strobing television screen every now and then, probably hoping for something to settle on so they can stop having to talk to each other.

No one notices him, though. He likes that, silently looking at these people, his people. He likes the rhythm of their conversations, flowing in and out of one another like trains passing, like the hum of a sleeping person's deep breathing, the quiet reminder of their existence. He likes that he doesn't know what they are talking about anymore, he has become too old for their conversations now to care for their small chatter. He will just listen and wait, catching glimpses when he can, or when he is called upon.

He feels happy, he thinks. Or, at least he thinks he is happy, that this could be what happiness is. He feels warm, he opens his palms one on top of the other in his lap, and he feels hungry again. He listens:

'Mum said that, though.'

'And where is Mum?'

'I dunno.'

He hears.

She is thinking about the first time she set foot in the only house they have ever managed to buy, the narrow home she has just left. She smiles to herself as she remembers holding a set of cold keys in her fist and finally feeling safe in the world, in having a place of her own, where she would belong. That was when Bedi surrounded her with his arms and kissed her so softly on the lips, like they used to when they were first married, and she had a flicker of hope, like this was the life she longed for when she was young.

She also remembers that warm spring day when they first met, walking in her father's garden and crushing crocuses with their feet. When he had those ridiculous trousers on and kept fidgeting around her, but their fingers still brushed and she saw a glimpse of their future, even if they were forever speaking at each other, always misunderstanding.

She feels a lurch in her stomach as she sees who she used to be, how determined she was to get out of her home and into the world, needing to find anyone willing to take her. She could never have known then how the world is merely a place to spend time surviving one moment to the next, finding purpose only in the brief moments of respite.

She manoeuvres herself past a small child careening on a tricycle and turns her smile to his mother as she struggles to keep up. There were all the things they said they wanted, all the things they believed they would find out – like if life is better shared, or if you have to keep moving in the face of catastrophe – and now that they had lived their lives, or the majority of them, she is still no surer whether she has the answers. She knows happiness when it comes but she does not know how to bring it into her life. Without meeting him she never would have had her children – those three she cares about more than her own life – but she still wonders how her life might have been different if they had never met. If she had remained alone.

If anything, she still feels somewhere, buried deep inside, that she yearns to get out, to be free and to wander. Where to, she has no idea. She has travelled – to Kenya, Spain, Italy, France, Scotland – and she has seen white faces look at her in exactly the same incredulous manner everywhere she goes. Each time she smiles back, not showing her teeth. Perhaps the wandering has always been inside her, a hope that things might turn out differently, even if she now knows they never will.

Besides, she could never leave her children, although they are truly adults now. She would never want to leave them because they need her – and she needs them.

She feels closer to her own father now, decades since his death. She knows he read his books to see things differently – to feel into a world he could never truly experience – and she thinks of her writing, how she had toyed with the idea of making stories when she left home and how she should have written more once she was married, rather than letting the weight of responsibility crush everything else. She was able to wander there – there was so much space. She will start writing again once she is home, she decides.

The biting wind cuts through the thick knit of her cardigan and she pulls it closed with her hands because the buttons have long since fallen off. She keeps meaning to sew on replacements but she always finds something else to do. She turns the corner at the end of their street and thinks of summer, of getting the inflatable paddling pool out for the little ones and watching as their soft limbs glisten in its cool water. She thinks of those cheap rectangular choc ices in waxy paper wrapping that she buys every time the ice cream van blares its siren, devouring them on her way back home to savour the synthetic taste.

She spots a pile of dog shit in the middle of the pavement and sidesteps it just before her shoes are ruined. No one takes any care anymore, she thinks, and remembers how her brother always wanted her parents to buy a dog. Her father didn't want the extra mess in the house or for any animals to knock over his piles of books. Pintu never forgave him for that – for always putting his possessions first.

She hasn't thought of Pintu in a long time, in fact she tries not to. She left home and he remained, insisting on becoming the man of the house and looking after their parents. When she came to England, their minimal contact reduced to almost nothing – they each had their own children, worries and lives to attend to. And then, as if it had only been days not years since they last spoke, he died. A telephone call told her of a cancer diagnosis she hadn't known about and reported that he was already dead. It was too late and too expensive to book a plane back for the funeral, so she lit her pooja wick and prayed for him, still seeing him in her mind's eye as a 16-year-old boy cradling a cricket bat.

She cannot wait for the birth of her second grandchild. She knows it will be another boy – she can feel it in her bones – and she is secretly pleased he will have an easier way in the world than a girl would. He will make his own choices and he will be able to make the most of his life in this country, she thinks. Things are changing now, finally, and these children will be the first to truly call this country home. They won't be stuck between continents, longing to return or to be begrudgingly accepted.

She makes a mental note to pick up some mint tea at Mr Shah's, as well as the semiya, since it will help settle Tara's stomach after the meal. Her eyes are bigger than her belly – even if she is eight months pregnant – and she will certainly overeat tonight. She is always tying up his loose ends, she thinks, but still she is strangely pleased he forgot the semiya, since it gives her a chance to leave the house for a minute, to be alone with her thoughts and to remember who she once was.

She steps over the curb on to the rough tarmac of the road as she wonders who she is now and what it is she will write about. She does not see the man driving at 48 miles per hour, far above the speed limit, drunk or high or running from something – no one will ever know – as he eats up the road towards her. She does not see that he is looking at her – perhaps he does not see her since his eyes are glazed and his lids are drooping half-closed – but he is looking right at her as he carries on, spraying loose gravel on to the pavement and shunting over the potholes in his way.

She is thinking about how her body has changed over the years but how she has kept that same smile and those same wonky front teeth – the ones she still feels self-conscious about. She does not see the two men on the other side of the road turn their heads a fraction towards the oncoming car, beginning to wonder if it can stop before she crosses or if she can cross before it hurtles past them. She thinks she should start smiling with her mouth wide now, it has been long enough. She has nothing to hide.

She notices a third man across the road and for a fraction of a second she sees Pintu's face in him, in the downward, sad slant of his eyes and his puckered mouth, as if this would be the man he would have become if he had been allowed to grow old. She is thankful to see him, even though she knows this is not her brother.

Her life now is full of experiences happening for the last time, without knowing it is the last time they will happen. She hears, but it is too late. She sees the other car, the one the speeding man will ram her on to as she lets go of her cardigan and rolls over the bonnet, cracking the windscreen to land on the wet ground, her head knocked against the curb. She remembers the smell of the sandalwood oil her mother would always dab on her wrists and drop into her hair.

Part II

She sees the inside of her eyelids. Lights flickering.

And it is like falling at the end of a long, bad dream. The suddenness of it all, like one moment she is moving forwards as she has done her entire life and the next the ground opens up beneath her and swallows her whole. She lies there, part of the earth now; not ashes to ashes but skin to dirt, flesh to glass, blood to paint.

Though she does not know this, she has three broken ribs, a subdural haematoma, ruptured spleen and a broken eye socket from blunt force trauma, a snapped femur, lacerations to 70 per cent of the skin's surface, a mouthful of broken teeth, a stomach full of blood.

If she had words left, she might ask: 'When you cut into me, what do you see?

'Is there some secret of me written into my bones? Is this the essence of me, dug deep into the bloody mess; the soil of home, pictures of memory, of time, of taste?

'Or, are there words written to tell the way back? Just enough to know that there once was a place, somewhere to belong, somewhere to imagine. The meaning made on every return.'

Part III

30 September 2019

Selena

'What was a culture for anyway?'

1

'No, that isn't how it happened at all. It was nothing like that, no.'

John's tone was just so pungently ripe these days, primed to piss me off. He didn't have to even say anything and I would be seething regardless.

This time he had said something, though. He had decided to start the day, at what I could only assume was some ungodly hour before 8am, for some ridiculous reason, by reminiscing about Mum's funeral. The chaos of it all, how we hadn't made it to India to spread her ashes, just my dad, heartbroken and still in shock. How could we have let him go alone?

'Your brother made the trip, I thought. I could have sworn he did,' he said, now with his hand resting on my lower back, placatingly. I shuffled over to the other side of the bed. Jay would be up soon, moping about in his hotel room.

'Don't you think I'd remember who went to spread my mother's ashes?' I raised my eyebrow comically, quizzically. I was dead serious. 'No, it was just Dad, on his own, without anyone. Don't you think I feel bad enough about that without you reminding me? And reminding me now when we're going to spread my dad's ashes too? What's wrong with you?'

The marriage counsellor had said that we needed to practice 'hearing' and 'accepting' each other's speech, no matter how ludicrous it might seem. But I was hearing – I had been hearing for the past 25 years of our relationship – and no matter how hard I tried, I just couldn't accept any more. I would snap at this easy acceptance. 'What's wrong with you?', 'Who do you think I am?', 'What's happened to you?' Just questions without answers, things I would say because I enjoyed how I couldn't take them back once they were out there. Like throwing a brick through a plate, no, a plate glass window. He would need to learn when to be quiet.

Let him hear that silence for once.

It's easy to think of life as something poetic, especially first thing in the morning. Going for your first piss of the day, feeling the cold bathroom tiles on your feet and looking out of the window to see the sun's early rays painted over the sky – the birds flecked through it like punctuation marks. But, really, you just look out to remind yourself that there is something out there, something outside the petty mire of your mind. Really, reality is just like reading a long and very boring book. One that once you start you feel like you have to finish in case things eventually pick up and grip you along the way. But hundreds of pages in, all you've had is endless descriptions and a few quotable lines, and then it just ends. And you think: what the fuck happened there?

Every time I thought of my mum, I became poetic, started looking at 'the bigger picture' – as if there were something to see there in the first place. Except all there was seemed to be senseless and tragic, like her death. I shouldn't think this but I wish Dad had died first, then we would have had her for another 25 years and we would all be making the trip to India to scatter her ashes. A homecoming and a celebration.

Part III: Selena

Instead, here we were on this dreaded pilgrimage. Our family thrown together like the world's shittest school trip.

I let the tap run so the white noise could maybe drown out my thoughts. The foaming water hit the basin like the applause of a standing ovation. But I could still hear him padding around in the bedroom, smoothing out the bed sheets and switching on the TV to watch the news. No matter where we would be, he always had this obsession with needing to stay in the know, to keep up with the constant scrolling through the news of every election, every scandal, all the debates. I could hear something about the worsening pollution in Delhi now, the shrill Anglicised twang of the presenter reeling off stats on the air quality index and how the city was reaching a 'critical point' with schools now closed in the middle of a public health hazard.

At least here in the mountains the air was thinner. It wouldn't kick soot into the back of your throat like in the cities; instead, it was cool and smelt just a little salty, from the Ganges and its thick, clogged flow of waste snaking down below. I could see it from the window, the bursts of the white rapids bubbling from just beyond our rickety balcony. Over the bank was the ashram the Beatles supposedly stayed in with the Maharishi, probably smoking a lot of weed and letting their hair grow out, knowing that it would one day be full of white tourists trying to replicate their experience, escaping the gaping maw of their lives with a theme park of spirituality, or rich Indians absolving themselves of their westernised sins with a brief stint of paid lip service. The demand was so huge that they were now building another just a few feet away, its white honeycomb structure ready to house the overflow of our hopes. A temple for the spillage.

I could hear him calling Jay's hotel room to wake him up, arranging to meet for breakfast downstairs in 20 minutes, as we had agreed with the others the night before.

'We've got a big day ahead, so make sure you're there, you need your strength.' I heard Jay whining an exasperated response on the other end of the line. I don't know why we still speak to him like a child despite the fact that he is almost 20.

Instagram was my new obsession. I'd only got it to spy on Jay once he'd gone to university and had stopped answering my daily calls, but now I couldn't stop scrolling. I didn't know any of these people I was 'following' but I still cared about them; I wanted to see what they were eating, what they were wearing, how they navigated the world through their shiny faces, flawless skin and painted smiles. More than anything else, I followed animals – puppies, wombats, red pandas, otters, capybaras. I wanted to take care of them all, to hold them in my arms, feed them with tiny milk bottles and squeeze the cuteness out of their impossibly tiny bodies. Every time the screen went dark and I saw my own gawping reflection I was horrified.

'Are you done in there yet? We should be heading off soon.'

I shuddered, pulled my pants up and walked out of the bathroom into the cold, dry bedroom. And there he was, stood by our little balcony, just looking at me and waiting.

'Well, go on then, you just said we haven't got all day.'

He scurried in, like an old dog sheltering from the rain.

Downstairs, I knocked on Jay's door. It sounded like he was galloping towards me when he finally opened it, bleary-eyed and with a tuft of his hair standing to attention on the back of his head. I licked my thumb and went to push it down as he backed away into the room.

'Have you showered yet?'

'Of course, I've showered, I'm not gross. It's just so early.' He yawned, theatrically.

I tried to think whether he had always been this camp or if it was an affectation he had picked up at university, along with his new friends he would tell me nothing about. Suddenly he was visiting home with gel in his hair, a little silver chain around his neck and wearing skin-tight t-shirts when he went on his daily runs. Even his laugh had changed into this ear-splitting cackle, as if everyone had to know what he found funny, and when it was funny, it was hilarious. There was always the one headphone in his ear, too, listening to something – or maybe it was nothing, just silence to drown the rest of us out. He glanced at his phone and went to put it in his pocket but looked at it again just before it slipped out of sight.

This was a nice hotel, much nicer than any of the hotels we would normally pay for as a family. There were fresh flowers at every turn, softly piping music and grand pianos arranged around the lobby where the well-dressed guests could loiter and gaze longingly upon each other. Even the staff were dressed to precision, wearing a language of clothing the guests could understand – dark linen suits and wafting long dresses – but nothing too personalised or expensive to leave them indistinguishable from those they should be serving. You knew exactly who worked here, even if they liked you to think they were quietly unnoticeable.

It was the other staff I always looked out for, the cleaners scurrying along the marble floors, backs bent to meticulously sweep every inch and unable to look up at the leathery feet passing by. They were everywhere and never once stood at full height, as if they belonged in the world down on the floor. These were the people my parents moved away from; this is what they never wanted me to be born into and to become. And I felt sorry for them now; I wanted to show them that I was one of them too, that I could help since I knew them – we shared an identity. I felt an unbearable need to get on my knees and hug them, to give them money or better clothes and to let them know I cared. But that would have embarrassed them. I'd just give the hotel a big tip at the end of our stay and hopefully it might make its way back.

I had a little scroll – someone was filming themselves making a clay pot while a dog sat on their lap. Watching it grow upwards through the grey muck in their hands was strangely calming. I forgot about whatever it was I was feeling bad about before.

Down at the breakfast buffet, we weren't the first to arrive. Nestled between a glistening row of pastries and a line of top-hatted chefs flipping omelettes were Tara, Sunil and the kids. They were each staring intently at their plates, tearing apart bits of paratha and slopping them in yoghurt or spooning masala on to their crispy dosas. Bits of the newspaper were splayed over the table, spilling on to Amar's chair and the floor, hiding bottles of sparkling water, orange juice and coffee. It was making me salivate.

We sat down at the table next to them and began the day's small talk: how we slept, what the food was like, what our morning shits were like (looser than usual across the board), what the weather was like (smoggy and hot), where everyone else was (not here). I ordered a masala dosa, a coffee with hot milk and then went to fondle some pastries with Jay.

I felt a soft hand on my shoulder. It was John.

'I thought you were going to get me before coming down, I was waiting for you in the room.'

He flashed me a half-smile so I could see the disgusting, gummy gap that housed the missing molar he refused to have replaced. I just looked up at him silently.

'Well, I'm here, aren't I?'

I wondered if Jay could pick up on the tension between us. I mean, you'd be an idiot not to see the resentment festering in this hot air. Maybe that was why he was spending so much time away from home, only visiting when he absolutely had to, like now? I knew what it was like to grow up in a house of silent grudges; its bitterness seeped into you, those glances and asides slicing into the way you saw your parents, until you were forced to pick sides. And it wasn't that it was so obvious with my parents – they never even argued, in front of me at least – but you could just see the desperation my father had to get out of there, to have been given a different life, while my mum had to be eternally placid and accepting. The best punching bag a husband could ever ask for.

Not that he hit her. Or at least I don't think he did. She was just simple and kind and never once said what her own wishes or needs were. Not in front of us anyway. Maybe she was a doormat instead. Growing up, seeing that, I knew I never wanted to be quiet and accepting – I wanted control of my life and maybe even someone I could control too. Fat lot of good that turned out to be; perhaps resentment was the inevitable aftertaste of love, that cloying reminder that too much sickly sweetness will eventually kill you. I took a bite of my danish, hitting the little pool of custard in the middle this time and feeling the crunch from the crystallised sugar. I decided to get another before they ran out.

My brother was a good reminder that things could always be worse. Seeing him lope towards us now with his wife in tow, her eyes fixated on the buffet, and his two children running straight into our table, made me shudder. He looked exhausted and it was only 9.15am. Things were worse for him because he didn't even have resentment, he just had an unrelenting acceptance of the shitty hand he'd been dealt. He looked like a man who had given up, or at least someone who had never even tried to be hopeful; he had never tried so he could never fail and never hoped so he could never be disappointed.

I wanted to take him out of his miserable life, to look after him, but that was wishful thinking. Largely because Sadia was so spiteful. There was no way she would let him live in relative happiness without her; she'd gut him first, leave him prostrate and begging for forgiveness, for at last using his own mind to act on how he really felt. I sometimes wondered what happened to that girl he had been dating when he was at university, the one he had to break up with because she was Muslim and her parents were going to disown her. He seemed so honourable at the time for putting her family first but I'm sure he woke up every morning now regretting it. I think Sunil had bumped into her in Hounslow a few years ago while he was shopping; I think he said she was married with children – although when she saw him it looked like she might faint, as if she had just seen a ghost from another life come back to haunt her with its possibility. Perhaps that was why Sadia kept such a tight grip on Rohan; she knew he wanted more and was capable of better.

What was in it for her to keep him trapped?

Part III: Selena

I wanted my boy to be loved by someone else at least. He didn't need to make these same mistakes.

Sadia and I had long decided to not even bother with the illusion of social niceties, so now when she walked past at the breakfast buffet, we just looked away from each other, as if neither of us existed. I could feel Jay watching, waiting for me to say something snide, but I didn't want to give any of them the satisfaction. Maybe I was becoming more reasonable in my old age.

When Sadia and I first fell out it was a disaster. It was the only time we'd had to have a family meeting, or a family shouting match, to try and patch things up. Mum had just died and I think we were still in shock, processing that image of her lying on the hospital gurney, cut to ribbons. And Sadia was the one to find out before any of us; she was the one who had stepped down from the bus because there was such a massive traffic jam backing up; she had been walking down the long Hanworth Road, nearing the blue lights flaring from the black windows in the distance, and as she got closer she could tell something awful had happened; people were gathered and gawping; she went to look and it was the torn crimson of a chunni she saw first, a brown arm lying on the wet, sticky black of the road, tufts of thick dark hair matted into the grit; she thought she recognised the thin gold bangle on the wrist, clean and untouched, and then she noticed that chunni again, its silver lining sparking a memory of it being flung over a shoulder in a hot, smoky kitchen, and then she moved closer to see a gashed cheek, a bloodied eye, and she vomited.

She ran the rest of the way without stopping and when she came into the house after hammering the door down it was me she saw first. I could smell the sick on her, I could see her skin was grey and dewy.

'It's your mum – she's dead, I think.'

I thought I had misheard or that this was some horrible joke. I just stared at her. 'Think what?'

'I think she's dead, I just saw her in the street.'

She pushed past me into the house and I could hear her repeating the words 'think' and 'dead' to the rest of the family, in front of the kids, over my brother's crying, my sister's shouting. I stayed in the doorway still, noticing how it was just starting to drizzle, the mist flickering through the street lights.

What got me was how she was the first to know. After we'd seen the cars, the body, the crime, the whole mess of it all, I couldn't forgive her for getting there first and then for leaving her. What if she had been alive still? She just let her lie there alone, helpless, without even finding out what had happened. She could have held her hand, she could have comforted her, but no, she just assumed the worst, stared at her like gory entertainment with the rest, made up her mind, and then ran away. I could never forgive her for that.

And the way she told us too; how she had to qualify what she had seen with that 'I think' because she couldn't be sure. She had bolted off before she could even know herself. I could have sworn she was happy to tell me, that there was a glint in her eye as if she knew she would always hold this power of having been the first. So, after the funeral, I told her exactly what I thought of her, that she had no place in this family and never would, that she was scheming and playing games for our affections, but she would never have them because the only person who could have seen anything redeeming in her was gone.

Part III: Selena

To be fair to her, she gave as good as she got, calling me conceited, spoiled, a brat who had never tried for anything and never would. I wanted to pull her hair and scratch at her smug face but I showed some restraint. Well, I called her an ugly cow.

Before we all met to reconcile – at Tara's insistence – John said I should maybe be nicer to her, that I shouldn't shoot the messenger. Perhaps that's where our resentment first began – when we were just newly married. I snapped back that he knew nothing, since he was happy to let his mother sit in a retirement home that he would visit once a year. What did he know about how I should deal with the death of my mother who I loved more than anything or anyone else in the world? A mother I would have seen a hell of a lot more of than he did his, if we had been given more time.

Anyway, that didn't set me up too well for the family ambush that came next. John was silent, implicitly agreeing with Sadia when she said how I had 'attacked' her and never made her feel welcome, that I had put her marriage and love for her husband in doubt. How I could have made someone doubt their love was beyond me, but I decided to sit quietly and listen as much as I could, to be gracious for the sake of my brother and sister who were so clearly and uncomfortably caught in the middle.

Of course, I was silent as long as I could be and then I walked out of the room, straight up the stairs. I was amazed that she followed me, goading me for a reaction the whole way. I wouldn't give her the satisfaction; I just sat on my mother's bed and felt the soft edges of her quilt. I wondered if it might still smell of her. I closed my eyes.

When I opened them, there was my father standing over me. I could see he was worried – his eyes turned down, pleadingly.

I had never seen him like this before, clasping his hands in front of him as if begging for money.

'Please,' he said, 'get along. We need to keep this family together.'

He looked like a sad child; a boy punished for a silly mistake. I wanted to hug him and apologise for my stubbornness, to tell him that things would be ok, that I would never leave, that I forgave him. I didn't, though, and so I didn't do any of that.

'Ok.'

I stood up, walked down the stairs, shook hands with Sadia like we were sportsmen, and then went straight out of the door. John came chasing after me with my bag and my coat.

'What happened? Is everything ok? What did you say to each other up there?'

In that moment I couldn't piece the words back together. But I felt the rock dislodge from my chest and work its way up the base of my throat to my dry mouth.

'I'm a coward. You have married an idiot,' I stuttered. I could feel it coming – emotion – and I cried in the middle of the street, letting my head fall on to his shoulder, his hand patting the back of my head before he passed me on to Tara who had now found us. She held me for what felt like the longest time, only letting go once I had soaked the shoulder of her thin blouse.

'You will be ok. We will be ok. We can keep going.'

2

The masala was already repeating on me; I could taste it in the back of my throat each time I burped. I made sure I had eaten as much as I could as I kept hearing that we had a long journey ahead of us and I didn't want to be hungry. I never wanted to be hungry. Hunger was the immigrant's inheritance and the fear of it was one of the few certainties of your existence. My parents grew up hungry, their parents probably almost starved, and so by the time I came along, they made sure to stuff me so full of food and the threat of hunger that I would never leave the house without something edible on me again.

One of my earliest memories revolved around it: my mum picking me up from school with a soft, squashed cucumber and mint chutney sandwich in foil for the 15-minute bus ride – just in case. I had eaten so many of them, I could think up the sweet, tangy taste instantly. It was an aluminium-wrapped gift I passed down to Jay ever since he was born, always keeping the fridge full so that throwing away rotting surplus brought me more joy than eating it.

How rich people could choose to stop eating and starve themselves for pleasure I had no idea; for me, the only marker of truly making it was having so much to eat you couldn't possibly finish it all.

From the look of the roadside hawkers on the way down here, I knew there would be nothing for us on the drive out.

Nothing unless you wanted to risk being hunched over a toilet bowl for the rest of the trip.

'Have you been to the toilet? We've got a long journey ahead of us.'

I could hear Sunil asking his boys, like they were still small children. They both gave a dramatic eye roll and stared back at their phones. The heat was so thick here I could feel it coating my throat every time I breathed in, like the dust from the dry soil would mark the insides of me by the time we left. It made me want to rinse my mouth out. I started glancing around for places I could discreetly spit and had a little scroll (a man was feeding apple slices to a tiny red panda while it stood on its back legs like a real, little person). Before I hawked anything up our driver arrived.

He was a short, greasy man with a name I couldn't pronounce. I'm not sure any of us could and we all felt a bit embarrassed about it – having spent all our lives facing the same problem – so we never addressed him. His English was patchy at best and our Hindi was almost non-existent so both parties weren't missing out on much. He mostly dressed like a schoolboy: navy polo shirt tucked into khaki shorts that rode up on his ashy thighs, while his shiny and hairless legs were capped off by rubber flip flops, his toenails overgrown and yellowing, brittle additions to his leathery feet. He was always smiling too – which might have been a company requirement – making himself seem overjoyed to be driving us four hours to the banks of the Ganges to dump our father's ashes in, like a busload of tourists hunting for morbid souvenirs.

I suddenly panicked. Who had the ashes? I looked through the bodies gently amassing around us – families waiting for taxis, porters trying to get our attention and bags, drivers leaning on their cars, smoking cigarettes through stained fingers and gappy teeth. There they were, boxed in a cloth bag hooked over Tara's shoulder. She looked tired.

'Want me to take them? You look tired.'

'Oh thanks for telling me, you don't look so perky yourself,' she snapped. She must have been tired.

'It's the heat – I can't sleep properly here. Anyway, want me to take them or not?'

She hefted the straps from her shoulder and into my hand. They were heavier than I had expected and I realised that this was the first time I'd actually held all of him. I had seen the coroners put the paper bag into the cardboard box and seal it, then place that in another, larger box and into the cloth bag. But I hadn't seen him or felt him. I had no idea what was waiting inside and in a few hours I would be tearing open those bits of sellotape and rifling through his remains, putting my fingers through every part of this man who I couldn't remember had ever hugged me, or said he loved me. When was the last time he had even laid a reassuring hand on me?

The heat and the diesel fumes and the thought of him were making me feel light-headed – I needed to sit down.

The coach was rust-coloured, rickety and far too big for just the 11 of us but I was looking forward to having a window seat to myself. I put my bag down next to me to make sure no one got the wrong idea that I wanted them there. I could hear the boys all laughing outside at the wonky signage above the number plate saying 'Amar' – our driver was smiling and taking a picture of our Amar, Tara's youngest son, in front of it. It looked like he might drop the phone, he was holding it so gingerly. Maybe we could call the driver Amar if that was on his coach?

Tara heaved herself on and was huffing and puffing her way to an empty seat. I could see the dark rings around her eyes and her soft, darkened knuckles that were looking more and more like our mum's hands every day. Maybe she was coming down with something; I hoped it wasn't because of something dodgy we'd eaten before or an infection the rest of us could catch. I hoped someone was looking after her.

Watching her shuffling to a seat just behind mine she looked so terribly alone, a bit too lost in her own thoughts.

'Are you sure you're ok? You're not feeling ill?' I asked, testing the waters one last time.

'Really, I'm fine, Selena.' She only called me by my full name when she was angry. 'I'm just tired and sad, I suppose. We are saying goodbye to Dad for the last time today, in case you'd forgotten. There is a lot going on, I just need some time to myself.'

'Ok, I'm sorry, I was just worried about you. Get some rest now.'

I tried to reach over for her hand but I ended up getting the back of my headrest instead. She found me though and placed one of her soft palms on mine and let it linger. I got a faint waft of her elderflower hand cream as I rested my head on the window, greasing up the pane. We began to move and I suddenly panicked that I hadn't seen Jay or John get on but I turned and there they were, sat together, John already asleep, Jay with his headphones in, staring at his phone. I wondered how long he would survive in the real world if I snatched it and threw it out of the window. Now that would be unforgivable.

I had a little scroll – a duckling was sitting on the back of a golden labrador while it slept – and glanced up to see how the city seemed to be undulating as we drove through it. It would be all stacked glass and thick vertical stripes reaching up to the sky one minute and then earthy iron and short, clumped tenements the next, and we weaved through as if we were just circling the whole mess. I had no idea where we were going. In fact, I knew hardly anything about this trip – it was Sunil and Tara who organised it all meticulously and I was merely along for the ride. I remembered my earlier conversation with John with a pang – how I hadn't gone to spread Mum's ashes all those years ago, how I hadn't seen or felt or held any of her once she was gone. It was enough to watch the coffin go behind the curtain and then that was it: I was motherless, left to make my own family now, one that she would never know.

Maybe that was why I was so adamant about us all coming on this trip. I wanted to make up for my selfishness and I wanted Jay and John to see it all, to bear witness to the whole complicated, confusing affair of saying a ritual goodbye. He wasn't coming back, and she wasn't coming back either – they had just disappeared without another thought for us, left here alone. We had to have the last word. But the goodbye was impossible, when you thought about it, because there was no one there to say it to – we were just saying it to ourselves. What good is a goodbye to the slicing wind or the banks of a river?

All that death really requires is our silence, that quiet sound of us packing it up and carrying it with us, knowing it will never, ever go away. It will always have the last word. And we'll be there, struggling to hear.

But what did I know? We were winding upwards now, climbing away from the city and into the hills. I had expected more greenery but all I could see was the grey of craggy rocks and the spattered gravel of the road tumbling off the sheer edge as we careened higher. I tried not to look ahead as truck after truck came jumping out of the corners, slamming on their brakes and then performing a delicate dance around us to make it through to the other side. Ever since the crash, cars had made me nervous, and India really wasn't the place for a nervous passenger. Looking forward, I reflexively began to hold my breath and gasp each time our driver pressed on his surely worn brakes, making the entire carriage squeak and churn. It was like the drivers spoke their own language through their bubbling jabs of the horn and their arms flailing out of the windows. But all I could hear was the adrenaline hammering through my ears.

Jay was asleep now too, his head gently bobbing closer to his dad's shoulder. In a different time, I would have taken a picture of them both – something cute, a memory. But why bother now, I had enough mementos. My brother was asleep too, his head tilted back over the headrest and his mouth open, almost dribbling. Sadia didn't seem encouraged by that scene and was instead talking to her son intently as he slowly nodded and his sister slept beside him. Sunil was awake, staring at the road calmly, keeping track of our progress.

I leant my head on to my hand and closed my eyes.

I kept seeing Dad's face everywhere. He was there as Robert De Niro in the film I saw on the plane, the one about an old man going back to work to stave off his depression after his wife died. He was there too in the kindly face of Dr Karl Kennedy in *Neighbours*, the silly Australian show I would watch religiously at university. He would even appear in the piggy pink of Jeremy Clarkson's bloated arrogance. It was funny how I would see him in others but I could never call up his own detail when I wanted to. The shape of him was blank and all I could remember was the mole below his left eye, the greying hair with tufts sprouting from his ears and nostrils, and a wideness that seemed immoveable.

I could still call up my mum's face each time I wanted to, though. There was Mum, always in her 50s, grey hair threaded through her thick bun, her eyes drooping at the sides, forever making her seem sad even when she smiled – which was almost all the time. Her faded, gold-rimmed, smudged glasses, the soft wrinkles of her neck folding out from the fringed edge of her sari, those dark rings under her eyes advertising a life of exhaustion, her teeth still wonky but brilliantly white.

I couldn't remember the last time I had seen my dad's teeth; he would always make sure when he smiled not to show the bottom row, those yellowing, thin stakes planted in the rubbery gums of his skull.

The bus rumbled and shook me awake. We were still climbing and the city was way off into the distance now, its existence an afterthought. I could barely remember the morning. What did I have for breakfast? It felt like I was still asleep, so I touched my face and pinched my cheek just to make sure. I wondered when we would level out as it seemed like we had been moving upwards for hours, winding nauseatingly to some peak.

There could be no river up here, surely?

I looked back and John and Jay were still fast asleep, head-on-shoulder, bouncing with the bus. I took my phone out for a quick picture. I hoped it wasn't blurry. I looked back at the others I had saved on there too – the emblem of Krishna I had for good luck, all of us in black for the funeral, those cygnets I'd seen in the park, nestled next to their mother so gentle and peaceful, all of us crowded on the rooftop bar on our first night in Delhi, the smog shining behind and the flash igniting our half-empty glasses.

Sunil was talking to the driver, distracting him from the road in his broken Punjabi, and the driver was nodding furiously, turning back to gesture to him, every now and then, and letting the coach veer ever so slightly towards the hillside when he did. I was gripping the edges of my seat with my fingernails digging into the dirty, discoloured fabric. I wanted to tell them to be quiet and just get us there safely.

We took a sharp left as the road started to level out, nearly bringing my head straight into the rattling glass window, and then we were on a dirt road, speeding straight towards a skewed building at the end of the way. I had that Bread song looping in my head, the one where he sings in a sweet falsetto that life was full of emotions, passing by. It was making me think of the '70s again, of being a child in the summer and that song on the radio, Tara humming along while cleaning the kitchen.

Maybe this is what he was singing about – that there are times when your life feels light, like every moment of sadness will pass and every piece of happiness is fleeting, but now things sink into you, like they are waiting. The resentments bloom like mould, the happiness stings with the afterthought of how quickly it had left, and songs always make you cry.

It had taken me the longest time to realise that Bread weren't black. They were one of the whitest bands I had ever seen.

3

I had to remember not to touch anything. The tiled floor was thick with dust and I could see the flies hovering above the grill in the makeshift kitchen. It should have been open and airy, this whitewashed bungalow filled with tables, but there were only two fans spinning lazily on the ceiling, pushing the hot, greasy air and its mosquitos ever closer to our mouths. There were trinkets for sale hammered on each yellowing wall – West African wooden masks, swords, Masai warriors sculpted from iron, statuettes of Hindu gods – and in the corner there was a table filled with tubes of Pringles, Airwaves gum and cans of Coke. Through a window in the wall I could see another brightly lit room, a maze of overflowing fold-out tables filled with plastic-wrapped sheets of paper, metal figurines and dishevelled books. A few men stood there idly leafing through the much-handled trash.

'Don't touch anything,' I barked at Jay.

His headphones were back in and he was glued to his phone, sensing his way to the long table that had been set out for us – a lone island in a sea of white European coach tourists.

'What is this place?' I asked my brother.

'God knows, I really hope we don't get sick eating here, though – it looks a bit ropey.'

'Yep, the last time I was here I got the worst shits, they lasted for pretty much the whole trip, I was so scared I'd be shitting myself on the plane home.'

'Mum! That's gross, stop it.' He was always listening.

'Oh, so you can hear out of those headphones then? Well, if you don't want to spend the rest of this trip on a toilet I'd recommend getting something that is vegetarian and don't drink anything with ice cubes in it.'

I could see Jay smiling at the corners of his mouth. It was impossible to look at him and not see a five-year-old still giggling at the word 'poo'. His father, meanwhile, was intently studying the laminated menu, trying to decipher the options.

'Chicken mince naan – don't get that; lamb chops – definitely don't get those; chicken wings – don't be stupid; butter chicken – absolutely not; masala paneer – maybe; eggs and chips – what?'

I settled on the plain naan and some black dal, Jay went for the chips and paneer, John for just the chips – he was a cautious man and I had to remind myself that I had grown to love him for it. For some reason Sunil ordered the chicken mince naan and the wings and his boys were shaking their heads in vigorous disapproval.

'Dad, didn't you hear Selena? You'll get so sick eating that, plus it's all so fatty, it isn't good for you.' They looked pointedly to his sagging paunch, spilling over the top of his unnecessarily high-waisted trousers.

'Oh you sissies, I'll be fine. You're speaking like true goras. I was born in this country, I know this food, my stomach is coming home!' He held his belly with both hands and shook it as he laughed heartily for effect. Tara was staring off into the distance, blankly.

'What are you getting, Tar?' I called over the others. She paused for a few seconds, as if it had taken that time for my words to travel across the table to reach her.

'Oh, nothing, I'm not feeling hungry.'

'You should get something, don't listen to me. I'm sure you'll be ok – plus, we'll need our strength for later.'

'Really, it's fine.'

She trailed off and looked back into the distance. Something must have been wrong but I knew by now not to say any more, this conversation was done. I decided to have a wander around the strange gift shop while we waited for the food to arrive. I picked up my Coke can and straw (to stop contamination) and manoeuvred past a table of tourists muttering to themselves as they pushed their chips around their plates and dunked naans into a dal as if it were a dip. I assumed they were Germans, since they were all dressed like Americans but they were being quiet and neat and making sure not to stare at the waiting staff as they handled their food like it was made of rubber.

There was everything in this place. Faux hand-painted scenes from the Kama Sutra where penises displayed themselves proudly under the folds of clothing, miniatures of Krishna, Ganesh and the other, lesser ones I never knew the names of, new copies of the *Bhagavad Gita* made to look old, and so many Bollywood posters – prints of the painted ones from the '50s and '60s where the hero and heroine are clutching one another in a romantic embrace, their faces just far enough apart to suggest a kiss without crudely implying it has already taken place – and then the photographic ones from the '80s and '90s where saris show a touch of midriff and cleavage, and the heroes' biceps bulge from their sequined short-sleeved shirts. It was all so kitsch and really the only appeal of the films was their unabashed camp; the frivolous dance sequences, the melodramatic tears, all that henna dye and botox, bosoms heaving in the rain.

I hadn't heard the word bosom in years and I had no idea why it had just popped into my head. It was the kind of thing my mum would have said, coyly referring to something us kids shouldn't know about or shouldn't have been watching. She was such a pure, innocent soul – the kind that deserved a soft, peaceful death, not being dragged over the tarmac like some ancient sacrifice.

'Can I help you, madam?'

I must have been standing there just staring at the table, lost in my own head again. The daydreaming was getting worse.

'Oh, no. Thank you.'

I could see the food arriving on the table and Jay was gesturing for me to come over and eat. I put my phone back in my pocket – I hadn't even realised it was in my hand.

It looked like those pictures of food you see on the walls of kebab shops back in London – plastic, shiny, yet somehow real. It smelled delicious, though, and suddenly I realised I was starving. Everyone else did too as the table was now silent, all of us with our heads down and focusing on our plates, the sounds of lips smacking, hissing burps and dishes being passed along so we could each have a taste. Even the chicken wings looked good – I bit the edge of one and its flesh was so salty it almost made me wince. I remedied it with a mouthful of cold, tooth-rattlingly sweet Coke, my stomach gurgling at the unusual combination. I probably still had all the dust and grit of those posters on my fingers while I was eating but it was too late now. I wiped my hand on my trousers and kept tearing off bits of naan to dunk in the piping hot dal.

The bill came to about £20 for all 11 of us. I thought it must have been a mistake but I was happy not to have to pay more. Not that I paid; Sunil did. And then we hauled ourselves back on to the bus after we each visited the bathrooms, which were a series of acrid holes punched into the floor. I couldn't imagine my mother fitting in here at all; I couldn't picture her squatting over the hard ground and pissing away into a murky cesspool. I could only picture her among the grey skies of suburban London, her bright yellow sari cutting through the scene like a burst of light, like a knife through a stiff canvas, her left hand bunching up the material of her pleated skirts so she could walk down the street, gracefully stepping over the smashed glass and sticky chewing gum, now somehow passing me hunched over her body in the road – that same sari torn into the black tarmac, like someone had tried to stamp out her radiance – she looks on the scene like her own guardian angel, me the mother now crouched by her as the dying child, and she just leaves us behind, walking off down the road, her sari still spotless, her posture firm, resolved to go somewhere I have never been, and as I see her leaving I want to follow her but I also can't leave that vision of her hopeless on the ground, peaceful as if she is asleep now –

'Mum, come on, the coach is leaving!'

I was standing in the doorway, staring out into the road. I should stop zoning out so much, I reminded myself, I needed to be more 'present' instead, whatever that meant. Maybe I should try a mindfulness app, but I hated listening to someone tell me what to do – even if it was just asking me to 'gently bring your mind back'. Surely I knew what was best for my own mind? Maybe I should let it wander if that's what it wanted to do; I had spent enough of my life concentrating on useless things.

I was sitting on the coach and I couldn't even remember getting up the stairs or crossing the road. I panicked and looked back to find John and Jay, who were already in their seats, John fast asleep, soon to be snoring.

I scrolled, my brain barely registering the new information the blue light beamed up to me.

4

I let my phone drop into my lap and I fell asleep immediately. I dreamt of my girl.

My little girl who had only lived inside me.

How I didn't want to feel her on me after they had to cut her out. How John had to leave the room once it was over and he had seen her from that bloody distance.

I was scared it would be too much to bear. That I would feel my brain and body flooding with love for something that was no longer real.

But she was too beautiful, the midwife said. And I saw her ten fingers and ten toes and perfect face, full eyelashes and head of hair. She was just asleep, still warm.

I could swear I felt her heart flutter, like she was just dreaming too. And I didn't want to go home, I wanted to stay there with her and wait until she woke up.

But I pressed on her cheeks and they turned to soft clay – each fingerprint of mine leaving a muddy mark. She was growing heavy and wet, heaving on my chest as I struggled to breathe.

I was sweating but all of the nurses had begun packing away their equipment, taking off their gowns and leaving me here, drowning under the weight of her, still cut open.

I didn't want to see what they had done to my body, I just held on to her as she began to slip through me, trying to move her as she broke apart in the force of my shaking hands.

I could feel my thumb pressing into her soft gums, tearing through her round face, her tiny folded ear and into her hair. Her eyes opened and I saw myself in their dark pupils, screaming.

The coach jolted to a stop.

'Hey, Sel, we're here. It's time.'

John had his hand on my shoulder. I must have looked mad as I could see the concern in his wrinkled brow and felt it in the little squeeze he gave me. It made me flinch at first, recognising the meaning of his touch, but then I put my hand on his and ran my thumb across his warm fingers and knuckles. I needed to make sure this was real.

'Thank you.'

5

The heat knocked me out of my daze and into the reality of standing in a rubble-filled makeshift car park. It stank of the bittersweet, clotting blood of hanging lamb carcasses that were being sold across the way and I could feel the looks of the surrounding men bearing down on us. We didn't belong here with our chinos, corduroys and patent leather shoes. I doubted any of us even wanted to be here. But we needed to be here, this was the only place we were meant to say goodbye.

An open-backed truck was packing in dozens of bodies – an overloaded, writhing mass of men. This is what you see on TV depictions of India: the dust, the heat, the overwhelming presence of people stuffed in every corner of the place. I had always assumed it was an exoticisation to show it this way, that there were in fact as many nuances to this colourful, sensory place as there were anywhere else. Now, I saw it exactly as I would have through the screen – somewhere entirely foreign, fearsome and enticing in its difference, except this time I could climb into that truck if I wanted to.

The boys were laughing while they used an open urinal built in the middle of the concrete field and their dads were taking pictures of them all lined up from behind while they pissed. They then rushed back, fishing out hand sanitiser from Tara's handbag and shuddering from the smell of their own waste wafting over. Sunil and my brother were speaking to the driver, working out the route to find our pandit so we could have the ceremony go ahead.

I remembered at dinner the night before how my brother had recounted Dad's experience of coming to scatter Mum's ashes here 25 years ago. Dad said he had to find the family pandit among the 3000 who had their 'offices' in this tiny town on the banks of the Ganges. Theirs were the little hovels in the walls filled with the handwritten records of family trees and presided over by holy men. It was his duty to find the right pandit with our Bedi record inscribed in a vast scroll so he could add our mother's name to the family line. Only then could he go with the pandit to the banks of the Ganges and place her ashes in her final resting place. And all the way he had to do exactly as the pandit said, buying rose petals from one roadside seller, ghee and spices to coat the ashes from another, and then making his way into the freezing cold water, his head submerged by the pandit's calloused hands while he recited from the Sanskrit scripture, allowing him up for breath to recite briefly with him the om shanti, and then finally digging his wet hands into the thick sand of her remains and tossing them out into the polluted foam of the water, washing them away from him so they wouldn't end up sticking to his white kurta like grit.

Dad had only described the place where the pandit was once – a hole in the wall backing off a large tiled courtyard – and that was all we would have to go on for now. Sunil seemed to think he could find his way as he had been here to put his own mother to rest only a few years after Dad, but his memory was sketchy too. Perhaps there was something about the place that defied description.

Standing here now it was almost like I could feel it; the heat cupping my head into a soft deliriousness, the taste of the dust being whipped up by the wind on my tongue. I ran my fingers through the silk of my shirt to steady myself on the rocky ground.

'Ok, the driver is going to come with us, to help us find the pandit. He knows some of them here.'

Sunil looked relieved. We had each avoided thinking of the logistics of how we would find this holy man but here seemed a small glimmer of hope that might see us through. I could hear Sunil's children cautioning my brother against going into the water, the eldest Amman, a doctor, concerned that the bacteria would give him an infection, or worse. Since he was my father's only son, we assumed Rohan would be the one to take on the burden of the ceremony and he gamely shuffled on, stooped over his gangly frame, his eyes downcast with concern about this newfound responsibility. Amman and Amar were carrying bags filled with towels and bottles of mineral water to douse him off once he was out. His own son Karan, only 14 now, running up behind, was playing in this game of duty and dragging his younger sister along by the hand.

I was wondering what it would be like under that silty water, disoriented and trembling as you trusted this unknown man's hand to keep you from drowning. A baptism in the death of another. There was nothing about this place that seemed holy, though. I took John's hand and made sure Jay was keeping up, his phone now cautiously in his pocket – as was mine. There were people everywhere, tour groups of schoolchildren, holy men – or at least men dressed to look holy – in their yellow lungis, paint marked on their foreheads, their bare chests cracking like old animal skin in the sun. There were visiting Indians making their pilgrimages to bathe in the water or scatter another's ashes, and so many children running everywhere, splashing around or trying to sell us trinkets, tugging at our legs, rubbing their thumbs and forefingers together in the international sign for 'give us your money'.

Where were the women? Everywhere I looked I saw men and boys, comfortable in themselves and in this heat, talking to each other, drinking their tea from chipped Styrofoam cups or jotting down notes on their large hands with leaking biros, passing glances as we tourists trundled through their streets, saying no to their children as we perspired. Whiteys on the moon.

It felt like there was no room to breathe. We were being led away from the banks of the river and into twisting, claustrophobic alleyways where mopeds would blast through, tooting their horns at us to shift sharply. We were preoccupied, anxiously looking back at our children following us, their expressions morphing slowly from giggling wonderment to boredom and then concern. Jay was talking to Amar about something seemingly serious, his head tilted to one side as he listened, Karan was talking to Amman, eagerly trying to keep his attention, and his sister Ayla was walking quietly with her mother, intimidated no doubt by the constant overwhelm of this place. Out ahead were the men – Sunil and Rohan – trying to make conversation with the driver, who now seemed even smaller than I had remembered when he was standing outside the coach this morning.

I moved away from John and went to Tara. I looped my arm in hers as another bike rushed by, the wind it kicked up whipping through my shirt, cooling the sweat on my chest.

'It's a lot isn't it?'

'Mmm, yep, it is.' She paused. I had nothing to say so soon. 'I wonder what all the kids are making of this. I thought it might be a fun adventure for them, something they would remember, a chance to reconnect with their "roots". But now I'm worried they won't ever want to come back. It might be too much.'

She said the word roots with such emphasis, such weighted disdain. It was like it was a dirty word.

'I was thinking the same. I mean, for Jay it'll be even more different because of his dad but I still wanted to give him the chance to see where we come from, even if it just means that when he's older he knows where to come back to, that he can remember something, you know?'

'Come back so he can scatter your ashes here too?'

'Oh God, no. Just tip me round a tree in the park or something. For God's sake don't go to all this effort to dump me in this place – what a rigmarole. I mean, we're no different from tourists here, you know? I wanted to come and feel something but all I can feel is indigestion and all this staring. I mean, would you want to end up here?'

'I don't know. I've been thinking about it lately –'

My heart jumped. 'What? Why? You'll have plenty of time to –'

'Yes, yes, I know, I was just thinking. I mean, Jesus, you asked me, Sel. I've just been thinking and I suppose there's this idea I have of India, of it being home or something, but being here I know I'm just as much of a foreigner as any gora visiting for two weeks of experiences. My "roots" are more with my people than a place, but when I'm gone I'll be leaving all my people behind.' She paused. 'Maybe what I'm saying is: do whatever you want with me because I won't be around to care anymore.'

'Exactly. Anyway, this is depressing, we shouldn't talk about these things. Are you hungry?'

'No, not really, have you got any water, though?'

I fished a cold bottle from John's rucksack and opened it for her. As we had grown older, I realised I had become more and more protective of my sister, like I had suddenly realised how much I needed her and with that came the attendant panic of not wanting anything to happen to make her leave me. My worst dreams were those when I saw her in the place of my mum, lying there on the road, eyes fixed open and helpless.

I wish I felt the same about Rohan, but Sadia had long since gotten in the way there. He would always be my sweet little brother and now he was someone who had to put his own family first. Maybe that was the way with men, that they needed to protect their own families rather than look out for those they had come from. I know that had been the way for Sunil, leaving his family to live with Tara as soon as they were married and then barely looking back since. But what of us sisters? We only had each other in this world and it would break me to have to live it without her.

'Thanks.' She smiled with relief. I smiled too.

The alleyway we were walking down opened into a small courtyard filled with cows sitting idly. Flies were buzzing over their mounds of shit and sinewy chickens ran through our legs. I could have sworn I saw a rat. None of us looked particularly comfortable as we were led to a small room in the corner of the courtyard where a pandit sat on a carpeted floor, playing on his phone. He stood up as soon as he saw Sunil and Rohan approach, bowing slightly to them as the driver translated.

'Come and have a look at this,' Sunil called after a moment.

Inside the hot, musty room was a rusted iron vault the width and height of the wall. The pandit was hunched in front, rifling through it like some storybook librarian. Teetering on the verge of crushing him were what seemed like rolls of wallpaper samples, folded in on themselves and snaking over each other.

'Bedi family, from Rishikesh?' he asked, mumbling.

We nodded as he gingerly picked up one stack and sat on the floor cross-legged. Here he unfolded the book and revealed hundreds of long onion skin pages of intricate Hindi script, each line I assumed detailing another life. The boys were leaning over and taking pictures on their phones while the ceiling fan whirred overhead, rattling with each footstep. I darted my eyes quickly to the corners of the room, making sure there were no mice or rats there to greet me as I went to sit down. The pandit licked his finger each time he turned a page, reading the lines as if it were the Guru Granth Sahib in a gurdwara, muttering names to himself.

'You should all be in one of these books too, you know?' Sunil said to his boys and Tara.

'How?'

'Well, your nana would have told the pandit the entire family tree when he came to scatter your nani's ashes and then when you all die he will make a note against your name, along with adding your children's names too.'

I could have sworn he looked pointedly at Amman when he said the word children, an unspoken nod towards his duty to get on with the business of child-rearing before it was too late. Yet another line to add to the long list of lives. It was nauseating to think that this was what a life lived ultimately came to: indecipherable script crammed on to the tattered pages of a notebook, stuffed in a prop vault, organised by no discernible method, and flicked through by the greasy hands of a pandit who had yet to clean himself up after his lunch.

It was becoming apparent that there were no Bedis in this

book. The pandit spoke to the driver, the driver spoke to Sunil, and Sunil looked at Rohan.

'Dad's family were definitely born in Rishikesh, weren't they?' he asked with a finger pointed at Rohan.

'Yes, his dad was born there and then Dad moved to Kenya when he was a young man to work on the railroads, that's where he got married and then he came to England.'

Two continental migrations in a lifetime – no wonder Tara shuddered at the mention of 'roots'.

'Ah, Bedi family, Nairobi and Rishikesh.'

The pandit took another tongue-like sheaf of papers from his cupboard, stifled a burp and ceremoniously tossed open the pages. I was aware that we were witnessing a show as much as a ritual. Ceremony was all performance.

I had a little scroll while the others watched on in boredom and anticipation.

I looked up after I'd exhausted the stream of nameless babies and bunnies on my feed – it felt like long enough already. The pandit was shaking his head in disappointment. Clearly there were no Bedis from Rishikesh by way of Nairobi and England in these scripts.

A whisper of hot wind touched my cheek as a fidgety young man emerged from the doorway and crouched next to the holy man, nodding as he spoke. I could see him write 'Bedi' in blue ballpoint on to the back of his hand and then he took out a phone from his torn top pocket and put it to his ear. Soon, another, lankier young man appeared, smiling at us as his hoop earring glinted in the light. He smoothed his gelled hair and gave a small bow with his namaste to Sunil. We followed him out of the courtyard and back along the narrow alleyway to the banks of the river again.

'Where are we going now?' I asked, to no one in particular.

'This man works with another pandit and apparently has some records of Bedi families in his books,' Sunil answered tersely.

'How do they even know this stuff? It's not like they seem to have any kind of organisational system going on.'

'Yeah, they could use a WhatsApp group or something couldn't they,' Amman interrupted. 'They could put a group message out to all 3000 of them saying "the gora Bedis have arrived, let's piss them around for a few hours then fleece them."'

'Alright, let's hope we're not getting ripped off yet anyway,' Sunil said, keeping the peace.

We took a sharp right turn through the silence of an ended conversation into another, larger courtyard. I was starting to realise that Dad's memory of a pandit's office off the side of an open courtyard could mean pretty much anywhere.

Overhead two kids were giggling and running across a balcony while an older woman slapped her washing against the wall and hung it on a sagging line. Another woman was in the courtyard, washing her feet at a glugging tap and glaring at us as we arrived. She pulled her chunni over her head and I instinctively checked to make sure my shirt was still buttoned and pulled up my trousers. I couldn't tell which places were houses or offices or public spaces here – it was all one thoroughfare: part moped-run, part market and part holy land. I was sure the Muslims were much better organised in Mecca. I couldn't picture the wealthy Saudis bothering with this kind of aimless wandering to find your man; they would have fast track passes around Mecca, like the ones you get in Disney World to get to the front of the queues for the good rides.

Sunil and Rohan loped off into another pandit's hovel and we waited, the sun beating down on our slumping heads. They really should have a WhatsApp group or something, shouldn't they? I took my phone out of my bag and snapped a picture of the square and the boys in the distance, Amar writing something on to a black notepad, Amman jabbing him with his finger in his side, trying to distract him, Jay alone watching the washing woman, Karan rolling his eyes at his sister as she skipped around him. I wanted to take a picture of this woman washing her feet, as it reminded me of one of those harem paintings you see, these half-naked dark women bent over and tending to themselves, dousing their skin with soapy suds falling on tiled floors while we look on unnoticed, gawping at their grace and voluptuousness. Maybe that could be one to add to my Instagram profile? Something to make me seem artsy.

I had to make sure I wasn't staring now, but she had the darkest eyes just faintly but perfectly outlined with kohl, a detail that made me think of her as someone calm and fastidious, a person who took care in her appearance, even if she could only afford a black pencil. I must remember to wear more makeup.

Gone were the days of making myself up for every occasion. I used to slip on knee-high leather boots and unladdered tights – now it was maybe a smudge of lipstick, a quick swipe of mascara, a dab of foundation on the cheeks. I had lost interest in the sagging face that looked back at me every morning in the mirror; there was nothing to see there anymore.

Maybe now was the time to live in this skin rather than searching it for answers and second guesses. Beauty is what's inside, that's what counts, I'd be telling myself. Or, maybe it's just money.

Part III: Selena

'Nope, no luck here either,' Sunil confirmed.

A round of sighs and groans emerged. The man with the slicked hair and earring patted Sunil's shoulder and gave him that head tilt I had been trying to master ever since I had arrived here – half 'we'll see' with a dash of hopeful uncertainty thrown in. No one ever said no, since there was always a way to what you wanted, or at least a way to lead you down the garden path to where you thought you had wanted to go. I remembered how Dad had always said to never trust anyone in India, that they'd all be out to get you, especially once they could smell that particularly British blend of politeness and naivety on you. 'If I go to India, don't even trust me,' he'd say with a flourish. I had never thought to ask why he hated his own people so much, why he held so much prejudice.

Another man arrived, this one with heavy gold rings on his fingers, a taut belly fighting to emerge from his kurta and the henna dye on his moustache staining the sallow skin surrounding its bristles. He, too, wrote down the family name on his hand and then made a call. For all we know they could have been calling each other – 'new ones for you to scam here, just keep them walking around until they tire' – some system they had going on. But we were moving again.

'Do we all need to stick together? Can't some of us wait until you have found the right priest, at least?' Amman asked.

'It's a pandit, not a priest, but yes ok, I'll ask the driver if there's a cafe or somewhere you kids can wait while we look.' Sunil sounded like he was reaching the end of his tether.

'I doubt there'll be any Prets around but just somewhere to sit in the shade would be good, maybe somewhere with a working toilet.'

Karan gave out a little laugh. 'Yeah, it's so dirty here!' But Sadia swiftly shushed him with a sharp blast of her breath before he could say any more. I'm sure she had wanted to tell him not to embarrass her, to be quiet and act like a good Indian boy instead, one who knew what to do in this place.

I knew she had always resented me for marrying a white man, as if I was dirtying our caste or the social standing of the family – whatever that might have been. I bet she thought that I was giving up on trying to keep our cultures alive by allowing myself to assimilate, to become one of them. With a name like Selena Stevens I could pass for white anywhere and I knew I did because of the disappointment in their eyes when those people on the other end of the phone line or email finally saw my brown face staring back at them. It was always palpable. It used to be funny but now I just wanted to ask them what they were looking at. I bet she was angry, too, that I had not only taken on this man's name but also had a child with him, one who would have his own mixed experience of our world. 'Half-caste' my dad used to call him, but I wasn't sure if that was allowed now.

If I didn't even know where to put myself in and among all these bodies, what hope did this child have? All of these children we had borne with us.

We wandered into a tight row of market stalls where we drew the attention of the sellers who were now hopping from behind their facades to follow us down the winding streets. They were trying to sell us metal holders for the ghee wicks Mum had used in her afternoon poojas, fanning their thick plastic packets of incense, draping wooden beads over our heads or, for some reason, offering packets of chewing gum to the kids. Sunil was up ahead shooing them like pigeons, telling them none of us were interested in their tat in his broken Punjabi. Although I quite liked the idea of having one of the wick-holders at home, lighting it each day and saying my prayers to bless our house. Perhaps that would bring me some kind of reassurance.

I remembered the 'spiritual' phase I'd had just over a decade before, dragging Tara to these women's meetings at a nondescript house in Hounslow where we would walk into a cramped front room of older brown ladies all dressed in white, where devotional music was being hummed and we overheard the talk of forgiveness, finding yourself and the dangers of eggs and butter. I think I liked how cultish it was, this coven of mysterious women all gathering weekly to resolutely ignore their domestic lives and instead focus on the bigger questions like karma, fate and, always, dietary requirements. We didn't contribute much to the sessions, nor did we really know what the ultimate point of it all was, but for a time it was enough to have a place to be and to have these people to belong to, these roots of one's own. But I can't remember any of their names now or why it was that we stopped going.

I think that was what I might have been chasing here – that natural feeling of belonging, even if it was only temporary. To just feel seen again, not stared at like a tourist, but to be looked through – ignored even – to be given back the invisibility of being. That was what it felt like to be truly seen. Or perhaps that's what I thought it was – I wasn't sure anyone's eyes had looked at me like that before.

They were looking now, but in the increasingly familiar sense of wonder and disapproval, as we gingerly moved past the outdoor tables to find seats in a small restaurant. Again, this place seemed almost exclusively populated by men, with each group sitting leisurely as they talked, sipped on their drinks and swiped their mouths with handfuls of deep-fried salty snacks and sickly sweet treats. I could feel them staring at me, unashamed and unembarrassed as they dunked their wet fingers between their lips. Of course, John was the one who really attracted the majority of the stares, being so luminously white as he patted the sweaty sheen from his bald head with the spotted handkerchief he always carried around. I doubt he noticed anyone, though.

Sunil briskly gathered the leftover soggy paper plates and cups from the table, stooping over while the rest of us sat and let out a collective sigh.

'Right, who's staying then?'

The kids followed with a cascade of groans, all wanting to rest, except for Amar who had said he might try and find the group later. He folded his notepad away and tucked his pen into its spiral rings. I wasn't sure why he was writing or what it even was that he saw, but the faint scratching of his pen made me feel like we were being watched. I didn't like the attention.

'I think I'd better sit this one out for now, I'm really feeling the heat,' Tara piped up.

She was taking on something of John's hue now too, her underarms marked by damp sweat patches and the rings under her eyes darkened by the early start. I was surprised, thinking she would have been the last one of us to break before we had seen this ordeal through. Instead, here I was, looking like the more responsible one for once. I was hoping to sit it out but I couldn't leave it all to Sunil and Rohan.

I asked if she wanted me to keep her company but she just shook her head like she used to when we were children, when I'd ask her if we could have one yoghurt to eat each, instead of having to share everything all the time.

'I'll stay if you like? I could do with a little break from this heat too,' John added, looking at me, as if to ask for my permission.

We all sat while they ordered miniature crispy triangular samosas, tall, cold servings of lassi served in metal cups, chips – again, for John – and steaming hot pakoras dished out on wet oval banana leaves. I could see how happy John was with his bounty, laughing while they passed around napkins and hand sanitiser, feeding each other morsels. It was a strange little scene, this stout white Buddha smiling among his Indian acolytes, a Desi last supper. I didn't know why I was fixating so much on him these days, surveilling him for every mistake and waiting for my chance to prove his short-sightedness or ineptitude.

His was a face that I had once found exciting and enticing. Then, it was like there was a universality in the whiteness of his skin, something that gave him a special access to power and belonging. His was the face that I would always see reflected on the television or in magazines and on posters, not the darkened irregularity of my blotchy brown arms and legs. Falling in love with him was suddenly to see his face everywhere, to be enveloped by this pinky whiteness.

Now, those ideas made me feel a little sick. They reeked of my naivety and willingness to jump out of my own skin in the hopes of being accepted by another. I was so blinded to myself and to those who looked like me. I had always thought I must be different. But it made no sense – I would always be this shade of other, no matter how hard I scrubbed. I would always be a Bedi even if I was now a Stevens. And now, whiteness disgusted me. John's face was that of all those piggy, bald men who would leer at me in the streets, those service workers who looked at me like I would never belong on the other side of the till, those sweating, throbbing heads gulping down pints and shouting at the football match on the screen. It was irrational, I knew that, not least because my son – my beautiful baby – was half white, but there were times I had wished he was all me, that he would really understand the unique beauty of our existence and that he could hate whiteness with me too. I had said as much to Tara not long ago and she had snorted back at me. 'You're only questioning your brownness now?' with a stifled laugh. 'None of us felt like we belonged, ever since we were kids, but we learned to live with that, not to pretend we were something else.' That had upset me and led to the first argument we'd had in a while. Apparently, I had spent so long trying to pass for white that I had come to hate the very thing I was trying to make myself.

It was exhausting work, all this thinking on being and belonging.

What a luxury to have been in this country for a week now and to have only seen a handful of white people. I wondered how they might feel to be the minority for once. It made me smirk to think of their awkwardness and insecurity before I realised that we were just as much outsiders as they were. And we had the added shame of not being able to navigate our own culture. We might have all looked brown in passing but linger closer and you'd see that we were just as white as the rest. Perhaps Jay and the boys would bring some of this understanding back home with them, a way to feel comfortable in all of their homes. But it was most likely already too late. What was a culture for anyway?

We heaved ourselves back on to our feet again, leaving the kids, John and Tara behind while the rest of us kept up the wild goose chase. I wasn't sure if Dad would have been laughing at us or finding himself deeply ashamed if he was still here. Instead, he was in that effeminate tote bag slung over Sunil's shoulder – something he definitely wouldn't have liked.

There were two stray dogs and three men following us: the driver, the second pandit's assistant and this third pandit's boy. He couldn't have been much older than 16 or 17, wearing ripped jeans and flip-flops, a striped polo shirt and a thick red tilaka on his unusually wrinkled forehead. We must have been on our fourth hour here as he led us through what I assumed was one of the main roads in the hellishly busy town, under low-hanging electrical wires hooked on to the main wooden mast, past yet more streetside sellers, children playing in the road and mopeds and rickshaws weaving through them. We took a sharp left and started climbing a steep set of stairs, being careful not to look into the tiny houses we could see crammed along each side, their bare front rooms adorned only with a cooker and maybe a single plastic chair and table. I glanced over at a woman standing in one, her smooth shoulder showing while her chunni was being pulled down by the baby she had tied to her hip with another piece of rough cloth. She patted the child on the back with one hand and used the other to flip a roti puffing up on the naked flame. When Jay was little, even making a jacket potato would sometimes have been too much of an undertaking, I remembered.

We reached the top, all five of us panting, and looked into a carpeted front room where several barefooted men sat silently, staring down at their phones. The boy rushed over to one who fished a pair of glasses from his front pocket, tilting his head while he listened. He pushed them on to his bulbous nose and looked up at us standing in his doorway. He spent a few moments taking us in, luxuriously.

'Aajo – come in.'

Sunil bent down to take off his shoes and the rest of us followed, neatly lining them up against the wall. I tried to stifle a cough with a hand cupped over my mouth as the dust and cigarette smoke in the air hit my throat.

We were all silent when we reached the back room. Metal shelves lined the four walls with scrolls of paper records wrapped in cloth and folded on to them like old film reels stacked in a projector room. In the corner sat a small man in the lotus position, one scroll already opened on his lap and flowing away from him like a stream of water pouring to the floor. I could see the different ink colours and scripts used to document these interconnected people, a living record of our togetherness and existence, something that would age and decay just as our bodies would. And once these sown strips of paper were smoothed into strands of fibre, we too would be entirely gone.

We watched on, our backs to the wall as the man flipped through the pages and followed lines of text with his nail-bitten index finger. He looked up and the boy soon crouched down next to him, nodding his head to the side before turning to our driver to translate. With this many intermediaries I wasn't sure if anything that finally got back to us was even half of the truth.

I wanted someone to address me for once, to let me know I was important, or just that I was also there. I wanted to check my phone but I knew I would be told off for missing something important if I did. I wished there were more people trying to reach me.

'Pandit says that he cannot find Bedis from Rishikesh.' A pause. 'Pandit says your record has been moved, or that pandit has passed on also.' Another pause – was he finished? 'He says to come back tomorrow and to look then.'

'But we can't come back tomorrow, we have to leave for Delhi then.' The vein in Sunil's neck was throbbing.

Yet another pause as the driver translated. Why we had decided upon only one day in the very place we had travelled thousands of miles to get to, I had no idea.

'Ok, pandit says he will do ceremony because it is getting dark and he will find your record to write in tomorrow.'

He probably thought we were idiots. Sunil looked to me and Rohan.

'Let's do it,' I said.

If he never found our record, what did it matter? If it had never even existed, it would have made no difference. This was going to be for us and by us and that was all. The wandering to find our man, the journey to be here together, the memory of this place and all its challenges – that was our rite.

6

Rohan and Sunil were fondling small wads of cash, trying to work out among themselves how much money the pandit would want and, more importantly, how much they were willing to give him. We had picked up the others en route and I could feel the collective relief as we edged closer to the end point of this monotonous day.

The pandit was leading us through the main street again, the vendors not bothering us with their selling calls this time as they knew we had a purpose now. The sun was beginning to float gently down through the sky and, as the road beneath my aching feet dissolved from a dusty brown to a muted gold through its rays, I kept hearing the same phrase in my head. 'Remember this.'

I held Jay's hand and told him to take it all in. 'Yes, Mum.' But my mind was wandering, back to my baby, back to feeling her weight on my chest for those few moments, and now to the fantasy of what it would have been like to bring her here, to hold her hand too. Or even to have brought her tiny box of ashes, to add her name to the list of our family records, to have her remembered by the pandits and anyone else who came to perform their rites. Had I made a horrible mistake by scattering her around the roots of a tree in the park I walked to every morning? Had I consigned her to existing only in my memory by not allowing her to be seen by others, to be pulled up into the family tree?

Part III: Selena

We never spoke of her anymore as it had only seemed to get more unspeakable as time went on. It was like she was never here. A hidden wound that could not heal.

The pandit was telling Sunil to buy a paper bag of rose petals as the sulphurous smells of the river began to reach us. Rohan shifted behind him uneasily, stooping down to his height to listen to the pandit's mutterings. Sadia took Rohan's arm by the elbow, whispering something into his ear – surely telling him to make sure the pandit knew he was the eldest son and that he would be the focal point of the ceremony, not his older brother-in-law.

I thought we would need to visit more stalls, picking up the spices and ghee that my dad had mentioned when he performed this ceremony all that time before, but after the rose petals, we found ourselves at the banks of the Ganges.

'Is this it?' Amman asked.

'I suppose so, be quiet so we can listen to the pandit.'

We stood beneath a vast bridge crossing the river, the sun now cresting just above its curve and a gigantic statue of Krishna defiantly bursting over a hill in the distance – something I had only just noticed. I also noticed prayers blaring from nearby speakers, ones I assumed must be attached to a local temple, and among their interweaving falsettos and clattering tabla rhythms I could hear the piercing squeals of playing children, splashing around in the water only a few meters away, the frothy water breaking on the three steps leading into its depths just ahead of us. There were slackened chains strung along the width of the river for people to guide themselves across and it was here I had assumed my dad clung on for dear life as his pandit – our Bedi family official pandit, I'm sure – said the prayers of the afterlife as he was submerged. I saw Rohan, nervous now, speaking to the driver, who in turn reached up and placed his hand on his shoulder, giving him a warm, reassuring smile.

'Turns out I won't have to go into the water after all,' he said, eventually. 'Maybe they've changed things since Dad was here. It's just me, you Tar and you Sel who have to go down to the edge of the water and tip in the ashes, and then we're done.'

I fished the black muslin scarf I had brought with me out of John's bag and draped it over my head, standing between my brother and sister as we gingerly made the three slick steps to the water. I took a sharp breath as it splashed on to my shoes and soaked my toes. It really was icy cold. I put my fingers around Tara's soft upper arm and felt her warmth through the fabric of her blouse, steadying me. I hadn't noticed that the pandit had begun his prayers since all I could hear were mumbled words, lilting in a nursery rhyme sing-song amid the shrill, metallic voices coming from the temple. Everyone was speaking at once and how very like our Bedi dinner table it was, with Dad always being the only one silent.

Rohan opened the white box of Dad and I saw him for a few lingering moments. He looked like dry, grey sand raked from the beach, like handfuls of experience poured into a container, like sandcastles rescued from being washed away in the surf.

We each took a fist of the rose petals from Sunil and placed them into the box with him, feeling the white marbles of bone that had not been fully cremated, like Jay's milk teeth that I had taken from under his pillow.

My heart was pounding at the sensation, realising that this was an entire life I could simply rifle through and would then toss away, never to be held again. I wondered if I might be able to keep a small piece of him.

PART III: SELENA

The pandit's voice rose.

We began to sprinkle him into the bubbling water and after each round we would watch as he dissolved like dropped candy floss in a puddle. The pandit was in a repetitive trance, building up speed with his utterance, and I made sure to take a breath with each handful, as if I was passing him through me for the last time, saying goodbye to everything other than his memory.

Rohan tipped the last crumbs of him from the box and the pandit motioned for us to swill the water by our feet so that the ashes would be carried by the current. I smiled, remembering that Dad had never learned to swim. He had always pretended to, while walking underwater in the shallow end. Surely he was swimming now.

I turned to look back at the others and saw children swarming us, putting their hands to their mouths and asking for money from the boys. Two men in uniforms then appeared from behind, shooing them away and proffering yellow forms for Sunil to sign while he fished in his pocket for the money for the pandit. I wanted to run at them all, to scare them into leaving us alone with our remembrance.

His voice was still so clear, booming in my mind: 'Never trust anyone in India. Not even me if I go there.'

I looped my arms into my brother's and sister's and we looked out on to the surface of the water. The sun was bouncing off its movement and now dipping just below the bridge.

In the corner of the sky a sliver of the moon was beginning to come into itself. For a moment, I didn't want to let go.

I didn't want to remember the myriad moments of the past that had made me so angry, so out of place in my own body now. I didn't want to see John, or Sadia, waiting, daydreaming. I didn't want to see my mum as I always did, her skin grazed with grit, her eyes open and lifeless. I wanted someone to pay, to give me an answer. I wanted to take Sadia by the throat and push her down into the water, feeling her thrash as she breathed it in.

I took a deep breath before I went to move.

'Is that it, then?'

Rohan

'Waiting is always the same, wherever you are'

1

The phone buzzed on the bedside table, right next to my face. I rolled over quietly to check that she was still sleeping, and she was, her mouth open just enough for me to feel the warm, stale breath fluttering on to my cheeks and to see the small pool of spittle gathering at the corner of her lips and soaking into the pillow.

Vicky has liked your profile.

Fuck me, if I couldn't work out how to turn off these notifications. But it was addictive – didn't I read somewhere that every time you got a 'like' or even a message it released a small dose of dopamine in your brain, like a dog who'd done a good job? Vicky, my Pavlovian tart. And what a voluptuous one she was, all cleavage and streaks of blonde hair, the camera angled downwards so it felt like I was about to fall between her pillowy tits. Must've been another fake account.

It all started around a month earlier. The divorced dads at Karan's school parents' group were talking about these apps, about how they had 'changed the game', whatever that was. I knew Sadia didn't like me spending time with these middle-aged, crisis-ridden men, but I liked hearing their stories of weeknight dates and getting handjobs at the Cineworld car park again – not that I had ever experienced that before – or about their shock at the sheer glut of women available to them now, these lonely fellow divorcees finally seeing themselves as viable partners rather than sad, sallow men chained to an existence they had never realised they had opted into.

I was curious. Opportunity seemed to be blossoming and for once my mind was open to it. Suddenly, every woman I saw seemed available to me, rather than just another mother or one of Sadia's potential friends – the 'informants' as I had begun to call them (privately). Perhaps I, too, should get a taste of this 'game', while I lived in the wet fart of a slowly dissolving marriage – one that my wife refused to talk about, let alone even acknowledge.

So, just out of curiosity, I downloaded the app they had all been going on about and moved it into a discreet folder on my phone's home screen – that much at least I knew of digital security. There was so much personal information to get through first – questions about my marital status ('single'– or would 'widowed' get me some sympathy?), age (could I pass for 40?), where I lived, my education, whether I had or wanted kids (why involve them in all this?), whether I drank or took drugs, my star sign, my height, my job. And then there was the option to answer questions about yourself, the kinds of boring conversation starters only people with no personality would resort to. 'What's your best travel story?' (managing to catch my son's sick in my bare hands while we were on a coach to the airport in Thailand?), 'what's your personal brand?' (sad dad, still married?), 'let's debate this topic?' (am I a terrible human being for being on this app?). I decided to leave those questions out for now.

I was starting to see this as a game, something like the ones Karan would obsessively play on the computer, building a virtual and carefree version of myself – the type of man I could have been in another life. I enjoyed picking out the photos to display on my profile – one of me alone in a suit at a wedding, another of me dressed in a shirt and shorts on holiday, also alone, and one more with a few (male) friends, just to show that I wasn't eternally unaccompanied. I felt a little flutter in the base of my stomach when I pushed on my phone screen to make my new life live. And then it began.

Was this a spiritual experience? All these bodies, all these curves and mounds and shades crammed into the rectangle of my phone, all governable by the flick of a finger. It felt like power – a rejection of the 3D world for the flatness between my hands. Now when I was on the toilet each morning, I would spend a few minutes swiping through, mostly saying yes, only saying no to those who looked too beautiful to be true or if there was that same apathy in their eyes and poorly constructed profile that I could see in mine. Then they came, a flood of 'hey's' and 'hi's' and 'how are you's?' filling my inbox like the best kind of spam.

I wasn't sure what to say back at first, all this attention was so uncomfortable and new. I had my curiosity fulfilled, the experiment was over; I'd seen this new game and I had very much enjoyed the taste of participating in it. But I couldn't shake the feeling that I still wanted more – I needed to see what all these hi's and hey's meant. Were these women simply curious like I was or did they see something more in me? Was there some kind of potential I had long ago put aside?

But mostly, the justifications came later, and first – I replied.
'Hi, how are you?'
'I'm good thanks, I like your profile.'
'Thank you, your pictures are very nice. Do you use this much?'

I knew the key to keeping up a conversation was to keep asking questions, ones that were polite but not so politely boring that you were held in that crushing vortex of small talk.

'Do you want to see my tits?'

I remember spending an entire morning reeling from the shock of that message. Jane, 53, brown-haired and buxom, offering up her breasts to me without question. Again, was this a spiritual experience? Of course, the answer was yes – to the tits and perhaps to the spirituality – but I was nervous to say so. What if this was all a scam, a ruse to catch me out with my trousers down (literally)? Or what if she wanted to meet – one naked picture might not constitute cheating but meeting in person might, and any further in-person heavy petting certainly would. Was signing up to this app cheating in the first place? Sadia would punish me with all the fervour of a cleric banishing a non-believer regardless, that much I knew for sure.

'Well?'

I wasn't expecting a follow-up.

'Yes. Please.'

It seemed important to stay polite. And there they were, only a few minutes later – slightly red from the light but voluminous and eminently touchable nonetheless. The first real pair of breasts I had seen in years. I mean, the women in the porn I watched were real but so many other men had seen those same brightly lit tits, whereas these were just for me, sent from someone who really existed. Or so it seemed.

Then the dread kicked in, seeping from the pit of my stomach and crawling up my spine to grab me by the shoulders and shake me with its paranoia. What if I was being scammed? I deleted the picture almost immediately. After another look.

PART III: ROHAN

And so it began, again. The same cycle of conversations – most ending in overtures for dates or petering out into nothing – and then the small few ending in another picture, or once a video. I would look at them, let the flow of flesh and nudity imprint into my brain, and feel that surge of momentary ownership (manliness?) power through me before it was replaced with an immediate dread and lingering shame. Delete and begin again.

It had been like this for the past three weeks and in that time I had deleted and reinstalled the app twice and I had also downloaded and then deleted another app. But I couldn't get enough of this spiral of excitement, intrigue and shame – I hadn't been this interested in anything since the last time I'd seen Misha. But I couldn't think of that, not now, not again.

Of course, there were certain unexpected surprises. Like the time I had seen one of my old colleague's profiles and had almost swiped her for a match before I realised. I realised later that she had probably also seen my profile too. Luckily, she had no way of contacting Sadia. Or when I downloaded that second app – at the height of my rabidity (stupidity) – and I must have set my preferences all wrong because there were men mixed in with the women I was rifling through, their hairy double chins and gappy smiles a horror among the smooth, considered appearances I was used to. The worst of all: coming upon young Jay on there, floral shirt open to show his surprisingly hairy chest and a silver chain around his neck, laughing with an open mouth and looking right at me. Perhaps he had made the same mistake as me? I swiped past him so fast from the shock that I barely had time to take it all in. Still, I couldn't help looking at him differently now. I wondered what he was up to, always scrolling through his phone and quickly tapping out messages. Poor kid would have a fight on his hands coming out to this family.

Anyway, it all needed to end now. This was no place for me; it was a young man's game. Or a sad divorcee's at least. I needed to decide if that's what I wanted to be – the first in the family to get a divorce, my father's only son, the carrier of his name. What kind of example would that set for my kids? But then shouldn't I teach them that happiness is worth pursuing, even if it meant sometimes going through difficulty? I needed to talk to someone about this, it couldn't just keep going around in my head, looking for –

'What are you doing in there? I need to use the bathroom.'

Her voice made me jump and almost drop my phone to the floor. I'd give myself piles by sitting on the toilet for this long, staring at it, into the abyss.

'Oh, sorry, almost done.'

I typed.

Hey, Vicky, how are you doing?

2

'Ugh, leave me alone.' That same refrain, every hour like clockwork.

I thought it would get easier with the kids as they got older, but it had all changed and yet somehow stayed the same. They were still unpredictable, difficult and disobedient – it's just that they could now dress and feed themselves and run away from home if they wanted to. That's what Karan tried last year – he must have been watching too many American films where the kids always run away for like a day and have a lovely adventure without ever getting mugged or stabbed or arrested – and we found him after only a few hours, sitting in the park with a rucksack containing his iPad, a half-eaten jar of peanut butter, a pair of headphones, a bag of jelly beans, a can of Irn Bru and a penknife. Real Bear Grylls. I supposed he was testing boundaries, or something else that might end up with us sending him to a £95 per hour psychotherapist. Come to think of it, we had never grilled him on the topic after we found him. We'd taken him home, told him not to do it again and then sent him, sulking, to his room. Sadia blamed me for not looking out for him, for not showing enough 'fatherly guidance', and I countered with the fact that she didn't show enough 'motherly love'. She barked that how could I say something so horrible to her, of course she loved her child, her firstborn son, that I didn't even know the meaning of love since I would never allow myself to feel it; I would rather stay closed off to the world instead, comfortable in my safe bubble of emotional distance. She had been reading too many of those *Chicken Soup for the Soul* books. Anyway, from that day – the running away, not the argument that we continue to have versions of – Karan changed, something hardened inside him. He barely spoke now, only opening his mouth to tell us to leave him alone, get off his case, or to stop talking. I assumed it was just another pubescent phase, one that would hopefully pass.

Ayla was another case. While her older brother had retreated into himself, trying to unearth a new identity from the muddy slop within, she had exploded out of herself. Where she was once an attentive and quietly curious girl, with a soft spot for me I had liked to think, now she was all lofty opinion, sarcasm and self-awareness. There was something truly heart-breaking watching her come into herself through recognising the eyes and opinions of others, how her walk changed from a shuffling run or stoop to a considered, elongated idea of poise, how her face needed to be made up now, her clothes her own (expensive) choice, her thoughts often closed to us where once they were written across her ever-twitching face. Strangely, the more she talked, the less I realised I knew about her, whereas Karan's silence I could understand perfectly – a calm amidst the inner storm, a mouth trying to process the brain rushing to reach the body. God, boys were slow. Still, getting them dressed and out of the hotel room took an age.

'I will leave you alone once we get to breakfast – we're late and we have a long day ahead of us, so come on. You won't want to eat anything they have once we're on the road, trust me.'

PART III: ROHAN

I used my best stern dad voice with a sprinkling of appeasement and it seemed to work. We were finally in the musty, air-conditioned fridge of an elevator down to breakfast. Of course, we were the last to arrive – Tara was sitting peacefully at the table, reading and eating with her family, Sel was staring silently at John's plate – and somehow both the kids weren't looking where they were going and almost crashed straight into them.

'About time – we need to head off soon.' Sunil spoke to me like my dad still.

'I know, I know, sorry – just getting the kids together, you know?'

'Food's good though.' He paused, as if questioning the reasons for our lateness. 'You should get the dosa. I might get another, actually.'

I looked at Sadia, who I knew was already looking at me. Giving me that look that said, 'don't eat that dosa for breakfast, eat the yoghurt and granola with fruit and don't you dare get fat like all the other men in this family.'

'Delicious, dosa it is.'

I didn't even feel hungry. My hand was in my pocket, fumbling with my phone, trying to manifest a buzz of recognition, the adrenaline vibration of a message received. I watched the kids while I waited and they ravaged the pastry and hot buffet sections, piling their plates with enough food either to make them sick on the coach journey, or enough to make them waste so much I would be embarrassed to see the waiter carry their remnants off to the bin.

The levels of poverty here had always made me feel deeply ashamed. I remembered the last time I was in India, when I must have only been about 11 or 12 – Ayla's age – and we stayed with Dad's cousins who had a boy servant who was my age too. They called him chotu – little one – this boy who would never look us in the eye, his thick hair matted over his forehead as he silently passed through the hallways of their marble-floored apartment, barefoot so as not to make any mess, this boy who slept outside on their balcony under a corrugated iron roof, always wearing a filthy and tattered t-shirt. It felt like something Victorian, being in the presence of that disabled kid from *A Christmas Carol* – even though chotu seemed fully mobile for now – while my family sat and feasted on their dinners in their suits and saris, waiting for him to clear the scraps after we left. This was real poverty, I had realised. We weren't well off back in England, all three of us kids sharing a single room and crowding around the single-bar heater when the frost started to cloud the windows, but at least we had changes of clothes and we could afford to eat three times a day – sometimes with a morsel of mithai thrown in for good measure. My mother was so horrified, she gave him a month's salary when we left as a tip – all of £15 – as well as most of the clothes she had packed for me to wear on the trip. The cousins were furious, telling her that he had never seen this much money before in his life, that we had been gone for too long and we didn't know how things worked here anymore, that it was a different, harder world now and that his existence as a servant to them was the best life he could ever hope for. He was lucky and he should never be made to understand that he could feel otherwise.

We simply left and moved on to the next town to see other relatives.

I kept thinking of chotu, though. Where was he now? Did he too have children of his own? And how, exactly, could life have become harder for him?

Part III: Rohan

This was a hard place. Everyone here was on some kind of hustle: the mothers with young babies strapped to their chests, weaving their way through the traffic-choked streets looking for cars full of tourists and then pushing their children up to the windows, fogging the glass with their breath and mouthing for food and money. Or the drivers who would tell us not to fall for these 'tricks', that these women made more money begging than they did doing honest work, that we should keep the windows rolled up, ignore them and instead go to their friend's place for lunch where the bottled water was filled with fetid discharge from the tap and sealed with clear nail varnish so it would still crack when you opened it, sating your thirst and leaving you shitting your pants only a few hours later. Or there were the police who would stop our car whenever they spotted our suspiciously white and wide smiles and careless, gesturing airs, and they would order the driver to show 'his papers' and charge us for the pleasure, regardless if he had them or not. No wonder Dad had told us to trust no one here, that even he would end up scamming us if he moved back. But I don't think we even trusted him at home.

I wondered what my children made of it all now. If they saw the kids sleeping on the hard shoulder of the motorway, their shaven heads only inches away from the scalping tyres of speeding cars, and then realised how lucky they were with their gadgets and games, that boredom was their only trauma – that and perhaps feeling like they weren't loved enough or attended to enough by their parents. But putting food on the table and clothes over their little bellies, that was love enough, wasn't it?

I looked over at them, sitting quietly and picking at their food, pushing it around their plates, and gearing up to ask us when they could leave, go back to the room and flick through the channels on TV. Sadia, meanwhile, was busy attacking her own plate with all the focus of a teenage boy attending to his first bra.

'Come on, you two, eat up. Nothing is free in this world, you know, so I won't have you complaining about being hungry later when there is perfectly good food here that you are wasting.'

I was turning into my dad.

They both let out lengthy sighs in response and I was glad. Sadia was still eating but I hoped she could feel my stare now, one that said, 'There's some fathering for you, making sure my children eat before I even get to my plate, while you're almost on to your second serving'. I had better heed my own advice and eat something too, since I'd need my strength if everything Dad said about the ritual to come was true. The dunking of my head under the freezing water of the Ganges while I tried not to be swept away or infected by the cholera that no doubt lived in that suspiciously brown water. I had tried to talk to Sadia about it before but she was having none of my equivocating anxiety. She was, instead, clearly excited at the prospect of me being the centre of attention in the family for once, rather than Sunil. I'm sure she had hoped some, if not most, of my light would find its way to her, even though Sunil had organised the entire trip.

I couldn't help but still be intimidated by him. Perhaps it was the age gap – something like 15 years between us – him and my sister getting married when I was only a teenager and then his being more of a father figure to me than my own silent, jaded dad ever was. He carried his own gravity, his own heaviness, in his practicality and silence. And in his protruding belly. He was the sort of man who, despite his tendency to hunch his shoulders when he walked and to wear his trousers too high up on his waist, people instinctively respected. If I was a quiet man, it spoke of my downtrodden, passive nature, but he made his quietude seem considered and eloquent; his silence was the pause between sentences that made you stop and listen to what might come next. And when he did talk, it would always be for some specific purpose, to ascertain where we should be going, what was happening, what needed doing. He didn't do small talk. For this, Sunil was a good man, I was sure of it. But I did wonder whether he had cheated on my sister, if he knew about the 'game' and if he, too, had developed a secret life to keep his own outward facade stable and reliable. A man like him must have some kind of outlet. One thing was for sure, though, he would be so fastidious if he did, there would be no chance of us ever finding out what it was.

I'm certain he thought of me as a failure, but I didn't hold that against him. I kept remembering the time I had asked him to come with me to a used car auction to buy my first motor and once we were there he ended up having to do all the bidding, as no one noticed when I raised my arm to put in an offer. If anything, I had now grown used to being almost invisible and had learned to use it to my advantage. If everyone thought I was too preoccupied with my own life and dissolving marriage to participate in theirs, then I could let them make all the big decisions for me and enjoy the consequences of their hard work in return. Of course, it meant I was silencing myself, but I couldn't have a say in each and every matter. Plus, my own life really was getting to be quite all-consuming. I wasn't sure how anyone had the time to engage in anything else.

At the very least we both knew that John was the real one to pity in this family. That downtrodden, bald Englishman who carried himself with the weighted gait of a man who knew his wife no longer loved him. I knew because I had to stop myself from slipping into it sometimes, too. When Sel and Sadia had fallen out, he had been utterly useless, shrinking further and further into himself as if he could eventually turn inside out and avoid all conflict by ultimately only living within his own spineless mass.

Ever since they had first got together, he had been trying to hold on to Sel – that much everyone could see – as he knew he was punching well above his weight and so he happily put up with her moods, her drama and her taste for a fight. 'Poor John', I had always thought. What a punching bag of a man.

'You're letting your food get cold – what are you thinking about?' Sadia asked sharply.

'Oh, nothing.'

'Well, it's never nothing. Are you worried about today?'

Her earnestness threw me. Maybe she was being kind because she was worried too, because the closest she had come to death was seeing my own mother strewn, bleeding out into the road, and ever since she had been terrified of death's eventuality, constantly checking in on her own parents and nagging me to one day allow them to live with us. I often wanted to ask her if that was the worst thing that had ever happened to her – leaving my mum there to die in the middle of the road.

'It's just so hot out here, isn't it? Even in this air-con I feel like I'm melting, like I can't really breathe or think.'

'If anything, it's too cold in here, they should turn down the air-con, it's like a fridge. Are you sure you're not getting ill or something?' She placed the back of her palm on my forehead, as though I were a child trying to stay home from school.

'No, no, I'll be fine.' I batted the hand away. 'I reckon I'm probably just a bit nervous about the ceremony later today, that's all. I just want to do it properly, get something right with Dad for once.'

'You'll be ok – it's not like they can let tourists go and drown in the Ganges anymore. At the very least the pandit will want to get paid first.'

She let out a hearty cackle and the kids looked up from their plates, bemused but unaware. I smiled too, I couldn't help it, it was the kind of joke my dad would have made.

'Well, exactly. We'd better get a move on anyway, all the others seem to be finishing up. I'll just get this boxed up for the journey.'

I felt a heavy, warm hand on my shoulder and turned around in my chair.

'Ready for this then, big man?' It was Sunil, smiling so I could see the horrible arrangement of his thin, skewered bottom teeth. For a second, I reached to put my hand on his for reassurance but thankfully stopped myself. That would have been admitting too much weakness so early in the day.

'Yes, boss.'

3

I could feel my tongue instinctively reaching for the soft, warm gummy gap at the back of my mouth, the source of the dull ache that was beginning to radiate up into the back of my head and down the base of my neck. As I pushed further into the confines of my own mouth, I could taste the faint bloody tinge of the metallic brace the dentist had installed to keep my surrounding teeth separated from this negative space, until she could drill in a synthetic replacement for the nerve-shot tooth that had once been buried there in my head. It must have been the humidity, or the nerves, that was causing this ache to flare, pulsing with my beating heart like my entire body was fizzing with the force of its uncomfortable being. I fished out a sheet of paracetamol tablets from my rucksack and gingerly swallowed two with a sip of water, tilting my head back each time to make sure they went down and didn't get stuck in my throat.

Everyone seemed to be off in their own world, waiting for the bus to arrive and take us on to wherever it was we were meant to deposit Dad. I looked for Sunil, his presence a reassurance that at least one of us knew where we were going and what we were meant to do, then I looked for Dad – his ashes – boxed up in a tote bag slung on Tara's shoulder, then the kids, both crowding Jay and his phone and whatever he was scrolling through, and then I reached for my own. Still no messages, just the screensaver of my children's faces smiling up at me, waiting to be defiled by whatever digital missive I was waiting for. It was probably the time difference, or lack of Wi-Fi that was to blame. I felt a kick in my insides and wished I had at least saved some of those digital treats for times like this, so I could pull up an image, a brief window into another world, and for a moment forget that I was standing on a filthy roadside, tasting the dust being blown into the back of my throat, the sun already beading sweat on to my greasy forehead, my boxers riding upwards into my ass.

'God, you're as bad as the kids, always on your phone.'

I'd always been suspicious of how little Sadia relied on hers. She must have a crutch of distraction somewhere else.

'I know, sorry, it's become a nervous tic or something. Maybe we should do one of those digital detoxes? You wouldn't find it hard, anyway.' I was only half-serious.

'Oh please, I've given birth to both of your children, giving up checking my emails and texts isn't exactly going to be difficult. Is it?'

I assumed that was rhetorical. My mind was already elsewhere, anyway. Namely on that act of birth and the two times that I had reluctantly witnessed it. The first was before I had learned to drive and had instead nervously spent months watching Sadia's belly expand and putting off the question of how we would actually make it to the hospital when the day came. Apparently calling an ambulance was out of the question, but maybe a taxi? Dad was a notoriously bad driver, so bad in fact that he hadn't been behind the wheel more than a handful of times since he had arrived in England. I realised I had no idea how he'd got Mum to hospital when the three of us were born, although he probably wasn't even there. I couldn't rely on him.

By the time Karan was ready to enter the world, there was still no plan for getting Sadia to the hospital – after failing two driving tests at the age of 18, I had panicked myself into a state of immobility. It was the middle of the night, around 2am, when I felt the warm, sticky wetness of Sadia's waters trickling along my calf, making me suddenly jump awake as I thought I had pissed myself while dreaming again about going to the toilet. Amazingly, she was still asleep, and for a moment, after the bedwetting fear had subsided, I thought she might not be conscious. A shaking of her shoulder sorted that out. She scowled as she awoke to the realisation that our baby was on the way.

'We need to get to the hospital.'

'I fucking know that – you should be sorting this out. How are we going to get there?'

Or she said something along those lines. There was definitely a smattering of fucks in there, targeted squarely at my ineptitude.

For some reason, the first number I thought to call wasn't that of the taxi service whose card we had pinned on the kitchen noticeboard but my dad's. Well, I wanted to call my mum but she wasn't anywhere anymore, so before I knew it I was reflexively dialling her landline and listening to the rhythmic chirping of the rings. I came to when my dad eventually answered, his bleary voice brusquely telling me to get to the hospital and to call once the baby was born, not give a blow-by-blow of the labour. I hung up and racked my brain for someone else to rely on.

The next thing I remember is being on the leather-trimmed back seats of Sunil's BMW, him speeding to West Middlesex in his button-down pyjamas, telling me I should really sort out my driving licence and telling Sadia that everything would be ok. She squeezed my hand until the nails dug in and left a line of half-moon imprints all along the ridges of my knuckles. Then there was the commotion of getting her into the ward and on a bed and into a gown and then everything seemed to come to a halt. Her screams merely joined those of the other faceless expectant mothers wailing in a primal unison through the walls. I wished I had brought a magazine or a book to pass the time but instead I busied myself getting her little cups of ice chips to suck on, rubbing between her sweaty shoulders and talking about anything to try and drown out the guttural cacophony coming from all directions. There was nothing optimistic about that place – it was a slaughterhouse of strip lighting and alcohol gel.

The birth itself was seared into my consciousness and I feared it always would be. It seemed to happen so quickly then. After all the waiting and watching the sun rise, suddenly the midwife was in the room and it was time. My legs felt like they might buckle beneath me, while Sadia had taken all the pain medication offered to her and it seemed to make no difference. There was a wildness in her eyes, a frantic fear mixed with anger as she kept screaming, 'Get him out of me.' I looked on in horror, uselessly, as the midwife probed between the folds of her legs, entreating her to push harder until she told us she could see the head. I peeked over the mountain of her knees to witness my wife shit herself into a small net as Karan's skull tore through her. He emerged, eyes open into the world and coated in a dewy fuzz, screaming himself from purple to pink.

At least with Ayla we thought we knew what to expect – our naivety formed a cosy buffer against a world-eating sense of uncertainty. Parenthood hadn't been at all easy with Karan but we knew we didn't want an only child, so the only thing to do seemed to be to try and get the second one out of the way as quickly as possible. I did my part, even though the way I saw Sadia had entirely changed. She was no longer a cold if alluring presence but a forgiving, vulnerable mess of emotion. Sex almost felt like I was taking advantage now, yearning for some attention away from the baby.

At least I had learned to drive. It was an automatic licence and therefore 'not a real licence' according to my dad, Sunil, Tara, Sel, and Sadia too, but it was a means of mobility nonetheless. When her contractions began to attack with a quickening force – this time in the afternoon – I drove home from work, picked up the pre-packed bag for both of us, dropped Karan off at Tara's and then made it all the way to the hospital in one piece. The maternity ward still radiated the febrile tension of a holding pen where unspeakable horrors lurked, but this time I had the latest issue of *GQ* to keep me company.

There wasn't much time to read, though, as it was clear something was wrong from the way the Indian midwife kept addressing me, rather than the woman whose prostrate body she was peering into. It was something to do with the baby being distressed and manoeuvring the umbilical cord dangerously close to her neck, the doctor eventually told us. I kept thinking about poor Sel and her miscarriage only a few years earlier, how she had told me they had to cut the girl from her and afterwards she still wanted to feel the body on her skin, even though it had long since died. Now they were taking Sadia to the operating theatre to cut her open too and I found myself vibrating my arms into a gown and fumbling with a bandana for my sweaty hair as I prayed to any higher power tuning in.

Part III: Rohan

Sadia seemed remarkably calm, resigning herself to the doctor's stern voice. His reassurance that a C-section was the best option washed over her head as she lay back into her pillow, looking upwards and counting her breaths, her eyes glazed and lacking the wildness that came with Karan's arrival. She didn't turn to me once.

I didn't want to know what had become of my wife's soft body beyond the makeshift curtain they had erected to separate the half of her that could still feel from the other half that was numbed and open to the probing hands of the doctor. So I heard her first, that tooth-rattling scream that delivered Ayla into my trembling arms.

When I finally got to hold Karan, I was nervous about experiencing that life-changing electric pulse of love that all new parents couldn't stop talking about – the realisation that now your life wasn't your own, it was entirely owned by another. Those thoughts only made me want to run somewhere far away and forget I had ever had this much responsibility. But when he came, there was a crackle of something that pushed through my body as soon as his squirming mass was placed on me, a charge that pulled my head down to touch his own, to feel the warmth of his miniature, yielding forehead. A primal togetherness. With Ayla, she was in my hands before I could ready myself, and it was there that she suddenly stopped crying and hushed to a whimper instead, her tiny heart beating so fast from the strain of being born I could feel it merging with the pulse coursing along the side of my neck.

I wondered if my dad had ever felt the same about me when I was born. If our blood ever pulsed the same; if he placed his forehead to mine. Or, maybe he knew he didn't like me from the start.

'Everything is going to be ok. Everything is going to be ok.'
I kept whispering the mantra as much to myself as to Ayla.

I should have offered to take the ashes from Tara but I could
see Sel had beaten me to it, the two of them now huffing on to
the orange bus we had commandeered for the trip. I wanted to
sit with my family, to be surrounded by their closeness again
– physically, if not emotionally – but by the time I'd made
sure our luggage was stacked deep in the bowels of the bus the
only place left for me was a seat at the front, by Sunil and the
driver, among the men. I could have playfully taken Sel's bag
from next to her and sat down there but I could see she was
exhausted. Tara, meanwhile, just looked like she could use the
space to think and be alone.

'Right, everyone on? Let's go.'

The bus let out a long hiss as we lurched forwards, pulling
out so abruptly on to the main road and into the oncoming
traffic that I let out a gasp and felt for my seatbelt. Of course,
there was none.

I opened the soggy box of lukewarm breakfast leftovers
instead and began scooping them into my mouth, my cheeks
puckering at the bitter spices while I listened to Sunil as he spoke
in broken Punjabi to the driver. I had forgotten how he could
engage someone in conversation for what felt like hours, only if
he was interested – a fate that usually befell labourers, waiters
and female shop assistants. I wished I could talk like that too,
filling the air with my confidence. Instead, I would run out of
breath before the sentences were over, sometimes mid-word,
while my underarms sweated and I gasped for air. I don't know
why I rushed every time I opened my mouth, but it was like I
had to speed through before the listener realised I was speaking.

'He's got six children, can you believe it?' Sunil turned to me.

'Who, the driver?'

'Yep, don't worry, he can't understand what we're saying. But he looks too young to have that many kids, don't you think? Must've had one of those village marriages when he was 13, his first child by 16. Can you imagine?'

I could not.

'That's mad. How does he even remember all of their names?'

Of course he remembered their names, they were his own children. I flushed with embarrassment.

Luckily, Sunil had shifted back to Punjabi, so I looked out the window, noting how the city's low-rises whipped past like the traces of a drying brushstroke on paper. The skyline was undulating.

I could have asked him: How many lives do we lead?

Jitana ho sakata hai.

What makes a life make sense?

Saans lena yaad hai.

But I had a line from a song stuck in my head instead, the one about dancing with tears in your eyes and songs making you cry. I couldn't remember the name or the tune, just that aching, foreign sense of wanting to be alone and to weep on a dancefloor. The fantasy that feeds a feeling. Was it the Bee Gees?

4

I had a sudden flash of my dad's body in the hospital bed, his torso sunken into the scratching sheets, his eyes milky and barely open, the machines huffing like he was so gently asleep. I just sat there watching, trying to be as silent as I could, marvelling at how this mountain of a man was now so small, so quiet.

Did I ever stop fearing him? Being back here meant always feeling the soft breaking waves of nostalgia in the pit of my stomach, those aching pangs telling me to endlessly remember my childhood, past relationships and just how I had come to be this gangly, corduroy-wearing man with a sallow face, salt-and-pepper hair and a continuing inability to grow a full beard. Thinking back as my head banged on the vibrating window and we wound our way upwards, I couldn't remember exactly when I began to fear him, but I had an inkling.

I remembered the geometric-patterned maze of brown carpet that covered every inch of the floor of the house in Bournemouth, an itchy close-woven pile that never got clean no matter how much my mum and Tara hoovered. It was a busy house, the three of us kids, Mum and Dad, Uncle Raj, his wife and their daughter, all squeezed into this terraced two-up-two-down. That was the entirety of my existence then. I didn't remember much about the outside world, apart from my dry knees freezing in grey shorts on the way to school and stopping at the corner shop on the way home to steal strawberry laces.

Call it boyish cheekiness, an insatiable sweet-tooth, or a willingness to do wrong – to be wrong – but I couldn't help myself. There was such a rush in dipping my hand into the plastic pick 'n' mix container directly under Mr Shah's counter and stuffing the laces into my linty pocket, not once taking my eyes off his wizened face. He had always seemed a nice, sensitive man, a friend of my father, and in hindsight I wondered if he had known what I was doing and simply allowed it to happen – better I steal here under his gaze than out in the real world where I could get into real trouble. Either way, it became part of my daily routine: obedience to the point of total silence at school, keep to my two or three friends in the playground, steal the laces on the way home and then store them in my pockets to savour after dinner each night, twisting them through my fingers as I sucked each one into my mouth, slobbering down my chin with saliva.

I remembered too, with the sharp force of realisation, the one time I decided to bring this kleptomania home. I must have been only seven or eight and my existence was largely overlooked in the general chaos of the household: Tara was being treated like a maid by our aunt, Sel had retreated into her own world of attention-seeking melodrama, and our parents were already at peace with the loveless trajectory of their marriage. There I withdrew into the role of a quiet observer, never wanting to make trouble, always too happy to be doted upon as the youngest. One year, the chocolate factory Mum worked at had a fault with a batch of their Easter eggs – something to do with a destabilised milk stabiliser – and so they chucked an entire line, hundreds of treats discarded thanks to the slightly bitter aftertaste they left. It was all free to take home for the workers, though, the bitterness seemingly no issue for their poor immigrant palates, and so I remember Mum coming back with an entire black bin bag full of chocolate, depositing one egg for each of us kids in the kitchen cupboard, only to be eaten at the weekend. Of course, I could not wait, so I devised what I thought was an ingenious plan: to sneak down to the kitchen early in the morning, before my mum would be up to make her breakfast tea, carefully pull the foil wrappers from the shells and run my teeth along the cold shape of them, scraping as much chocolate as I could from each one before packaging them back up. For days I did this, looking through the kitchen door into the back garden and listening for noises upstairs, eating tiny shavings from each egg, mindful not to break through their structure, before gingerly placing them back on the shelf and returning to the warmth of bed, sated with the knowledge that I had done something only I knew about, something that would satisfy only me. I never thought about the consequences, that come Saturday morning my sister would rush to the kitchen – not Tar, she was too old to care – tear off the now-sticky, brown-smudged foil and look on in horror as she saw that something had gnawed at her smooth gift-egg, reducing it to a gnarled, flimsy mass. Sel squealed as if she herself had been violated and dropped hers to the floor, sending my dad straight down into the kitchen where I looked on sheepishly, my own egg, of course, untouched, preserved for its full enjoyment. He took one look at me, put on his glasses, looked at me again and grabbed me by the scruff of the neck, dragging me into our small back garden. I'm not sure why he wanted me outside but half way down the cracked pathway he stopped and turned my face to his, asking if I had eaten my sister's eggs. I let out a nervous giggle in response, so he threw me down and kicked me once right on the meat of my buttocks and then again on my side below my ribs. I whimpered on the wet grass, shocked by his force. He grabbed me by the neck once more but Tar ran out and shouted at him to stop, and for some reason he did, breathing on her and then huffing his way back into the house.

I think that might have been the last time I can remember him touching me. After leaving me there, hunched over the damp grass, crying into my sister's shoulder, I couldn't recall a hug, or a handshake, or even a pat on the shoulder from him.

I don't know why I was the one to eventually take his hand when he was lying in the hospital bed, dying of cancer. I was shocked by how soft his palms were, recoiling reflexively as if I had touched the burning blue cone of a flame. Tar and Sel just looked on, holding their own children.

That regimented, chocolate egg-eating cycle of denial, satisfaction and pleasurable guilt has since followed me into the rest of my life. My eating has remained routine: breakfast always a small bowl of cereal, lunch a sandwich at 12.30pm and dinner by no later than 6.30pm, with each meal confined to a single plate or bowl. Those gnawing pangs of hunger have become a satisfaction in themselves, a bodily reminder of my self-control, my ability to override even the most primal of functions. Meanwhile, I made sure my kids had whatever they wanted, whenever they wanted it. No matter how angry they made me, I only ever hugged them.

Here, though, routine was a foreign concept. The days swam by in a soupy heat and uncertainty, while I allowed myself to indulge in whatever I wanted, along with the kids; an entire curry for breakfast, beer for lunch, jalebis and gulab jamuns and rasmalai with dinner. Perhaps that beating had brought with it the first fear of consequence, an understanding of the 'real world' trouble I had flirted with at Mr Shah's, as well as an awareness of my own shifting body – its wants, needs and pains.

Maybe the hunger for self-control, for hunger itself, was just a defence against the unpredictability of the world outside – a need to retreat to the safety within.

A time to feel.

Here and now, I might have finally been free to do as I pleased. To be brave again.

'Right, we're here, time for lunch,' Sunil announced. The coach heaved to a stop next to a squat roadside building.

Or, it was just another way to say fuck you. For the first time.

5

It seemed to take an age to get everyone awake and off the bus, each of us in our own little dreams, fantasising. It appeared this was the only place fit for tourists like us to stop for lunch, but nothing about the whitewashed bungalow looked sanitary.

Sunil was walking ahead, with the driver looking like his child next to him. I noticed he had begun to hobble, with his hands clasped behind his back making him stoop forward over his belly like a concerned priest surveying the parish grounds. I could tell the kids felt uncomfortable since they rushed up to walk next to me. I wasn't sure what protection I could provide – the two men crouched either side of the doorway, smoking and spitting idly into the dust were intimidating enough already. My shoulders began to tense.

'What is this place?' Sel asked.

'God knows, I just really hope we don't get sick eating here – it looks a bit ropey.'

'Yep, the last time I was in India I got the worst shits, they lasted for pretty much the whole trip, I was so scared I'd be shitting myself on the plane home.'

I couldn't help but let out a belly laugh while Jay complained. Shit humour still tickled me.

She was right to be cautious; walking into the humid dining hall it was clear we were about to be ripped off. The first tell-tale sign was a rickety table full of packets of Airwaves chewing gum, Pringles and bottles of shining, lukewarm Coke drawing the kids' attention like a beacon of familiarity among the mess. I had to physically pull Ayla back from grabbing at the packets of crisps, conditioned like the little consuming robot that she was. I'd like a packet of gum for myself but I knew Sadia wouldn't allow it now the kids were pleading; one wrong move and the floodgates would open for purchases.

There was no one sitting at the kiosk, though, and no one seemed to be watching it either. The waiters were either loitering in the fly-infested kitchen, their teal shirts untucked and their bare feet flicking off their sandals to rub their calves, or tending to two tables of rotund white tourists sipping their soft drinks gingerly through straws and picking at a plate of green sludge with shards of naan. I was moving before I fully understood what I was doing. I brushed past and palmed a packet of Spearmint sticks, feeling my heart flutter into my throat and my chest heaving for a big gulp of air. I wasn't sure what I was trying to prove but, at the very least, I could still steal.

I was hesitant to touch the laminated menu, let alone sample its wares, but I knew I should probably eat. I heard John reel off the various options and was tempted to order a big bottle of Kingfisher and slowly sip it from the tiny milk glasses they had on our table, letting its fizzy coldness sting my teeth as the others rolled the dice on meat and dairy. But I guessed I had to keep my body purified for whatever ceremony was to come, at least physically if not mentally. I desperately wanted to check my phone to see if Vicky had messaged me back, to feel that rush of reciprocity, to get back to my real online life. I wondered where she might be and what she might be doing right now. She would be just waking up, willing herself to leave the warm bubble of her duvet and to get ready for a day's work; slipping off her nightie and running the shower, testing its temperature before stepping in, soaping herself, lingering perhaps for a moment and feeling the water rain through her hair, towelling dry, putting on her makeup while the radio played softly in the background, pulling on a skirt. Or, getting out of bed to sit on the toilet, aching for a shit before her children ran screaming into the room, demanding her attention, piercing her need for peace and adding to the trace of those dark bags under her eyes.

Was there a man sleeping in her bed too?

'You're off again in your own world – you haven't said a word since we got here. What is it with you today?' Sadia barked.

Was she thinking of me?

'Oh, sorry, I was just thinking. I'll have the dal – that seems safest, doesn't it?'

Probably not.

'Better just get some cokes for us all too; I'm not sure the water will be ok.'

I had never really been alone. First, I was surrounded by my family and watched over by my mother and sisters, then there was Misha, young and naive and hopeful, then I retreated back to my mother, wishing all women would be more like her, never wanting too much, never reaching too far, and then I latched on to Sadia, both of us trying to stoke the embers of a romance dampened by its impossibility ever since. Did I really know what it was like to be in my own company, to rely only upon myself? I had always defined myself in relation to – or in addition to – others, wanting to lose myself in my partner, making each decision like it was a consultation, never leaving anything to spontaneity or chance.

But something changed when Mum died. And the only person I thought I could rely on to help bridge the gap between 'before' and 'after' was Sadia – the new constant in my life, the only person to actually see her die, and to be self-interested enough to walk away. A person who could still pity me and help me suffer, rather than expect support for her own problems. I suppose I hadn't supported her since either, emotionally at least. I just expected to remain the centre of my own universe, never alone.

I didn't know what loss was as I'd never taken the time to let it sink into me, to understand why it wanted to pull my entire being deep into itself. I had just put it aside in a box, something to be unwrapped at unguarded, quiet moments, nibbled on, and then put back, safe in the knowledge that I would never have to fully confront its bitter reality. But here was another loss, one that I thought I was ready for – hoping for? – and it was one that felt different, that just gently took its fat finger and knocked that box off its shelf, spilling the damp, rotting contents over the carpet and leaving me to sift through the pieces. I had never spoken this to anyone, never thought to open my mouth and let that brokenness out, to let myself out.

Maybe I wanted to. Maybe I at least wanted to know how.

'This looks alright, you know, Dad.'

'Yes, it'll be ok. Everything will be ok.'

6

I wondered about my name. Between shakes of the bus making burps of garlic-tinged dal crawl up the back of my throat, I began to think of its meaning. A name strictly for boys – unusual when it comes to the typical androgyny of Indian naming. I remember the pandit once telling me as a child that in Sanskrit it translated as 'ascending'. Climbing, rising – to where I wondered? It seemed a name full of hope and potentiality but as I had grown older it also became laden with a pressure to achieve its promise. It was a name to evoke the sensation of climbing upwards to the thin, lonely air of our grey skies. Because once you named something, it was fixed forever. Or, it became fixed once you figured out what it was supposed to mean. Then, you hardened yourself to it; you looked at it differently and coldly, as a challenge or an 'other'. You realised that this label didn't fit with the unnamed body you had grown into, rather it was an advertisement for who your parents had thought you could be. Now, who you would not be.

In fact, I didn't like labelling things at all. With Misha, for instance, the possibility of sex – that fraught tension between flirtation and intimacy – was what made our immature love work. Once the naming of a relationship, and especially marriage, was spelled out, something solidified in us. Suddenly we weren't floating anymore, we were walking down the same path our parents and their parents had – the future was heavy, weighed down with responsibility and the difficulty of acceptance. I swore after Misha that I would keep things light to free myself from all the baggage that was stopping me from living out my named existence. Then I got sad and lonely and settled for the first person who gave me the slightest bit of attention.

When I named my children, we just chose whatever sounded nice and would be easy to pronounce. I wasn't sure I even knew what theirs meant.

'Beautiful, isn't it?'

I looked out of the window to follow Sunil's gaze. The Ganges was weaving into view, somehow less grandiose but still more intimidating than I had imagined; a choppy bottle-green mass bordered by thick clumps of washed-up detritus and the specks of bodies bending into it, bathing or crawling along like marks on the chalky gravel of the shore. I thought I saw a boy who looked just like me.

'Finally, we reach the end.'

'Well, not quite, we need to get you in that thing first – if what Dad had said was true.'

It was almost imperceptible but Sunil had started referring to my dad – his father-in-law – as Dad. Sadia had done this since the day we got married and it never failed to make me cringe; each time her tongue hit her teeth it was a grovelling, shameless attempt to keep in his good books. I don't recall her ever calling my mum Mum, though.

I suspected Sunil was closer to my dad than his own – he was my father's golden boy, the responsible, reliable man I am sure he had wished I would be – whereas I had never even met Sunil's father. He had lived somewhere up north but died by the time Sunil was 19, just after he met Tara, and he had hardly mentioned him since. Tar had implied that he was a quiet, stern man – even more silent and foreboding than our own father, it seemed – and that his death when it came, silently in the night, was something of a relief, an act that could release Sunil from the pressures of his family life into a new adulthood. That was with his widowed mother in tow, of course. Her, I had met, and all I could remember was her consistently unsmiling presence as she sat in the spare room of Tar's house, watching TV, flicking channels on anything and everything from the *Ramayana* to *Big Brother*. There was something calming about her quiet predictability though, knowing that there she would be at every family function, placed in the corner of the room and talking to my dad in Punjabi, both struggling to hear each other over the noise and neither having anything in particular to say to the other.

I wondered how Tara felt about her husband's new dad, or about how our dad softened to her when he accepted Sunil into the family – as if her choice of husband had suddenly made her worthwhile. It must have been so tough for her being the eldest, having to essentially parent the rest of us and look out for our mum while he was out god knows where, passing the time betting or just walking to remind himself that he was capable of still moving, that there was still somewhere to go. Maybe he was so absent because he wanted us to want him, but all it achieved was to make us realise we were much happier with him gone. The door closing as he left was a weight lifting. Then Tara could take over, her and my mother a pure force of maternal protection, and when Dad returned it was like he could feel it – taste our resentment thick in the air – and he hated us for it. This powerless man who had felt no respect or appreciation from the world and who thought it was his right to be shown it at home, now realised he would have to earn that too.

It was better just to sit back and let it not happen.

Sunil couldn't have known all of this – he wasn't there – and instead, he might have been the only one of us to truly love our dad. Perhaps he even understood him. At the funeral service back in London, he was the one nodding his head solemnly, shaking everyone's hands and thanking them for coming. He was the one who sobbed when we played the *Hanuman Chalisa* and the coffin withdrew behind the velvet curtains. The other three of us just looked down at our shoes, digging our nails into the palms of our hands, trying to muster up the spectacle required of us.

'You're an orphan now, Dad,' I remember Ayla telling me. And that made me laugh, a little too loudly. It was the way that she said it so cheerily, as if it was a special badge of honour I had now, something to set me apart from all the other dads, rather than a confirmation of my eternal aloneness.

'Hey, thank you for organising all of this, by the way. I don't think I've said it before but I know it must have taken a lot of work and I know we all really appreciate it.'

I felt an overwhelming need to thank Sunil for being the only one who had loved my dad, the only person who showed him some appreciation while he was still alive. All I could do now was feel an immaculate, burning guilt for my neglect and hope to repent through this ceremony I was scared to take part in. Or, if Dad wasn't around anymore to forgive me, maybe Sunil could.

'Oh, of course, it's no problem at all, you know that. Happy to help.' He smiled, like all he had done was pick up milk from the garage on the way home.

'Can I ask you something?'

A pause. 'Yep, sure, go ahead.'

'Where do you think he is now?'

'Who?'

'Well, Dad. I mean, do you think he's still around us somewhere? Or even reincarnated?'

'He won't be reincarnated until we put his ashes in the Ganges, apparently. But I'm not too sure I believe all of that really – I've never given it much thought – I suppose he's just gone, isn't he?' He waited, I hoped not for an answer from me. 'Yes, he lived and he had his children and grandchildren and now he's just gone, he's in a box back there, and soon we'll be putting him into the river near where he was born where he will sink into the soil and become part of the ground he used to walk to school on when he was a kid. Remember that story he always used to tell, about walking barefoot with the biscuits in the bin? Or, was that in Kenya? I can't remember.'

'Yes, Kenya I think, but I know what you mean. I suppose that means he's just in our memories now – the longer we talk about him, the more we'll keep him alive, in some way?'

'It's like with your mum – I didn't know her for too long before she went and the kids definitely not, but the way that Tar talks about her always, it's like she's with us still. She's living in the house, in the photos, in our heads, you know? Maybe that means her spirit lives in our talking and in the stories we tell each other. Once we stop telling those, what else is left?'

'The photos, I suppose, but then no one would really know who it was in them.'

A long pause. The coach narrowly avoided heading straight into another lorry turning the corner, both drivers tooting their horns like Morse code, signalling their existence.

'What about your dad?'

'What about him?'

'Well, I suppose, I've only ever seen pictures of him... You don't speak of him much.'

I wasn't sure why I had blurted that out and for a second it felt like I had crossed an invisible line – a boundary between men, one that smothered unprocessed, unspeakable feelings. I couldn't tell with Sunil. He would radiate calm placidity with an authoritative force, or he might occasionally explode.

'That's because he was a difficult man. He was quiet, he never really let anyone get too close to him – especially not us. I suppose I never got to talk to him, to properly understand him. I just left, got on with my own life and then he died.'

Sunil's kids would joke about his propensity to explode, comparing it to those old cartoons of rage billowing as steam from a man's ears, his reddened face hot with blood. I had seen it once myself and realised it was no laughing matter. It was something to do with a wrong booking on a family holiday years ago, nothing that couldn't be resolved pretty easily, but there was a way that the (white) manager spoke to him, a certain tone, and then they were standing almost nose to nose, bellies touching, Sunil thrusting his finger in the direction of the manager's chest, speak-shouting and saying that this was unacceptable, ridiculous, a total joke, a waste of time, to never speak to him like that again. I just stood aside with Tara and silently started to sweat. The other man flushed pink, gently shaking his head, careful not to make eye contact. Everyone was staring at us.

'To tell you the truth, I barely think about him anymore. Sometimes I forget I even had a father. It's funny really, how you can just learn to never think about who or where you came from,' he continued, calmly.

'I suppose I don't spend much time in the past either.' I felt I should share something since he was being so open. 'Although, I feel like I need to more and more these days, especially with the kids getting older and asking more questions.'

'Like what?'

'Well, just what my childhood was like, what we were all like as kids, how I could ever stay sane without the internet. I think they see me as more of an actual human now, rather than just their dad.'

'It's a responsibility that, to be seen as a person. I don't think I realised it for a few years, not until Amar came along at least, and by then I might have given too much away. Maybe I should have protected them a bit more from my life, from how it really was, and just stayed their dad, you know?'

'How do you mean?'

'Just my moods.' Another pause. 'How I'd let the world outside the house sink into me and become part of me. I couldn't let it go. I couldn't give them the image of an easy adult life they might have needed from me. But then, what does that even mean? Shouldn't they just be happy they were always provided for, that I never raised a hand to them? It's much more than I can say about my dad.'

'They have to understand the world at some point; it's no bad thing that you were honest with them at least. It's better than my dad ever was with us.' My face was getting hot. Sunil was, unusually, beginning to meander.

'He was almost too honest, though. Maybe you were too

young to see but I could read it on his face – how everything in his life that was out of his control had become personal, a failing specially made for him to always carry around. People talk about some men carrying the weight of the world on their shoulders – that was your dad. And it was slowly crushing him, pushing him further and further into himself, into that silence.' Sunil was looking ahead at the road, never once at me.

'Nothing is really in our control, though, is it? We just have to accept that.'

'If we all thought like that, there would be no way we could ever achieve anything. Some things you have to fight for, surely. Otherwise, what's the point? May as well just sit back and let life happen to you. You must have fought for lots already in your life?'

'Yes, you're probably right.' I wasn't sure.

'Anyway, at least your dad was much kinder to me than mine ever was. At least he had that decency in him.'

'And now he's gone too.'

'Yep, that's just the way. We'll all be gone soon.'

'Do your kids never ask about him? About your dad, I mean?'

'Not once – he really is just a relic to them. A picture.'

I hadn't noticed that Tara had moved up the coach to sit behind us but now I felt her shift forward in her seat. I wondered how much she had heard. Surely she must have known more about Sunil's father and what his death had meant to him? She had at least met the man.

'What are you two talking about?' she probed.

'Oh, nothing, Rohan was just asking about my dad.'

'Oh really, why? Digging for something?'

I blushed instinctively. 'No, no, just thinking about our dad and dads in general I suppose. Like what it means to be one.'

'I wasn't sure what I'd be like as a mother – if I could be as loving as Mum was. But now I see that the kids just take over your life and make nothing else really feel important. All of the bullshit we used to worry about doesn't matter anymore because now it's all about making their lives as abundant as I can. Like they can just go out into the world and pick whatever they want.'

She looked tired. Tired but determined to speak.

'Pick from what?'

'From anything. From the tree – of life? I don't know, but just to feel confident out in the world, not to always be taken for a mug or to be looked over as soon as you're seen. You know what I mean anyway. To feel like they can just do it.'

'Like Nike,' I added, uncomfortably.

'What?'

'Oh, just a joke. Anyway.'

That had killed the conversation. But I felt like Tara was right. The only thing we, as parents, could work towards was to give our kids a sense of freedom to be whoever they wanted to be, to follow their desires, rather than feel the pressure merely to make the decisions they needed to make to survive, as we and our parents had. There were no choices in that past. But some things, like this freedom, are so far from the realm of our imaginations that when they happen, they still seem an impossibility. When would we know our kids really had room to breathe? To be able to step into themselves and out of us?

For now, anyway, I was wondering when we would ever arrive at our destination. We had been on this coach for what had seemed like hours since lunch, winding queasily up hillsides then back down, cutting through greenery and into the brown dust of these ramshackle village towns. I wanted to ask when we would get there – wherever it was we were meant to be going – but I was scared to awaken that impulse in the kids too. We were rattling along a flat, open highway where small men worked the fields on either side, hunched over and hacking at the prickly grass. They seemed impervious to the heat and humidity, focused only on the ground in front and the meagre wage waiting for them. We could do with more of that work ethic back in the UK – put a white man in work and he'll always find his way out, Dad used to say – and I couldn't remember the last time I actually saw a white man sweat, really put his back into something and feel its consequence. No, they just waited for everything to be brought to them instead. Even the poor ones, they felt the world owed them something, and the arrogance was breathtaking. Maybe that was the real difference between being brown and being white: we knew that no one owed us anything. In fact, anything we had managed to stake a claim to we knew they would try and take away, whereas they saw everything as their God-given right and us lot as thieves. I hadn't done much backbreaking manual labour myself, but that was beside the point; at least I had to fight for what I had achieved.

Just thinking about the state of it all made me clench my teeth with anger and now the bases of my thighs were throbbing into the muscle. I could feel something aching in my stomach, a familiar, unavoidable fizzing that was causing my left leg to shake.

'God, you know what, I actually really need to pee. Sorry, I've just realised but is there any way we can get the driver to stop quickly, Sunil?'

Part III: Rohan

There was, of course, no functioning toilet on the bus and, as Sunil spoke to the driver, he nodded and proceeded to jerkily pull over to the side of a brown field, lifting the creaking lever to open the doors. The men stopped working to peer over at me curiously as I gingerly stepped out, feeling the warm air envelop my throat. I couldn't just set down here and piss on the side of the bus, but there was nowhere else that might give me cover from these prying eyes. I hoped they wouldn't come over and say anything. Surely everyone just pissed wherever they liked here – something about having fewer social norms?

I paced down to the rear wheels, where everyone inside might be able to see me least, turned my back to them and then fumbled with my zipper to pull out my flaccid dick, making sure to try and cover it with the palm of my left hand as I did, my thumb keeping the waistband of my pants down.

Pissing used to be such an enjoyable, carefree experience. I remembered how I would purposefully hold it in when I was at home, almost to bursting, knowing that there was a toilet nearby for me to use when I absolutely needed it and playing with the tension between restraint and satisfaction. When I did run to the toilet, I'd release that steaming stream of urine with a deep sigh – it was almost orgasmic, almost my first sensual experience. Now, though, pissing was a fraught matter, much like everything else. Even if I was bursting to go, like this very minute, for some reason my sphincter would clamp down as soon as I needed to release, as if my own body was playing a game of wills against my mind. When this had first started, maybe two or three years ago, I would panic at the urinal, squeezing with all my might and becoming increasingly nervous that someone would see me just standing there, dick in hand, waiting like a pervert. I soon realised that the key was to try and relax, to think of something else entirely, and then it would come – first tentatively and then full of warm, spraying force. It was no different standing in this heat, knowing I was keeping everyone on the bus waiting, feeling the eyes of those workmen judging me for my impotence as I tried to defile their land. I had never pissed on an Indian field before. I scanned the horizon in front of me, trying to focus on anything that might give me some distraction, but this was a soulless expanse, a flatness of dry grass and air, a place in which you felt none of the softness of nature nor its wonder, just the largeness of it bearing down on you, crushing you into your own small presence.

I thought about how I had never felt safe or welcomed out in the natural world. I took a certain comfort in the greyness of the city, how its fragmented chaos was navigable – there I knew my place and everyone acted accordingly. Out in the open, the potential for unpredictability seemed ever-present and any moment could be engulfed by wildness as the chaos was no longer of our own making. Only white people seemed to really enjoy being out in nature, supposedly losing themselves in the beauty of trees, flowers and sprites while making sure that this was still a space where their unrivalled self-confidence continued, where they felt safe in the face of any danger. I didn't really see much beauty in nature, even in our manicured parks and gardens. All I could see was the only consistent truth of our existences: everyone and everything fighting with itself and each other to survive; branches trying to colonise the sky and forcing their way upwards; grass threatening to ensnare our every step; insects aiming for our mouths and ears, worming their way into our warm, safe bodies. I wanted to get back into the air-conditioned safety of the bus before the outside could penetrate me, before I could smell its wind on my hair and clothes. But at least I was pissing now, a stream darkening a curved line into the raw earth of the roadside. I hadn't seen that a sizeable spray was also fanning out from the tip of my dick, misting my crotch and trousers with its excess, gushing with a misguided force too powerful to be contained.

'Fuck. Fuck's sake.'

I tried to shake the last drops of urine from my veiny foreskin, zipping up and buttoning my trousers and smoothing down their front, with dark patches of moisture blotching both legs. I sheepishly stepped back on to the bus, hoping no one would notice my embarrassment, or my suspiciously damp hands. As I sat down into the cool, itching felt of my seat, I could smell the sweet musk of my trousers wafting up to me. A rush of saliva surged from the back of my throat and my tongue thrust forwards as I gagged into the fist of my hand.

7

Finally, we arrived. Could a country have its own smell? If it did, England's was a mix of fresh laundry, gritters' salt and clods of damp mud – something homely, earthy and manageable. In India, the smell got everywhere. It was close to the inside of old books, the waft of dust that came with a spine cracked for the first time in years, mixed with a touch of sweet rosewater and an acrid kick of diesel; the type of smell that would embed itself in your clothes, hair and skin, surprising you with its presence when you opened your suitcase back at home. It reminded you where you had come from.

That smell thrust my face into its musty armpit when I first stepped out into the makeshift car park. Makeshift since it was a dozen or so buses and cars parked among what also looked like a local market. There was a set of brownish-pink meat carcasses hanging on one side by a man smoking on a camping chair. Another was cutting hair under a tree with a pair of what seemed like tailor's scissors, the flat plates of metal scything through streaks of black. The three boys had run off the coach to find a toilet as soon as we parked and were now lined up at an outdoor urinal, twisting towards Tara's camera with their backs to us as they pissed freely into the trough. Sunil, meanwhile, was talking quietly but insistently to the driver, trying to work out where we needed to go to find our pandit.

Part III: Rohan

I noticed a misty cloud smudging up against the back of Tara and Sel's legs, one that moved as I turned my head to the side and faced Sadia, now softly fogging her cheek. I took my glasses off and lifted them to the light, noticing that they were covered in greasy fingerprints. I placed the base of each lens into my mouth, breathing on them gently and rubbing them with the tails of my shirt between my thumb and forefingers.

I had always hated wearing glasses as a child. First, because the kids at school would call me four-eyes and because I hated how they made my eyes look so big and buggy in proportion to the rest of my face. Then, as I grew older, I thought they made me look effeminate and bookish, since every time I went to clean them, I had to do so delicately, knowing that if they ever broke I would have to sellotape the pieces together rather than be able to buy a replacement pair.

I remembered the first time Misha and I kissed; she so confidently lifted the frames from my nose with her vibrating hands and put her arms over my shoulders, pressing her lips on to mine as I felt the twin mounds of her bra push into my chest, like two things fitting together so easily. But I was only thinking that I needed my glasses back to see and that I hoped she hadn't squashed them in her hands or dropped them accidentally. I was thinking other things, too.

Once I had earned some real money, I began buying contact lenses and was amazed by my limitless field of vision and equally frustrated by but also fixated with the nightly ritual of dousing them in a mystery solution and placing them in a submerged case in my bathroom cabinet. After years of living with small children, routine became both a sanctuary and a curse and then I found myself going back to my glasses. They were the first thing I could find to allow me to see when they would come screaming into the room or when I heard them cry out like small animals in the night. Now, I quite enjoyed the limited sight contained in these two rectangles and the ability, like at this very moment, to take them off and see only the blur that lay in front of me, this destruction of detail. It was like watching the air, rather than everything sitting in it. My glasses were a prop, something to be flourished and waved around. Perhaps I had embraced my effeminacy.

That was something I could tell had always repulsed my dad too. The way my hand would sometimes bend forward at the wrist when my arm was resting and relaxed, or the way I might throw my head back when I was really laughing, or how I could never quite look him in the eye. One of my strongest memories as a boy, apart from Tara stepping in to stop my beating, was of him talking to Mum in the kitchen, saying he was worried they had raised a 'sissy boy' because I spent too much time with her, always clutching the folds in her saris and pulling at her chunni, asking to be held by her. I tottered into the room and she saw me; she swept me up in those strong arms while my dad just looked at me and walked away. I think he wanted me to hear exactly what he thought of his only son. And as I came to know what a 'sissy boy' really meant, at the height of the AIDS fear, I too joined in with the other young men I knew, shouting slurs at anyone we thought might be gay and who had the audacity to be seen outdoors, rather than staying at home and living in their shame as they should. Of course, when I was alone and I saw the rare sight of two men holding hands or just being together in that way you knew wasn't only friendship, I wished I could have been as brave. But I was also so thankful I didn't have to be, that the only person I needed to become was one who could stand up to his own father. That was something I still hadn't managed to work out.

I wondered what I might do if Karan turned out to be gay. How would I hide the disappointment in my only son? My fear for his protection and safety? My envy of his realisation of who he really was, or at least his confidence in who he thought he could be? And I thought of Jay again, his smile reaching out of my screen like a terrifying vision, knowing that I had seen something I had no right to bear witness to. A taboo.

We were walking now. Sunil must have been privy to some sacred knowledge and I shuffled up next to him and the driver who had decided to accompany us. Not for an additional fee, I hoped.

'Does he know where we're meant to be going?' I asked, tentatively.

'Well, apparently we have to find our pandit by asking but there are thousands of them here, so it could take a while.'

'Surely they'd just lie and say they have our family records, take our money to do the ceremony and we'd be none the wiser?'

'Have a little faith, come on, we can't travel all this way and just go for the first person we come across, can we?'

I was becoming agitated. My heart was thumping and my underarms were sweating, probably from the nervous anticipation of having to go through the ordeal my dad had described to me when he did this same journey for my mum. I had recounted it to the others last night over dinner, how Dad had spoken of finding the pandit with our family's records of births and deaths in a hovel by a tiled open courtyard, how they had then both walked down to the banks of the river, picking up ghee and spices and flower petals along the way from market sellers, and how he had had to wade into the freezing water himself, gripping a chained railing so he would not be swept away, with the pandit dunking his bald head under while he spoke his Sanskrit prayers and only letting him up occasionally to breathe before thrusting him back down into that filthy torrent where he clamped his eyes closed and heard the sounds of its constant movement. I had sworn my dad had told this story to all of us, but for some reason I was the only person who remembered it. As I spoke it into existence, I began to doubt the details while I saw my children's eyes flash in fear and delight at the challenge I was about to face. Sunil had also been here to spread his mum's ashes but his memory was patchy too. He only told us that he walked in up to his waist, then tossed the ashes into the water as the pandit stood on the shore, mumbling. It was all over in five minutes, he said.

There seemed to be something untrustworthy about this place, something that left it unfixed in our imaginations.

'We packed as much mineral water as we could carry and some towels for you, just in case you need to get in. We'll need to make sure none of the river water gets into your mouth, or anywhere else, as it looks filthy, so you'll need to wash yourself down with this after.' Amman handed me a heavy, lumpy bag.

I couldn't quite believe that he had grown up to become a doctor. When did he get so responsible? I still remember him as an overweight, pre-pubescent child with a hatred of authority and a worrying appetite for finding women attractive, staring at them through the window of the bus when I would take him on our semi-regular trips to the Treaty Centre. Then he would make me buy him two-litre bottles of Coke and white chocolate Magnums, stuffing them into his mouth as he asked me about girlfriends and alcohol and what it was like to 'go out'. Then, when he was 16, he just decided that he wanted to be a doctor. Suddenly he listened to his teachers and started handing in his work on time, tucking in his shirts and letting his female fantasies only occupy 60 per cent of his brain, or so I assumed. We always had a connection, I guessed because we were the closest in age in the family, and so I had done my best to act like a big brother to him. But since I had started my own family and he went off to study and then got married himself, we drifted into a strange place. If anything, he seemed older than me now. Or, at least more sure of himself. I could see Karan looking up to him, asking what it was like to be a doctor, implying that my work was unworthy in comparison. It really was.

'Did you bring your swimming trunks, Dad?' Karan asked now, eager to help with the others.

I had not. I had forgotten.

'Oh, I'll just go in with my boxers on, or maybe naked.'

'Dad! You have to take it seriously!'

'Ok, ok, I'm sure the pandit will have a kurta or something I'm meant to wear, don't worry.' Although, when I thought of it, I wasn't too sure that he would. I should have planned better.

It was like an alarm had been going off in my head – in all of our heads – ever since we landed here. At first just a faint ringing, it had grown louder into a shrill, rhythmic droning, pulsing in our skulls the closer we came to reaching the purpose of our journey. Now it played like a siren bouncing between my ears as we snaked our way past the stone-paved banks of the river, crowded with people washing themselves, children playing and selling toys, and groups of shaven-headed devotees, cutting further into narrower passageways where the beginnings of light would break through the overhanging clouds. We jostled among speeding mopeds, waiting cows and throngs of men – this place seemed to be all men – forever pushing forwards in the same singular direction. I tried to make sure everyone was sticking together, craning my head around to catch glimpses of Tar and Sel together bunched up with the kids, visibly stressed by the sheer mass of bodies we were having to negotiate and no doubt worried by the stares of men, questioning their presence, who sweated freely into their yellowed vests and slurped hot tea through the aerating gaps in their teeth.

The sickly smell of dung slapped me as we turned the corner into a brick courtyard full of skinny, fly-flecked cows and yet more men, idling in the crushing heat of the afternoon sun. Sunil had disappeared through what looked like a solid wall with the driver and I rushed forward to find him in a tiny, dark room, speaking to a small man sitting cross-legged on a worn carpet and picking at his toenails. Once he saw me the man stood up and Sunil popped his head out to call for the others to come over and take a look. I wondered whether I should have taken off my shoes, as a sign of respect.

We all began to crowd his doorway. 'Bedi family, from Rishikesh?' he questioned, mumbling.

He then stepped over to a giant iron chest in the corner of the room and heaved open the door to reveal what must have been the scrolls of family records my dad had spoken of. I couldn't quite believe that he had been telling the truth. I was used to his exaggerations and embellishments, those little tricks to make the monotony of his life seem more bearable – like how his dad had once shot a man for reneging on a bet, or how he had tried to smuggle gold bullion from Kenya over to the UK when they first migrated but customs stopped them at the border, having been tipped off, he assumed, by his jealous sister-in-law. I had always thought these stories to be another way for him to buy himself into our imaginations. But maybe they were real. Perhaps he had lived the life he said he did. Either way, there was no way we could know for sure now.

Sunil was answering the pandit and ceremoniously explaining to us the origins of our family line. I wasn't even sure my dad was born in Rishikesh – how could he have known so much?

'Ah, Bedi family, Nairobi and Rishikesh.'

I heard the distinct rumble of a stifled burp as he tossed through another sheaf of pages and then began to shake his head slowly in disappointment. I wondered whether he was playing this up for his audience. Was he expecting some kind of tip for his bookkeeping services? This was not the pandit we were looking for.

I yawned and felt an acidic tear in my upper lip that my tongue immediately darted to, discovering the saltiness of a pitted ulcer that must have been silently growing there ever since we had arrived. It ached deeply and pulled the corner of my mouth down, like a theatrical mask of tragedy, like my body was entering into its own revolt.

A sweaty, skinny young man jostled past the others into the room, crouched by the pandit and whispered into his ear while he continued to shake his head. He went to summon another with a call from his flip phone and this one arrived with a diamante earring and slicked-back hair, giving a small bow only to Sunil as he entered the room. The first young man had written Bedi on the back of his hand in a shaky blue ballpoint and the second was copying it next to the om tattoo on the back of his, each branding themselves with our family name.

'Who are these kids?' I asked the room.

'I think they work for the pandits, looking out for people like us who are trying to find their family records.'

I didn't like being known as 'people like us' but now we were following that glinting earring and shiny hair as the boy bounced back into the courtyard, weaving through the cows and their shit to the river once more. I felt the gentle spray of a mystery liquid on my cheek as we tucked back in among the market stall hawkers, shuddering as I began to imagine what it could be.

Sadia pulled me sharply aside as a spluttering moped rushed through, carrying two women in full saris on its seat.

'Pay attention!'

'Sorry.'

I hoped my kids hadn't heard that exchange. Thankfully, they were tailing behind, gazing slowly at the brass incense holders and curved little dishes for pooja on sale, probably assuming they were ashtrays. I silently prayed that no one would need to stop to find a toilet soon, as I could only imagine the horrors that awaited us there, and then I looked for Dad's ashes, momentarily panicking that we had left them back in the pandit's room. Sunil had them slung over his shoulder in the tote bag, like a giant carrying a bindle. My whole body felt like it was vibrating.

Into another hovel: a line of folded plastic chairs stacked against the concrete wall, a humming fan pushing warm air around the room, a man sitting cross-legged with his trousers riding up to reveal a pair of suspiciously hairless calves, resting his hands on a taut belly and staring into the blue of his phone screen, a yellowing poster of Krishna looking both ridiculous and intimidating, the faint whine of a Bollywood falsetto coming from a TV, a standing man flicking his big toe under the frayed edges of a carpet, the smell of talcum powder and damp, Sunil and the driver holding court beneath the fan.

I checked my phone for messages. Still no signal.

I realised that we had lost one of the pandit's boys along the way, but he was swiftly replaced with a new arrival as we left the hovel and its courtyard full of women washing their feet and clothes. This one was an older man with gingery henna dye on his hair and thick gold rings on his fingers, like one of the men my dad used to go and meet in the local shopping centre after he had retired, sitting on a fake marble plinth and talking the afternoons away in front of Woolworths. I would see him there sometimes if I happened to pop into town after college for an errand, and it was strange to quietly witness him removed from the power he would radiate at home, now just another person trying to make himself heard, forever hunched over when he sat, staring at his feet and into his thin shopping bags. It was the first time I had really noticed that he was getting old. He had become another man with no working purpose and only time to kill. I had never seen him speak in that setting either; he would just sit there and listen, nodding imperceptibly and waiting until it was acceptable to return home for dinner where he could see out the rest of his evening in the forgiving company of his TV, hoping for sleep to come before another day began.

This henna man wrote our name on his hand too and then made another call. I wasn't sure I believed who they were calling or what they were saying – there was clearly no system in place, just a process of casting around in the dark – but all

I needed was to put enough effort into looking, then we could be satisfied we had tried our best when we inevitably failed or realised this was all some scam. None of us read Hindi anyway, so who knew what was even written in those scrolls?

'Do we all need to stick together?' We were already beginning to break apart. 'Can't some of us wait until you have found the right priest at least?' Amman asked.

'It's a pandit, not a priest.' Sunil corrected his son with the exasperation of an underpaid teacher. 'But yes, ok, I'll ask the driver if there's a cafe or somewhere you kids can wait while we look.'

'I doubt there'll be any Prets around but just somewhere to sit in the shade would be good, maybe somewhere with a working toilet.'

I heard the burst of my son's laugh. 'Yeah, it's so dirty here!' Followed by the hiss of Sadia immediately shushing him. She was embarrassed and, judging by the heat that was coming through my cheeks and forehead, so was I. There were some things you just didn't say. We should have at least kept up the illusion that we were home, that this was where we belonged.

But it was the boredom of it all that had caught me by surprise. The overwhelm and the stress and the heat and the exhaustion I was expecting, but the long periods where everything plateaued? Where I felt transfixed by my inability to engage with anyone or anything around me – simply waiting? That I was not expecting. I felt like a child again, being dragged around the aisles of the supermarket as my mum looked for the best deals for us, knowing that there were no distractions for me here, no time at least to imagine we were somewhere else, as we moved forever forwards, circling closer and closer to the place where we had begun.

Part III: Rohan

I was following Sunil in a wake of unfamiliar men, pressing my body through the architecture of this haphazard place, appearing in rooms and alleyways before pausing only to listen, look and then move on, dragging my body where it was told to go. I had thought this would be more exciting, more of a treasure hunt for our ancestry, or an adventurous story for the kids to base their own growing identities around – one where I figured at the centre of it all – but it was just one long queue. Waiting is always the same, wherever you are.

At least we had found ourselves somewhere to rest now and as I sat in the small booth we had taken, I felt the familiar, satisfying warmth of coming indoors after a long walk, smelling the wind on your skin – or the faint tang of urine on your pants – and sensing the need for sleep pulling you further into yourself. Walks were only worth it for the smug accomplishment of returning home.

I realised I never knew what it meant to feel safe. Now I was surrounded by this family – John tucking into a plate of soggy chips, my children making goldfish faces as the steam from the crispy samosas they had bitten into too quickly escaped their mouths, Tara and Sel sharing a glass of lassi like they were kids again, sharing everything, Amman sanitising his hands and cutlery scrupulously, Amar gingerly sipping on a Coke, picking at the pakoras on the table – I hoped that this was it, what we were all meant to be striving for.

I felt Sadia next to me and I remembered when we first met: her forever in a pair of gold hoops and washed blue jeans, the little gap between her front teeth that seemed, somehow, so exotic and unfamiliar. How you could always see the pink of her gums when she smiled properly and wide. I couldn't understand how you could feel so sure of someone and then one day realise they no longer made any sense to you.

'Right, who's staying then?' Sunil had decided to break up our feast.

'I think I'd better sit this one out for now, I'm really feeling the heat.'

Tara looked like the day had really got to her. I could see the bags under her eyes, greying against the pale damp of her skin.

We left her and John and the kids behind, surrounded by their detritus on that sticky table, while we added to our harem of followers with two persistent stray dogs and the third pandit's boy, phoned by the henna man as we ate. This one really was a boy, with his torn jeans and flip-flops and the worried look he seemed to wear permanently on his face – that teenage consternation I now recognised in Karan and in the old family photos of me loping in the backgrounds of celebrations, my corduroys obscenely high-waisted and my head bowed over my bony shoulders, trying my hardest to dissolve into obscurity, to be left alone.

We followed the rhythmic slap of his sandals against the stony roads, spending what must have been our fourth or even fifth hour in the town, looking up to see electrical wires cutting through the murky skies and watching for running kids and careening rickshaws on the ground. I almost reached for Sel's hand, like we used to when we crossed the road as kids.

'You know, this trip has made me think about the strangest things, things I'd forgotten I could even still remember.'

Sunil was talking, perhaps just to pass the time.

'Did you know I went to school with another kid who had my name? I mean, I know it's not the most unusual Indian name, but for a kid in Leeds in the early '70s at a comprehensive school, there weren't too many Asians or even Black people around, never mind someone else called Sunil, spelled the same too. He was a year or two below me and, of course, everyone would lump us together, mistaking us for each other even though we looked nothing alike. He had these buggy eyes that his face still hadn't grown into and he was so scrawny and angular, like a scrunched-up piece of paper, whereas I, well, I just looked like me, didn't I? Anyway, he had this awful stutter and he couldn't get through a single sentence without tripping over his b's or d's or t's and, of course, this was back when if you had a stammer you were seen as "simple", like you were just thick and good for nothing in the world. But the amazing thing about this Sunil was that he was just so clever, such an intelligent, eccentric little kid, always wearing these sleeveless jumpers like he was a geography teacher, and keeping his shoes impeccably polished. It was just that he couldn't speak properly to show the other kids how smart he was, he could only do it on paper, and they didn't care about that. You know there was a lot of bullying going on back then – most of it racist – and he would get pretty picked on, name-calling, people shoving him in the corridors, the odd fight, things like that. I felt some need to look out for him at the beginning – probably because of our name or some kind of "brown kids stick together" thing, I don't know – but I would step in when I could see the other boys emptying out his rucksack on to the floor and saying that he stank, and I would march over and tell them to piss off, hoping they didn't have the energy to actually fight, and then help him pick up his stuff. Then he would just put his tongue between his teeth, fighting to get out a "thanks" before he went on his way. After a few rounds of that, I started to think that maybe he didn't care that I used to try and help, and his little "thanks" had begun to piss me off too, making me believe he thought he was better than me or something, so I stopped. And I soon realised that without me trying to keep off the bullies, he was attracting most of their attention instead and so they would leave me and my few other friends alone. For that, I was thankful, and I'm even ashamed to say that I joined in making up rumours with the other kids about him behind his back – that he was an orphan and dropped on his head when he was a baby which made him look and talk so strange. I was only 10 or 11 – we were just dumb kids trying to get attention – but I should have known better. And one day I heard this slam come from outside my classroom and it was Sunil being thrown into the lockers again, this time with extra force, as he had decided to fight back, and the others just laughed as they pushed away his flailing arms and slapped him in the face with his own hands until his cheeks were raw instead. Then they picked him up and carried him over to the end of the corridor, folded him in half so that his face was sort of between his legs and threw him in the bin. They left him like that, with his limbs spilling out like banana skins and him wriggling to try and set himself free. We all laughed and then gradually, silently turned away, leaving him there on his own.'

He paused. I couldn't see his face because he was walking ahead but it seemed like he might be about to cry behind those broad shoulders. I took a sharp intake of breath to try and break the lingering silence –

'And then they just sort of left him alone after that. They must have found a new weakling to target, I think. Maybe he had grown too boring, too accepting of their punishments or something. And I forgot about him really. I went off to college and then left school to do my apprenticeship before university and met Tar and moved to London and that was that. But it was when I met up with a few of my school friends towards the end of my time at university and we were reminiscing about old times – or as much as you could reminisce once you realised you didn't enjoy any of it, that you just survived it – and one of them asked if I'd heard about Sunil, about my namesake. Of course, I hadn't, but that question alone was enough to make a brick of guilt suddenly thud to the pit of my stomach. He told me that apparently not too long after we'd left school he'd finally learned to stop stuttering but he had also developed some kind of cancer, a rare one in the spine, and he'd become really unwell. Apparently, his older sister was special needs so his parents were so busy looking after her, they hadn't paid proper attention when he'd said his back was hurting him, and they only took him to the doctors when it had spread much too far. Then he'd started chemotherapy but that was just a shot in the dark and only made him feel worse. So they took him off that and he died. He was only 19. That was it, he died, and no one even knew about it – my friend had only heard because his grandad was apparently friendly with Sunil's uncle or something and word had got back to him about the funeral and how sad it all was. It must have already been two years since the funeral when they told me. And, of course, I felt strange and sad about it all, about not having looked out for him more or kept in touch or taken any interest really, and then I forgot about him, again, and became absorbed by my own life. It's only been since we got here that I suddenly remembered, thinking about whether his parents had made this journey, or if anyone had cared for him. All that cleverness he had, all that shit he had to put up with, for what? What was the point of it all? It seems like such a waste.'

I didn't know what to say to that and neither did Sel it seemed, so we stayed silent, walking up a steep set of stairs alongside the main road.

What was the point of it all?

You could see into people's houses on either side of the steps and I focused on not letting my curiosity get the best of me, only glimpsing a mother with her child wrapped in her sari as she flipped a roti and another, older woman hanging a crumpled set of discoloured whites on a washing line. She looked straight at me as I huffed past and I instinctively turned away, somehow ashamed by what I had seen.

We reached the top, all of us panting, and looked into a carpeted front room where a series of overweight, greying men had gathered, all sporting various stages of male pattern hair loss and sitting silently and staring into their phones. Every place here seemed to have a room full of these men with nothing better to do, nowhere else to be.

Our boy rushed over to one with a particularly large and reddened nose, who fished a pair of glasses from his front pocket and then looked up at us standing in his doorway while he listened to the boy's explanations. He spent a few moments taking us in.

'Aajo – come in.'

8

There was no record of ours, but what did it matter now? I was tired and my mind had long since drifted from the meaning of this quest to the prospect of getting back on my phone and feeling the exciting unfamiliarity of its images being beamed to me. There was still so much to discover – it made my stomach tingle.

The sun had begun to dip in its arc of the day and we had decided – or Sunil had – to put our trust in this pandit to confer the ceremony on us and then to find the right scroll to inscribe Dad's name on later. Or, we would leave him unknown. Either way, we'd get him into the river, which is all we had come here for. When one of us died, we'd have to start this entire process again and I certainly didn't have the energy for it.

We had laboured back to the restaurant to pick up the others, Sunil had palmed me a wad of worn notes to pay the pandit with, as if I hadn't brought enough of my own with me, and now we were heading down the main road, passing through the toffee-gold light that seemed to paint over the surrounding vendors as they watched us – in curiosity or amusement, I couldn't tell.

My chest was lightly aching each time I took in a breath and I felt my ulcer once more, stinging with a curious poke of my tongue. I realised I hadn't been to the toilet since we had stopped on the roadside and that revelation caused my sphincter to spasm intuitively. Was there a religious rule against urinating in the Ganges once I was submerged?

Best not to. It was probably a bit too harsh to send my dad into the afterlife wafting on a cloud of my own piss. Half-arsing it without the proper pandit was punishment enough.

This pandit, the one with the big nose, was for some reason only addressing Sunil, perhaps assuming him to be the eldest in the family as he instructed him to buy a plastic bag of suspiciously pristine rose petals from a toothless, crumpled lady. I was relieved that I might not have to undergo the submergence ceremony, dissolving instead into the background and settling for spectatorship like the others.

I felt a sharp pair of nails pincer my elbow. 'Make sure he sees you and knows who you are. This is your dad after all.'

I wanted to shush Sadia like a petulant child but she was right. Now was the time to take some ownership of the occasion, even if it was just another way to play the game of one-upmanship that had been a fixture between her and Sel ever since Mum died. Then I had been too young to see the subtle shifts of power and affections around me. I had just wanted my mum back, for her to have the time to see me fully grow into myself. And maybe her dying when she did stopped that growth altogether; it was a moment after which I became determined to stay attached to all that had come before. There could be nothing new now. But I didn't want to think of that.

We really were each the centre of our own universe, I supposed. I touched my pocket and felt my phone, hoping for service and Vicky's enthusiastic reply.

It turned out that all we needed were the odourless rose petals and once we got them, the pandit kept walking down to the banks of the river, us trailing in his lopsided gait. We stopped in front of three steps leading into the water, its frothy scum trailing on the white stone as it splashed from the movement of the bodies floating in it. Above us was a bridge, framing a giant statue of Krishna that I had only just noticed crowning a hill in the distance. The scale of it all made me feel a little unsteady – the alarm began to sound once more through the cavern of my head – and I focused instead on the noises filtering in around me. There were the shrill calls of prayer playing through a loudspeaker, tablas beating out a rhythm, children splashing, voices.

'This must be it now.'

Jai Hanuman gyan gun sagar
Jai Kapis tihun lok ujagar

I recognised the sounds of the *Hanuman Chalisa* playing on a speaker nearby.

'Just here?'

Raghupati Kinhi bahut badai Shri Raghupati
Tum mam priye Bharat-hi sam bhai

It was my mum's favourite prayer – the one we played at the house when her coffin was there. It was kept closed because her injuries were too much for everyone to come and see and mourn.

'Those chains leading into the water look familiar.'

Durgaam kaj jagat ke jete

It felt like everyone was speaking at once.

'This feels maybe the same as before.'

Sugam anugraha tumhre tete

At least it meant I could remember her as she was in life, full of hope.

'Can we go back after this?'

Sub sukh lahai tumhari sarna
Tum rakshak kahu ko dar na

'This is it?'

Ram Lakhan Sita sahit

I hadn't noticed our driver had tucked himself next to me, bobbing beneath the throng. I turned to him as he placed a reassuring hand on my shoulder and smiled.
   'Now is time, just brother and sister with papa.'
   'So I don't need to go in? Just me?'
   'No, all together, just follow pandit.'
   'I don't need to get changed?'
   He walked off without answering, leaving the family gathered.
   'Turns out I won't have to go into the water after all – maybe they've changed things since Dad was here. It's just me, you

Tar and you Sel who have to go down the steps to the edge of the water and tip in the ashes, and then we're done,' I told them.

I knew Sadia would be seething that I no longer had the central role as the son of noble duty but, for once, I was relieved that Dad might have lied. It was simply another story of his that none of us would ever know was true, one to add to the list of murky recollections that made up the cold, resentful man I would always remember him as.

The girls pulled their scarves over their heads and I felt the sudden urge to take off a hat, or bow, something to show respect for the ceremony. Instead, I heaved the box of ashes out of its corporate-branded tote and picked the lid open, peeling away a thin film of plastic to reveal the grit and bone and mess of our dad. There was so much of him there. I dug my fingers in instinctively, like a child testing clay, and I felt how he was cold and how the water too was cold as we took the steps down to its edge.

The pandit had begun mumbling his prayers under the metallic calls of the nearby speakers and we each took a fistful of roses to place into the ashes before letting handfuls of both drop into the water. I looked to the pandit for instruction but his eyes were closed in recital; I followed Tara instead, who was emptying him with all the care of a shaky, futile gesture – like returning sand to the sea. Clouds of him disappeared under the surface as the milk sank in the cups of half-drunk tea he would leave scattered around the house.

I heard his baritone calling me beta – I had forgotten about that – and I felt my throat tighten and my gut kick, like my body wanted to make itself cry. The pandit's voice rose as his chanting picked up in pace and we began to feel the slick bottom of the box with our fingertips and the grain of him digging itself under our fingernails. Our three hands came together to tip the remnants of him in as the pandit gestured for us to swill the water so he would be carried out in the current. I smiled and I remembered that he had never learned to swim.

The sun had sunk below the bridge and it was impossible to ignore. All I could see when I looked ahead was light, the reflection of my own retinas. There was some commotion happening behind us but I chose not to turn around, instead feeling Sel's arm loop through mine and the soft fabric of her headscarf tickle my cheek. This must have been the closest we had been in years and I felt a pre-emptive urge to pull away, before our closeness took hold and I spent my time wanting it again.

I realised that, if I was lucky, I would live long enough to see most people that I knew and loved die.

But that didn't make sense.

Surely, we could not all die?

I felt a reverberation as Tara unhooked her arm from our chain.

I sensed a buzz down my trouser leg, but felt no phone in my pocket.

My mind raced: had I dropped it? Did Sadia know?

Was this a spiritual experience?

Tara

'I begin'

1

And I could see the streaks of brown I had painted over the bottom of the canvas, the way I had begun with just one stripe, its thick mahogany dripping on to the floor below, but then had kept going, pushing ever further into the picture's space above, wanting to cover the whole thing. Then, I had stopped. Taking the pointed bottom of my paintbrush, I scratched into the wet oils: *Spirit for the highest good of all.*

And I saw in the paint my favourite trees: the twisty one with big roots for sitting in in Osterley Park, the tall, straight one with space for just my feet in Bushy Park, the broad apple tree at the back of our garden – I did not know their names but I remembered what I would go to them for. To sit beneath them when home was suffocating me and I had my schoolwork to do, when I could take their energy as I had emptied my own, when they provided the soft music I needed in my head to drown out the silence. I saw myself sitting at the turn of autumn, when the leaves looked like they were on fire from a watercolour sun, wrapping my scratchy wool coat around me and opening the greasy pages of my biology textbook, willing the chapter on the replication of DNA to embed itself into my mind.

And on the wavering edge of the brown, in the grain of the paint, were the shapes of numbers bleeding into white; the numbers of years, good and bad: 1994, 1956, 1966, 2018. Each year passing into the next, hoping for something new. And yet it always ended up the same, or worse. The only resolution worth keeping was one of survival, the constant movement forwards.

And I felt the meat on my bottom lip thrumming with the force of my own blood, beating out a rhythm through the damp side of my neck, my chest, my gut. I kept looking, upwards, at the faint buckling of this ceiling, the cracks breaking out along the edges of the smoke alarm, blinking red at me with each shallow breath taken.

And I thought:

who will know me when I cannot tell them?

So, I begin.

I couldn't remember how long I had been awake for. Visions seemed to merge from dreams and memories on to the off-white of the hotel room's ceiling, its texture lit now by the stripes of sunlight fighting through the edges of the curtains. I had been waking up at stupid hours – 4am or 5am – ever since the kids had been little, but I enjoyed my morning routine of wakefulness to see me into the safety of the day. It felt like I better understood the importance of each morning by being in the kitchen and watching it miraculously come into being through the window – from black to blue to purple and orange – each time a surprise.

PART III: TARA

I had been with Sunil so long that there was no need to say much to each other anymore. It felt like everything we needed to get out of our system we already had, perhaps more than once.

My eyes opened and I stared, marking time through the huffing of my husband's breath and the automatic switching on and off of the air conditioning unit.

There was a lot of breathing going on in this room.

I had felt unmoored ever since we arrived. The little threads of repetition and activity I had so carefully woven around my life, to give it enough structure to carry me when I could not carry myself, had unpicked. Where there was once silence and paint and distance, now there was a chaos of voices and bodies and warmth – everything felt new and uncertain.

Questions kept coming to me, asking me who I was, what my life was for, and who would know me when I was gone. I needed time and silence to answer them. To tell myself.

And I couldn't escape this sense of simmering panic, one that would erupt with the breath-catching force of a missed stair while we were queuing at the omelette station at breakfast, or when I sat down to pee. It was like my body was unearthing the past my mind had spent so long burying. Now, I remembered again.

It was recalling the beating I had stopped for Rohan when he was a child, Mum's endless coughing, that cold night when she had died, and Dad's constant unthinking and unfeeling. I still wasn't sure whether he ever loved me. And I was questioning what it had meant to love him, too.

Recently, I had found myself going back to the records of my youth in the soundtrack of my mind. Donny, Diana, Marvin, Stevie, Michael. I had Stevie Wonder's *Don't You Worry 'Bout*

A Thing reverberating through my head. An ironic refrain to haunt the over-thinker.

I had been thinking about death, too. Not the mechanics, but how people might remember me once I was gone – the ways in which everyone would then have a claim to who I was, their own version of the myriad acts that make up a life. Was I kind enough? Was I too kind? Was I there enough or did I define myself through my kids? Did I have a good enough career?

Thinking about my memory after death, while I was still alive, was like looking for the sea and forgetting that I was already underwater.

The mechanics were more certain. A stage four neuroblastoma, a child's disease found in the smooth abdominal muscle tissue of a 56-year-old, a metastatic fire raging through my insides, threatening to escape at any moment. Within the next 18 months, if I was lucky.

It had all happened before I had a chance to explain.

The ache in my belly was a kind of guilty secret, one I hoped would one day disappear. It didn't, and so I had to tell Sunil, then the kids. I watched their faces crumple into fear and concern. It was the look I had worn in the sun-damaged pictures of my childhood. I could feel their innocence being whipped away. This was proof that their lives would never be easy, that no matter how they might claw their way into joy or stability, there was always a crisis waiting for them.

By the time cross-clinical meetings on the allocation of my care had been arranged, my arms were moulding into patches of purplish bruising and the pain in my belly had reached around to my spine, gripping me from inside.

It was the word 'terminal' that made everything come

sharply into focus. That word conferred an extreme purpose on the rest of my life, a guarantee of things coming painfully and quickly to an end.

Things had been changing in the months since I had told the kids. Where there was once defiance and a sense of independence, I now felt them fighting their way back to childhood, back to my side as if from there they could stave off the certainty of time. I did not need the rest of the family adding to the chorus. While my body was in open revolt, I took control of the only thing I could. I kept silent.

The first omissions of truth were like injecting myself with sparks of hope. If I could pretend this was not happening, it would not become real. It all felt too impossible to put into words; all my speaking was done for me now. I was not in denial about my condition, rather I had moved into an inert acceptance, one that plucked me out of the forward momentum of life and placed me instead into a holding pattern of a slow spiralling inwards. It turned out that death, like much of life, was just a matter of waiting.

Let's have some semblance of normality on this trip. One last dose of ignorance before I allowed the onslaught of everyone else's emotions.

Sunil rolled over, his eyes slowly blinking open and pulling me back into the room.

'Morning, are you feeling ok?'

am I living, or am I feeding time?

2

My memories of childhood were all full of hands and faces, happily feeding each other from the same plate. There would be the chewed plastic on the tips of the thin straws Sel and me would pass between us to slurp up sticky-sweet Fanta at the cinema, or those tiny pots of Petits Filous we'd scrape with our teaspoons and lick clean – even apples we'd take turns in biting, going right through the core and the seeds. Nothing belonged to anyone, everything was ours, or nothing at all.

I never knew what it was to confidently call something mine until I met Sunil. Not that he was mine, he just never shared and had never learned how to either. His upbringing was one of fighting for scraps, a battle for the loveless affection of objects at the expense of the humans he was surrounded by. Every man really was for himself. Suddenly, when I was around him, everything I had was mine. And it felt weirdly powerful, it was like I was beginning to realise who I was outside of the brother and sister and mother I had spent my life providing and worrying for.

Once the kids came along, they were parts of me. Everything that was mine was theirs – it was my uncertain blood under their soft skin, my genes bursting in multiplication, my cancer they could inherit. It was all unguarded mouths and slackened faces populating my vision – squeezable hands to place my morsels into – there was no question, I existed for them.

Part III: Tara

And Sunil kept a distance. He would protect and provide but he could only feel safe if he still knew that some things were unquestionably his, things he needed to fight for. That routine had worked just fine, a dance we had improvised to. Until a few years ago, when I realised that both kids had stepped out of me and grown into their own sure selves – so much surer than I ever was. It was like there were so many things I was now no longer allowed to do. No more feeding them new tastes at the dinner table, no more kisses on the softest bits of their cheeks, no more holding hands when crossing the roads. We had become so professional in our contact.

So, I missed sharing. I missed being wanted. I missed being needed. Most of all, I missed the unspoken understanding that I would always leave a spoonful for you in whatever I had, just in case you had wanted it too. And I knew you would do the same – or, at least I would hope.

3

Lee had massive, gnarled hands sprouting sausage-like fingers and sporting purplish tattoos of blurred swallows on their veiny backs. He used to cup his mouth with these fleshy appendages when he spoke because, I later found out, he was ashamed of the huge black gaps between his teeth. He never smiled in public. But he had a wicked sense of humour, the kind that only emerges after being filtered through the misery of a childhood that saw him sent to a borstal where he would bare-knuckle box for sport and drink the jug of water meant for showering to sate an endless thirst. It was the type of humour that keeps a person alive.

I knew his mother was Polish and a terrible cook but that was all I knew of his parents. He had a younger sister who had moved to Australia as soon as she had the chance – one of the first people to take up the £10 ship passages – and an older brother who he'd long lost touch with, whose son was now a heroin addict, often slumped over the bar with a whisky at the African Queen in Hounslow. Lee had kids of his own – a son and a daughter. The daughter had special needs and had for a time run away from home to live in a semi-detached house in Slough with a man who had advertised himself as a 'spiritual conduit' on Facebook; Lee had eventually managed to bring her home, but he never said how, and his daughter had retreated even further into herself ever since. His son was part of the family business –

construction – living in an industrial town near Swansea with his girlfriend and two kids, and Lee had a wife – for a very long time – but she died from a cancer that had sprouted on her nose, which she ignored until she could no longer get out of bed. There she stayed, smoking to keep the walls yellowed, comforted by her two dogs and Lee bringing her trays of Iceland ready meals.

Lee came into my life over a decade ago. One Wednesday I had arrived at my dad's for our usual, dutiful weekly lunch with Sel, and the smell of stale tobacco stung my nostrils as soon as I walked in the door. He was slurping a too-hot tea through his front teeth, trying to explain to my dad the cost of ripping out the kitchen units and laying new tiling. His baggy grey sweatpants were daubed with flecks of off-white paint, while his t-shirt was too tight, showing the red burned back of his neck and a stripe of beige where his skin had never seen the sun. Dad was in his corduroys and a tucked-in, button-down shirt – clothed to the extreme – standing and gesturing like an old man lecturing an imbecile.

I was surprised to see him and his lanky co-worker Jim back and tearing apart the kitchen the following week, making small talk with us after he learned Sel was a pharmacist ('is it bad if I'm now addicted to the Nicorette chewing gum and still smoking, but smoking like a couple less than I usually would do?', or, 'I've just been eating prawn baguettes from Greggs for lunch this week – that's healthy, right?') and with me he seemed to take a genuine interest in my work, in the way that I used paint impractically. 'Our work isn't so different, you know,' he'd say, smiling with his lips closed. 'It's just mine helps people – and yours just confuses them.'

who would tell me?

I knew what men wanted from me. Or, I learned that as soon as I had got a job. It was a summer stint at the Lucozade factory my mum had started working at to bring in extra money after Dad had retired absurdly early. I would stand with her on the production line, a straight row of brown women with their hair in buns and nets, wearing lab coats and screwing on bottle tops, all day. It was obscenely boring work, so I made a game out of it, tapping a rhythm with my foot as the bottles passed and making sure to screw a lid each on the third tap. When I was in perfect timing, I was a triplet-tapping machine of efficiency. But sometimes the belt would skid or slow, or someone further down the line would place their bottles too close together, and then my entire rhythm would be set off and I would have to adapt. Because the work was so monotonous, we only worked in 55-minute bursts, with five minutes off each hour, a 15-minute break every four hours and a 45-minute lunch break. These breaks were sacred and almost all of the women – the factory floor, for some reason, was all middle-aged women – would spend their breaks in a polite silence, sitting, massaging their temples, gently closing their eyes or clasping their hands to restore circulation.

Upstairs, in the stale corporate hum of the office, were the men. I could see them, their sleeves rolled to their elbows, pencils tucked behind their ears and their shirts all a uniform white, as if to counter the effeminacy of their jobs which were spent writing and typing while us women downstairs were doing the manual labour. I would always take my lunch with Mum, both of us unwrapping our soggy, foil-covered sandwiches of cheese, cucumber and mint chutney while we sat on the brown patch of grass laid behind the factory. It was a searingly hot summer, one where we spent the days grateful for the sun but wary of the thick humidity that gathered in the air, waiting for the coming rainfall. When it did come in heavy sheets and gritty droplets, Mum had to take the day off because her asthma flared, leaving her wheezing on the sofa in concert with my dad's sighs. I felt a simmering anxiety without her by my side. I heard the thunder outside syncopate with a loud slap to my bottling rhythms and that day I ate lunch in the canteen alone.

All the men in the building seemed to make a point of ignoring the women, or at least the brown women who worked on the shop floor, and it made no difference to me, as I had managed to pass through life so far unnoticed, invisible, unremarkable. I walked through the factory's bowels with my head bowed, just like at school. At the Formica table in the airless canteen I sat alone and I remembered gingerly unwrapping my sandwich when I saw a hunched, pot-bellied man standing opposite me. He had a whorl of hair flicking up from his head and thick bifocals on his nose. In his heavy hands he was holding a tray with a plate of mince and peas and rice and a small glass of water. His nails looked shiny.

'May I?'

I can't remember if I said yes before he sat down, but the atmosphere had something of the head teacher's office to it when he did. He introduced himself, told me he worked in the marketing department and then we ate the rest of our meals in silence. The following day, when my mum again stayed home, her chest rattling as my father complained that really I should be there to look after her, the sun was burning through the damp mist of the previous rainfall and I decided to eat in the canteen again.

He appeared and sat at the table, this time not asking permission. I felt nothing towards him except the small flattery of being paid some interest by someone new, and I was curious to know why he was interested in me. I couldn't remember the last time someone other than my mother or sister had paid any attention. Certainly not a man. It made my cheeks feel hot when he asked me about my plans for university, my mum's work at the factory, even my art. This time I managed to ask him how long he had been at the company and in London and he answered, letting me know that he had a wife at home and two daughters in primary school too. The thought of his family reassured me.

For the next two days we kept up the same ritual – on the second with him buying me lunch from the canteen and me, when faced with it, feeling nervous to eat in front of him, all the while knowing my perfectly good sandwich was mouldering in my bag. And then on Friday, he didn't show up. I waited, keeping my head firmly focused on the table and the clacking feet of passing people until I glanced up at the clock and realised I only had ten minutes left to eat my lunch. I had no appetite anyway.

On the way out of the factory at the end of the day, stepping into the bronzing afternoon light and smelling a hint of garlic in the air, I saw a pistachio green Volvo pull up by the exit to the car park.

'I can give you a ride home if you'd like?' he asked.

I don't remember saying anything, I just found myself getting in, putting on my seatbelt and listening to his apology for having missed lunch because of a meeting. My cheeks felt warm again, my stomach tickled with a liquid response to his attention. His belly was almost touching the steering wheel. I cracked the window and felt the hot air slice through my fringe as I looked out at the optimism of a Friday afternoon in summer – I swear I saw a child letting go of an orange balloon and watching it float up to the clouds. We drove in silence with the radio humming softly between our breaths. His car smelled of hot plastic. Then, he brushed my leg with his hand as he went to change gears. I glanced at it, the nails still pared and shiny. He kept his hand on the worn leather of the hard gear stick for a few moments and as we made a turn, he let it float down to my knee, pausing there for a moment before beginning to inch its way up my nylon tights and towards my inner thigh, keeping his eyes straight on the road ahead.

All I could think was 'does he know what his hand is doing?', like he might have temporarily lost control of it and would be so embarrassed when he found out. As he reached higher, where no one had felt and even I had avoided, and I felt the clammy heat of his palm almost tickling my thin, cotton underwear, I panicked and reflexively clamped my legs shut. He let out a faint whimper – and I thought a wry smile – before he carefully removed his hand and placed it back on the gear stick.

Neither of us spoke except for my telling him in a scratchy voice where to turn to get to my road. When we pulled up to my house minutes later, my dad saw the strange car and swiftly came out of the door to meet me. He had seen him.

I tried to pass it off as a friendly lift home but, for once, he was perceptive, and went to reprimand me without raising his voice, forcefully telling me never to accept any lifts or any kindnesses from these white men again, to keep my head down and to call him if I ever needed a lift for some reason, and otherwise to walk.

'Don't ever come back here like that again', he said, and I could feel the uncertainty in the way his voice shook. He knew the reason I was being paid attention to and I briefly wondered if he had done the same to some other unassuming young girl. Then I banished the memory of that shame, fear and embarrassment to the back of my mind, where the rest of those experiences would come to live.

The rest of the summer at work continued as normal; Mum came back, we stuck together, and I only saw him once more – looking out at the two of us from the window of his bile-coloured car as we left one day. He drove off as soon as he saw that I noticed. It was years before I could stomach a mint chutney and cheese sandwich again.

I knew what men wanted from me. But Lee was different. He had done a decent, if slow, job of Dad's kitchen and from then he became a semi-regular presence in my life, making odd repairs at my house or at Sel and John's new place. Our contact was always fleeting and professional, a slurry of small talk and greetings punctuated by invoices and the exchange of money. Just before my 50th birthday, I decided to rip out our kitchen and start afresh – completing a long-held promise to myself to never cook facing a sauce-splattered wall of tiles again and to instead angle the hobs towards the window, so I could do the boring work of meal-making while daydreaming with a view. Lee and his two builders spent almost every day at the house for the next two months, spraying dust into each room, drinking ungodly amounts of sugary tea and leaving piles of Greggs' sandwich wrappers and crumpled issues of *The Sun* behind them when they left each evening. It was during those eight weeks that I realised our line of work really wasn't so dissimilar. While I would be in my makeshift studio at the back of the house, covering another portrait of my mum in black paint, then white and starting again, Lee would be drawing in the rubble space of the kitchen, sawing curved shapes that would make our granite worktop somehow liquid, improvising with these raw, frangible materials as if they were such pieces of soft clay, waiting to be formed and reformed by the guiding warmth of a hand. I would sometimes walk by while he worked and pause to witness the methodical process of pencil, blade and thought, taking mental notes to try and make my own process more intuitive, rather than staring at the canvas until the urge for a violent change overcame me. It was in these pauses that I gradually learned about his childhood, his wife, his family and his own particular views on the world. 'There are vibrations we don't feel,' he would say after a period of silence, 'ways that we're moved without really knowing it – we just have to learn a way to tune in. Doing my work is that way and I'm guessing it's the same for you.' I had always assumed he was something of an idiot. I was wrong.

After the kitchen, we kept up a friendship of texts and the odd phone call – updates on my work (I was trying a series of portraits from memory, which had all become Rorschach blot testimonies to my relationships), his plans to move to Wales to be closer to his son and the sea – and I was pleasantly surprised at how Sunil took it all in his stride, seemingly unthreatened by our friendship, even staying on the line to talk shop with Lee once we were done. Trust was the unexpected benefit of a long marriage, and I was pleased to realise that a friendship could be exactly that and nothing more.

When my diagnosis was finalised – the 'terminal' pronounced – it was to Lee I turned after the kids and Sunil finally knew. I told him I had always wanted to try marijuana ever since I'd discovered Bob Marley and how I had envied the other kids getting stoned while I was at university, knowing full well I'd be banished from the house if my dad ever smelled any of those 'funny cigarettes' on me. I assumed he might know where I could buy some. And so, on one of those fiercely sunny yet bitterly cold late spring mornings, Lee rang our doorbell and fished out a crumpled box of Marlboro reds from the inside pocket of his torn bomber jacket. Ceremonially lifting the lid, I saw three tightly wrapped sausages of brown-green knocking against each other. 'I think you can take it from here,' he said. 'Not really my thing but I hear it calms the nerves very well.'

With the same effort I would apply in dragging Sunil along to a strange display of Rachel Whiteread plinths at the Tate or to sit inside a mountain of cardboard boxes at the Serpentine, I used the leverage of our relationship to make him smoke. Here was a man who, by his own admission, had only puffed on a cigarette once and coughed so hard when he tried to inhale that his eyes streamed, declaring from then on, 'I just don't see the point.'

I looked through the drawers and cupboards in the (now not so new) kitchen for a lighter but only found a damp box of Cook's matches and a gas lighter. I took both out into our back garden where Sunil had set up two canvas chairs, a small wooden table and a couple of glasses of wine. A scene of perfect tranquillity. My hands were vibrating with excitement when I fished out one of the joints, hearing the thunder of a passing plane overtake the crackling of its fat tip when I lit it. It smelled like burning sage and the plume of oily smoke I took into my mouth made me want to spit. Sunil, again, took a tiny drag, held the curls of smoke in his mouth with his cheeks puffed and then spat the vapour out into the dusky air. The sage smells had mixed with a hint of lager and curry leaves now to make a pungent aroma and I worried in case the neighbours caught on. After my second toke, I could feel my heart racing up to a peak and then dissipating, conferring on my limbs a sleep-filled heaviness and warmth. It felt like the contents of my brain were gently dripping out of my head, like the pleasing pop of a blocked ear when coming up from water for air, and I could see the trees shimmering above me, like they were all waving hello. We were so much smaller than ourselves, I thought, and the things you think will matter never turn out to matter at all.

'Are you alright?' Sunil asked, draining his wine glass down to its final sip.

I mmmm'd a pre-verbal response, swallowing the pool of saliva that had now surged forward into my cotton mouth.

'You haven't said a word for the last five minutes – that thing is almost burned down to the end.'

From then we entered into a kind of unspoken pact, that I would continue to enjoy a little smoke every other day in the garden, blunting the ever-sharpening realities of my condition, while Sunil would potter in the flowerbeds nearby or join me to sit quietly and watch the undersides of planes flying by. I had asked Lee, with genuine concern, if this now made him a 'dealer' and he just laughed – showing teeth, or lack thereof – saying it wasn't dealing if he wasn't accepting my payment. It was a secret gift – one I had decided not to tell the kids about.

I had undergone a few months of this ritual and decided to purchase from a neon-coloured, bubble-font website something that looked like a USB stick with a small bowl at the end so I could concentrate my dosage into single hits of substance, unmuddied by tobacco and nicotine. I could be doing without more cancer anyway. And before we set off for India, I fastidiously washed it out, hiding it in my carry-on medical bag along with sheets of painkillers, gels and gauze, praying that it would pass unnoticed. I wasn't feeling self-destructive enough to bring substance across the border and gathered instead that some of the younger relatives we were meeting up with might be able to sort me out, discreetly. I would need something to counter the frenzy of this trip.

It would all work itself out – and, for once, it did. My cousin Nisha had stayed with her parents in India while the rest of her aunts and uncles emigrated and now had two impossibly beautiful daughters, Serena and Kitty. Kitty was married to a man who wore shiny suits and headed up his family's rubber business, while Serena was still highlighting her hair a gingery blonde and living at home, studying for a graphic design degree before she inevitably married and never worked again. On our second night in Delhi, while we were eating thick, spicy pasta in the gravel garden of an Italian-fusion restaurant, I asked Serena where I might find something a little stronger than drink.

'Like bhang, you mean?' she asked, giggling into her hair.

She explained bhang was a milkshake concoction with hash mixed in. 'Bhang without the drink, ideally,' I countered.

She gave me a side glance, sceptical, then conspiratorial. 'I know a guy.'

Part III: Tara

She made a few taps on her phone and at lunch the following day she palmed me a sticky brown briquette wrapped in greaseproof paper. What was I supposed to do with this?

I figured it out, in the dank bathroom stall of that yolk-coloured restaurant, hoping not to trigger the fire alarm. Crumbling a small corner into my USB-pipe produced a dose of herbal calm, a momentary glaze to coat the next hour's proceedings with. And with the others having rushed downstairs to wait for our bus to take us to the banks of the river, I stood by the open window of my room, took a small cube, placed it into the bowl and lit it with my trusty green Bic, watching the ember glow in response to the long pull of my breath. I drew in the slick smoke of restitution. I thought of Lee, at home in Wales with his dogs, letting them run out on the seafront, his contentment unearthed from a secret place.

I noticed the paint-smudged tote in the corner by the door. They had left Dad behind. The box was heavier than I thought when I went to pick it up and as I carefully opened him, revealing the sandy mass of bone and grit he had become, I felt the urge to dip my nose in and smell. But there was nothing, just the waft of my own cloying perfume radiating from my neck. I closed him, placed him in the bag and heaved it on to my shoulder.

Downstairs, on the tarmac, in the angry sun, the tiredness hit me like a joke slap behind the knees. I could feel Selena edging closer to me.

'Want me to take them?' she asked, pointedly. 'You look tired.'

She could tell something had been wrong with me these past few months, I knew. We were too close for secrets this heavy.

I relented, then snapped, and gave her the bag – she could have the responsibility.

When did she take my role and become the big sister? I remembered telling her when I was first pregnant with Amman, pulling her into the front room of our tiny new house, and her giggling like a little girl – an involuntary response to intimate knowledge, or nervousness at the sure change of our relationship. Even when she was pregnant with her own, she would call me at all hours asking for advice, fear shaking her voice, knowing she would never be ready until her body forced her to be. And afterwards, when a new love filled her life and opened her eyes to something much bigger than herself, she would ask about my meditation and Deepak Chopra books and spirituality. Then we would go together each week to that terraced house just off the Hanworth Road and wear all white and sit with the other women on the sheet-covered floor of the living room, not speaking or feeling, just being together and breathing. When we grew tired of that – and their strange rules about food and dress – we started to sing together, joining a choir to tunelessly belt out Carole King and Stevie and Joni, enjoying the rush that came with making a sound so instantaneously, hearing only the buzz of our own voices reverberating through our heads, the rhythm pushing through our feet as we tapped along. But now it was like we had exhausted our hobbies and ways to be together. Perhaps we had finally become our own people, or we had lived long enough to run out of things to say to each other.

who would speak of me?

Increasingly, I just wanted to be left alone.

4

I managed to drag my feet on to the coach but as soon as I collapsed into my seat, my eyes closed.

I slept hard and dreamt of nothing, only hearing two lines repeating and sending me deeper:

> In time we all float,
> to forget where we should be.

5

Of course, being a painter was never the first choice. I assumed that was a profession for white people with long hair who didn't wash. No, my future was going to be surrounded by books, pens and paper – the detritus of an accountant's or lawyer's office. Those were the heights to which I would aspire. I was too young to really know what those roles meant, but judging by the way my dad would say them, slowing reverentially around each vowel – doctor, accountant, lawyer, engineer, pharmacist – I knew these must be holy things. The only acceptable professions for a good Indian child.

The issue was that I was no good at maths. Numbers scrambled themselves in my mind until they became shapes to be regurgitated on to the page in a random sequence. And words had a habit of untangling themselves from their sense; either hardening into page-long blocks that my eyes would glaze over and then have to return to again, or becoming liquid in my mind as I read aloud: here/hear, there/their, word/world. Still, I was smart, I knew how to play the game of question and answer, revision and release – it was just I could feel each passionless moment as it went by, dreading the eventuality that my life would ultimately become a form of rote learning. Learning how to work and how to be.

At home, our objects were reliable. Everything existed in sameness and normality. The squeaky faux leather sofas in the back room were silent presences, geological formations bolstering the very framework of the house, the lacquered wood dining chairs were cursive and scratched, the kitchen worktop somehow plastic yet unbreakable, the windows etched with lead piping that cut the view of our back garden into diamonds. I can't remember the first time I noticed we even had any pictures on the walls. They were just always there: a faded drawing of children skating on an ice rink, a couple boating on a lake, a cartoonish scene of two multi-coloured gods intertwined, all blandly dissolving into the periphery.

While between us things always seemed to be changing in increasingly chaotic ways – Dad's evening absences, Mum's worsening asthma, the simmering competition between me and my gormless cousin – these objects became comforts to me, a cosy ugliness to believe in. And they imprinted themselves into my mind.

I hadn't paid attention to the things themselves but the image of them lived in me. When I found time for myself, away from the chores I was forced to complete by my uncle's vindictive wife, I would walk to my favourite tree in Osterley Park with my pencil and pad of paper and, sitting beneath it, I would sketch a version of that image. Except what came out wasn't exactly a picture, it was more like lines shaped around the feeling the picture inside gave me – my own private sense of safety. Looking down at my page, at the dance of light and dark and movement, I felt satisfied. Then I would return home, ready to face the uncertainty once more.

And as I grew older, more images sunk into me: the gnarled angle of my mum's hands when she would roll out rotis, like the mess of a tree's roots forcing their way into the ground for warmth and sustenance; the slit of afternoon light across my dad as he napped, his face always threatening to awaken from its momentary peace; Rohan's rocking himself to sleep each night, back and forth, until he toppled over with tiredness. I wasn't sure what these all meant but I found myself growing more and more agitated to get them out on to the page, otherwise my body would be filled with their information, fizzing at its seams. And each time I would feel the same satisfaction, the same deep exhalation of energy and completion once I had allowed each image to say what it had wanted to. That was when I realised that no matter what I did with my life, this was something elemental, like thirst, hunger and touch, something that would need to be fulfilled regardless of everything else.

I was smart. So I knew coming out to my parents as an 'artist' wasn't an option. It was still a dirty word, even in my mind. My mum, in her infinite kindness, wanted me to be happy but it was beyond the remit of my dad's comprehension. It wasn't for us, it was failure. But things progress in their own way, I grew to learn, and I soon left home to live in Manchester to study pharmacy, where I met Sunil when he handed me a plate of mithai on our first Diwali in our halls of residence. As I came to know and then love him, I started painting in my spare time. I would pay for sheets of rolled canvas and tubes of cheap acrylic from the art school and silently attend their weekly life drawing classes, always leaving before they brought out their wine and began comparing their attempts with each other. It was just exercise for me, a means of release.

The people that did see my work – Sunil, a few close friends, and a couple of art school lecturers glancing at it – either thought it was nonsense or quietly interesting. But their responses didn't matter to me, it was the doing that counted. And for all of Sunil's practicality, there was a softness in him that implicitly understood what this meant to me, that even though I could tell he had no idea what these thickly applied sheets of colour meant, he was happy for me to continue as he could see it was something I needed. It all flowed: once I had his support, I painted more, the distance between the image that was inside and the one that came out shortened, and my confidence to share it grew.

Painting was still a private activity when I became pregnant with Amman. It was my own wordless communication and silent, perfect understanding – the ideal form of therapy – while work was still, begrudgingly, locum shifts at local pharmacies, fulfilling prescriptions for powerful anti-fungal creams, morning after pills and methadone. After my baby was born, though, it was like something gently clicked into place inside me. He was the most perfect picture I could have hoped for, he was a soft, soap-smelling little gift, and while he huffed, all bundled up on my chest, I kept asking myself:

what are you waiting for?

I had hundreds of finished canvases at the house – so many that we had built a shed in the garden to house them – and I would tear off the tarpaulin to rifle through them hungrily, remembering the moment of each's making and the feelings it captured: the shining black of my dad's portrait, austere and unreachable; the absurdity of a man eating a banana in the rain; the blast of light when I had tried to paint my mum. I resolved to put on a show.

Since my painting had remained largely in my own head, I had no idea about the commerce of creativity, about how I should sell myself far more than my paintings, as a 'new mother', a 'late bloomer', an 'undiscovered talent'. Instead, I wrote to the Hounslow Community Centre and asked if I could hang up some pictures in their hall, just so people other than myself could see them. They eventually replied, accepting if I gave them a 20 per cent commission on each one bought. One crisp Monday morning, I turned up with Amman gurgling in the pram and set about tacking the paintings to the walls. I had placed a small advert in the local paper and the following day I declared it open, simply by propping the double doors wide and setting up a small table in the corner.

I enjoyed sitting there and watching the people pass by. Some would stop in out of curiosity, politely walking past the paintings and then sauntering off after they felt they had given them appropriate thought. Others came to talk to me.

'What are these about?' they would ask.

And I would flatly reply, 'Whatever you want them to be.'

That usually produced silence, but if they persisted then a simple 'I don't really know,' would do the trick.

I liked their confusion, their inability to let themselves go and really feel what all of this meant. Or maybe they were just entirely unintelligible, in which case that made me happier since it vindicated the fact that this truly was just a gift for me to enjoy. I had tried to let others in but this would only be a world of my own making.

Several days passed in the same way without a single painting sold and I enjoyed the meditation of sitting there with Amman, feeding him when he was hungry, talking to the sweet, elderly reception staff, sketching in my notebook and listening to my music. The songs never failed to make the time pass, to provide me with a certain flow to guide my hand. And when Sunil, Sel and Rohan all came in one late afternoon, they each bought a picture – perhaps out of pity – and then Sunil later brought my mum and she spent minutes in front of each one, trying to understand. In the end she sat with me and held my hand. She told me she was proud.

Towards the end of the show's two-week run, a middle-aged white couple dressed in floaty silks and sharp shoes stepped in. I had only sold four pictures – all to my family – but after at least twenty minutes of browsing, they offered to buy all of the rest. I thought it might be a joke but they were deadly serious. They introduced themselves as Peter and Shirley Leon, they were both artists and former art teachers and had just sunk their life savings into opening a small shopfront gallery on the Teddington High Street. They had decided to pop into my show after catching my advert at the back of the paper. They said I had promise and talent and that I should come to the gallery one day and perhaps talk about representation.

I never went back to the pharmacy after that. Sunil was making enough to support the kids by now, so each year I would spend nine to ten months painting silently in the house and then around November I would drive over the best of my works, which Peter would hang in his tiny gallery for a winter exhibition. That was the best time for my pictures, he thought. In the first year, there was a small interview with me in the local paper and a review. I didn't care to read either but the Leons seemed happy. Our opening was busy, almost everyone I knew came – even my dad who looked terrified to be so out of place and who stayed for half an hour in an itchy suit and then left without saying a word. I sold around two thirds of the pictures and the others Peter and Shirley bought, for 'future investments' they said. They believed in me but they never made me feel as if I was doing them a favour – they knew the works would be worth far more than what they had paid, they said. I just needed to keep working, to keep translating those images to canvas. Until their true worth kicked in, my pictures mainly served the purpose of decorating local houses and being given as gifts. I doubted anyone outside of a ten-mile radius of Hounslow would know about them at all.

When I thought of my work, it seemed a peaceful experience. But there were always moments the mind would happily skip over. Like when Mum died so suddenly and I didn't pick up a pencil or a brush for almost a year. I didn't set foot in the gallery then – even for that year's show, which was made up of all my previously unsold pictures. It just felt like all the pictures in me had emptied out. I had come to terms with the fact that I might have said everything I needed to, or that there was no more paint left to speak. Perhaps she was the driving force behind my creativity, the voice that had told me all that time before, 'What are you waiting for?'

She was the only person who made me believe in an innate kindness in the world, in the fact that it could be a place where the best sometimes happened. If not, how come I ended up in her arms, in that sanctuary, out of all the other mothers I could have been born to? I hadn't realised how much I still needed her smile and her easy reassurance, the soft down of her sagging cheeks, the squeeze of her rough, darkened hands. And there was still so much I wanted to ask too, like how married life felt before I was born, what her childhood had been like, how to make her saag, who she actually was as a person and not just my mother. She had died and taken my right arm with her – there were no marks left for it to make now, no questions left to ask. It was done.

And then it wasn't. As quickly as she had gone and landed me with a lack of purpose, so I woke up on a bitter January morning, the sky laden with clouds, and stretched a fresh canvas on to a waiting board. I had spent all night dreaming of her as a young woman, with us both at an unusual house party, conspiratorially laughing together and enjoying the free food, knowing no one else but each other. And then she left me alone and I abruptly woke up.

'What are you waiting for?' she said.

I needed to paint her, properly this time. I primed the canvas with a heavy, reflective black and then began scratching in her outline with the edge of my palette knife. I wanted her from memory, from the pictures I knew inside of me. Once I had finished the outline, the paint had settled and begun to dry. Then I daubed on a brilliant white, bringing the shape of her to life, the smoothness of her forehead, the deep furrows of her laughter lines. Working on the white, I added her flesh tones: the browns, yellows and blues of her mottled skin, the dark green of her eyes, a speck of white on their pupils to bring her gaze into the room. There was the hint of a smile curling at the edge of her lips, her neck was long, straight and eternally graceful. I was sweating and exhausted by the time I was finished – but there was a liquid warmth that came round my stomach when I looked at it. It wasn't the feeling of dreadful anticipation that she might still be alive and forgotten and walk through the door at any moment, but an understanding that she was here, again.

Each day from then onwards, I prepared a new canvas, or painted over an old one, with images of my mum until her faces were all that surrounded me in my studio. And ever since, hers has been the only form I have returned to – a constant space of inspiration when I have been drained of everything else.

Those first pictures of my mum seemed to shock the Leons when I eventually showed them. They stood silently and then Shirley hugged me and left traces of her Opium scent on my lapel for days to come. 'This is something new and beautiful,' she said. Peter entered the first one into the National Gallery's portrait competition and it ended up reaching the final. Two years later, another was included in the Royal Academy Summer Exhibition, and gradually my pictures started acquiring a life of their own, away from me and from their instilled meanings. Still, I kept up my yearly show, gave no interviews and stayed off any social media. This was my own internal world, after all, my own reason for being.

I hoped that this lineage of pictures would one day include my dad. But now that he was gone, there was still nothing there – no real sadness, no real regret, just a simmering anger that he had never once told me he was proud, never told me he loved me or that he understood me at all. Maybe he had died a long time ago.

I felt a need to turn him into something solid and fixable, something I could control with my brushstrokes, but there was no image waiting inside. Nothing could be released.

Maybe I was feeling relief.

when will I release?

Or, if I didn't speak him out, that meant it wasn't real.

6

'What are you two talking about?'
      I had heaved myself to the front of the coach, away from the post-prandial sleepers, where Rohan and Sunil were yammering away at each other.

'Oh, nothing, Rohan was just asking about my dad,' Sunil said, with the brusque tone of voice he'd use with the kids when they had not put something back 'in its proper place'. Rohan was being brave.

I wanted to see how far he would go. 'Oh really, why? Digging for something?'

'No, no, just thinking about our dad and dads in general I suppose. Like what it means to be one.' He blushed, just like he would when he was a cheeky little boy realising he had done something wrong.

Just because I didn't yet miss our dad, it didn't mean he wasn't grieving. I still couldn't quite believe he was a dad now too and I immediately felt bad for teasing him.

I had only known mothers and a mother's love in my life. To me, that was simple. That was foundational to everything. Dads just existed on the periphery, passing through like a dangerous undercurrent, or the unexpected bridge in a song – all key change and modulation. There was no sanctuary there, just something to get through.

'I wasn't sure what I'd be like as a mother – if I could be as

253

loving as Mum was. But now I see that the kids just take over your life and make nothing else really feel important. All of the bullshit we used to worry about doesn't matter anymore because now it's all about making their lives as abundant as I can. Like they can just go out into the world and pick whatever they want.'

I hadn't meant to say so much but once I started, it just flowed. I felt myself welling up thinking about leaving my kids without me, leaving them like I was left. None of it was fair.

'From what?' Rohan asked, always clarifying.

'From anything. From the tree – of life? I don't know. But just to feel confident out in the world, not always be taken for a mug or to be looked over as soon as you're seen. You know what I mean anyway. Just to feel like they can do it.'

He tried to joke away the earnestness, but I didn't get it. I had spent my life worrying I'd be taken for a mug – my softness something to be taken advantage of – just as I had seen happen to my mother. And I wondered if that was something men ever had to think of or was it just something that ran in the Bedi gene? My dad, for all his anger and bravado, was essentially a man built on the principle of timidness, one who used to try and exert his power at home to make up for the lack of respect he was shown by everyone else. We would tiptoe around him like a petty king, but I would see his bowed head to others, the way he would come home reeking of fear after a shift on the night bus, willing himself to be made invisible. Later, I realised this was all self-preservation – the powerless enacting their own subjugation on those who would come to experience it for themselves. That filthy cycle of shame. Poor Rohan had it the hardest. He lived in the impossible position of being the infantilised youngest of the family and yet also its most valuable member – the continuer of this messy line. It was a weight I watched turn him from a pliable and hopeful kid into an unravelled, rudderless man, one always clutching for support in the sea of his life. Like all men, he missed his mother and he yearned for his father, even while he was still here. Maybe now that he was gone it would free him somehow and allow him to find himself again. Or, he would continue the tradition and ensure his insecurity was passed on, making himself a stranger in his own family's presence.

'Just a joke. Anyway.' He trailed off into silence.

It was like he was my child too – another one to leave behind.

Our mum's silence had always been so accommodating.

I shuffled back to my seat and fished my iPod from my bag. Headphones on, I scrolled through its selection of artists – Amy Winehouse, Bill Withers, Bob Marley, Coldplay, Donny Hathaway, Erykah Badu, Fela Kuti, George Benson and George Michael, Janet Jackson, Jimi Hendrix, Lenny Kravitz, Luther Vandross, Marvin Gaye, Michael Jackson, Nusrat Fateh Ali Khan. I rolled my thumb back up the wheel and settled on Marvin Gaye.

Although we had first met through the exchange of sweets at a Diwali party, it was *What's Going On* that really brought me and Sunil together. Released only a few years before we both arrived in Manchester and found ourselves sharing the same kitchen, the cover still leapt out as it appeared in a cube on the screen now. Marvin's boyish slickness was gone; instead, here was the upturned PVC collar glistening in the rain, a beard populating those carved cheekbones, a thoughtful gaze into the distance – a remembrance, or finding something worth looking for. It was like this was something you had to work towards, rather than an object to be enjoyed and thrown away.

And then, there was this lanky, pockmarked boy with knotted curls and corduroy flares holding out a brown cassette with that same image, asking if I wanted to listen all those years ago. We plugged our headphones into his splitter and sat on his lumpy, boy-blue sheets, close enough to touch but not close enough that we were. He clicked and started the rhythmic whir of the tape. Marvin's pleading 'mother' sent chills radiating around the back of my head, that yearning falsetto crying out for comfort – the universal call to home – and then the liquid sequencing bleeding into the earnest, shaker-shuffling of *Right On*, before the open expansiveness and choral harmony of *Wholy Holy*, and I looked out of the window and realised it had begun snowing. Thick, fluffy flakes puffed their way past us and the light radiated that brilliant white of the biting cold and its first snowfall. I thought about how none of us chooses where we are born or who we are born to. How you can't always get what you want – in fact, you hardly do – and anything that happens to you has always happened before. We are all just repeating ourselves, trying to be heard, and only some of us cut through the noise.

I can't remember either Sunil or me speaking at all that afternoon when we listened. We let the tape play out its sides, felt the beauty of Marvin's voice, the depth of his meaning, and then I left for my room. The connection was made. I had grafted the tenderness of that song and its richness on to the shape of this stretched boy and it was for me to learn later that he was a person of his own, one with a kindness and a soulfulness that we unearthed together, in time.

Part III: Tara

Much later, when we heard the news that Marvin had died – shot by his own father – we cried at the unthinkable cruelty. Some things were so sudden that they made no sense at all.

And there was so much fun too – people always forgot that. There was the cramped heat of an overstuffed dinner table, sitting on the sofa and laughing until we cried, the drunk buzz of singing in a crowd so loudly you couldn't hear yourself, dancing with my kids, holding hands in the sun and the rain, jumping up and down for no real reason, knowing together without saying, crying at something beautiful, finding each other and sharing each other. There was so much to be had. And I always forgot.

7

Still, I felt nothing. The air here was like syrup, warehousing me in its humid thickness. We had decamped from the coach into what must have been our destination – a rubble car park full of waiting, staring men.

I worried I was spending too much time in my own head, not taking in the presentness of this moment, not making a lasting memory for my children with my aliveness. But what was there really to see? These goodbyes were always the same, the ritual theatre to massage ourselves with, something to counter the anger we felt at being left so soon, or a public repetition of something we had said to ourselves long before: 'I no longer need you.'

I couldn't help the solitude unfolding over me, a longing for a past that had already been used up, and an understanding that each moment was being drained as I lived it.

We walked.

I could feel a new image settling into me, one that I would need to exorcise soon. I saw a mahogany streak cut with blue, an arc of strobing white breaking out above, and the violent movement of flesh tones in the foreground, all set amid a dusty smog populated by the soft brush-flicks of bodies. It was a feeling of intimacy and unpredictability as we weaved between the people filtering through us.

Part III: Tara

We stuck out here but I didn't mind. There was a comfort in being surrounded by people who looked the same, even if we knew we were entirely different. Their existence, their bulk, was enough.

Looking at them, I realised I knew nothing about my history. I always thought I would come to it naturally, like a realisation of some greater belonging, but instead I had got on with the stuff of life – that constant running – and still I was none the wiser. My identity lived in my head – 'Indian', 'African', 'British' – and my skin was just a housing to confront each face and mirror. Both kept me from being known by a stranger in a strange country, that recognition of ourselves in each other. It kept me from getting the nod I saw the Somali kids give each other when they rode past in Hounslow, a flick up of the chin, an understanding.

I wanted my people. But even with them around me I realised I felt that same sensation of aloneness that had followed me through life – not loneliness, just the constant belief that I was alone, an alarm gently sounding through my body. It told me that I could look after others, I could love them and they would love me in return, I could rely on them when I needed them, but ultimately they were malleable and moveable – the only thing that was fixed was me. It was a pulsing that was getting louder in its rhythmic certainty.

I wished I had asked more when I had the chance. But now I was something rotten, decaying from the inside out like fruit. I wished I had seen my parents as people too, people crushed by their surroundings, just trying their best to bring us kids out alive. I hope mine knew that. I hope they knew that I had poured all of myself into them.

I would have liked to just sit down and cry, to let it all out, but there was something solid inside me that wouldn't allow it – a buffer of decorum. The refrain that everything was ok.

We walked.

'Are you feeling ok, Mum?'

We had reached a hovel of ancient papers and what looked like seated pandits in the corner of a fetid courtyard. I could feel the sweat beading down my back, rolling its way to the waistband of my trousers. My boys closed ranks around me, shielding me from the sun. Their concern was a constant presence.

'Yes, I'll be alright, don't worry. You should pay attention to what's going on – they might have found the pandit.'

'You should drink some water,' Amman said, offering me a bottle like a child.

'Maybe you should sit down,' Amar followed.

'I'm fine, really. I'll take a break when I need to.' I took the water, a compromise.

A deep inner sigh radiated through me. I could remember the moment my own mother had turned from parent to child. It was when I was on my Easter break, studying for my O Levels, focusing on a future finally away from the family and still terrified to leave them alone with my dad. I remembered him sitting at the bottom of the stairs, lacing up his steel-toed London Underground boots, shrugging on his padded beige coat like a second skin and walking straight out the door. It was only 3pm – he had no work to get to – but he left my mum lying on the bed in the front room, spluttering and coughing through another bad asthmatic episode, without saying a word. I remember walking in and her gasping to pass the inhaler, a knotted arm reaching out to me. I sat with her and held her upright as she took her dose and breathed deeply, her lungs rattling as she closed her eyes for a dark moment. Then she asked me to put the *Hanuman Chalisa* tape in the machine and play it for her. That was when I knew I would always have to look after her, that no matter the shape of my coming adult life, I would always go back to her and repay the debt of care she had given me when I was young and defenceless. Perhaps that was always the way with parents and children. And I wondered now if she too had felt that same aloneness, that even with me there to hold her, I would eventually leave, just like everyone else she had been taken from – her mother, her father, her brothers and sisters. I had hoped my own children would not have to come to that realisation so soon.

We walked.

I had been spending a lot of time excavating the emotional loam of the past. After my diagnosis, it had been gently suggested that I might want to find a therapist to talk myself through the end of my life. I didn't think it would be much use, but I had been fascinated by the idea of therapy ever since I began to see divorced friends seeking it out after their eldest children left home. Could you really pay someone to listen to you moan for an hour a week? It was a luxury I could not afford. Plus, that was what sisters were for.

But then, the opportunity of six free sessions on the NHS arose and I found myself in the airless waiting room of an empty annexe in Hammersmith Hospital. I spent most of the first hour reeling off my life's injustices – racism, an emotionally absent father, the diagnosis – getting them out of the way early on, and trying to work out if Richard, my therapist, was gay. He had greying hair and a thick middle, spilling over as he slumped in his puffy chair, and his eyes angled down at their edges, giving his stare an entreating kindness. His questions had a camp lilt to their upturned endings, ones he flourished by tilting his head as he waited for a response like a true Indian. He wore a wedding ring that my eyes would drift to when I waited for the answers to his questions to arise.

Questions like, 'And how did that make you feel?'

Each time I would try to explain anything – like not remembering my dad ever hugging me – I would only be left with the most basic language: sad, angry, confused. Words were meant to expose you but here they opened up a gap between the life in my mind and the one I could share. It filled up my mouth with the ache of possibility and doubt.

Still, I kept going back. I liked Richard's gentle way of listening without judgement, his validation of my experiences, his reassurance that my life had indeed been hard. It wasn't that I had sought out suffering, we just learned that its bitterness was something I had been marked with. Now I was passing that legacy on to my children. It was almost too much to bear – I still needed to be sure that they would be ok. That was the least I was owed.

At our last session before we had flown here, Richard asked me about death. I talked around it with platitudes on the fact that we all die – it is an inevitability of life – it was just that mine was coming sooner than most. What I wanted to really say was that we all thought we could control our lives, that we were owed at least 80 years, but tell that to my friend Sharia whose daughter was playing in the street in Iran and who brushed past a live wire and was electrocuted to death at the age of eight – there was nothing just or guaranteed about that – or, what about those who live far past 80 in a prison of their own senile minds, what kind of life was that? Surely they had died many years before, when their ability to think and be in the outside world had left them? Really, I had done well to last this long and I was escaping the possibility of a demented, useless old age. My time was my time and there was nothing I could do about it.

I was furious when he asked me again, 'But how do you feel?' I seethed that I wanted to get it over and done with, that what was the point of living when you knew your death, a painful one, was just around the corner? Of course, I didn't want to die, I didn't want to die yet, but if I had to, I wanted to die now. Let me be in control for once.

This was like one of those dreams where you're just eternally falling, living in the sickening gut-churn, and I hoped that I would wake up before I hit the ground and exploded.

He looked at me with that sad, kind silence. Really, I was terrified. Angry, yes, but scared. What was waiting for me? Some thick, eternal blackness? The end of consciousness, the end of all of me? I just couldn't think of it, I had to put it out of my mind, it was forcing my weakened heart to palpate up my throat, squeezing my escaping breath.

It was simpler to think of becoming the paint in my brushes – material applied, formed and reformed. Forever new. Bob Marley asked if we could be loved and perhaps I would become love, something wafting through the invisible fabric that held us together, an unstoppable force. Perhaps there would be a party waiting for me with Bob, Marvin, Michael, Donny, my mum.

I liked that. That's what would be left. Just a soft sleep and then one big, happy celebration, full of food and music, with Mum smiling there, her arms always open.

and how does that make you feel?

For now, we walked.

8

Even if I had no appetite, there was something inescapably comforting about sitting at a table together. There had been many memorable ones: the nail-rapping, plastic-sheeted surface in Mum's first London kitchen; the thickly varnished wood of our childhood dining table, only used when company was over; the endless, uniform MDF of the school canteen; the Formica island of our shared kitchen at university, a space for the furtive holding of hands; our grey-brown drop leaf design at home, the site of many spilled first meals and tantrums; the wheel-up, L-shaped moulding of the hospital table, home to my array of post-operative mascots; and now this, a steel protrusion extending from a street-side booth, a place of respite from the heat and chaos of the day. I was sure this would be a table we all remembered.

Sunil had gone off with Sel and Rohan on their quest for the correct pandit, leaving the rest of us to try and find some fun in this day of waiting. I was glad for the warmth of the concrete we were sitting on, radiating up the backs of my legs, while the boys fastidiously rubbed their hands with sanitising gel, like a cartoon imitation of glee, and turned their noses up at the wet menus slapped down on our table. The men stared openly at us, their eyes lingering on the spectral whiteness of John's bald head while they slowly licked their fingers and slurped up their steaming, sweet tea. A white man among us. One I imagined had never been so noticed before.

'How are you finding it here, John?' I asked, prompting Jay to look up from his plate in a reflexive panic.

'Oh, it's been interesting, hasn't it? Busy but fun – there's just so much to take in, like it's always changing.'

I had always liked John, his sweet lack of self-worth and gentle incredulity at the world. It had made him an entirely unthreatening and largely invisible presence in our lives, a necessary one to cushion the chaos of my sister's ever-changing moods. So unthreatening, I often forgot he was actually white.

He Ain't Heavy, He's My Brother. That song that always piped up when I thought of him.

I could tell things weren't going well between him and Sel at the moment. The pointed looks she gave him when he asked a question or made a sound, his constant, awkward gestures of reassurance, like squeezing her shrugging shoulder with a clammy hand. But marriage was a long, unfolding conversation – this may have just been an unexpected tangent, an interruption, a moment of silence. It would pass. It usually did.

'How about you? Does it feel different to when you visited here last?'

The last time I was here, I had spent two weeks in silence. The latest instalment of my spiritual explorations had seen me become increasingly drawn to the soft, meandering voice of a bearded guru who would lead afternoon meditations of laboured breathing on one of the Indian cable TV channels. There was something about his glee at the world and the calm survey of his gaze that made me feel at ease, even through the screen. As his broadcasts increasingly became a part of my post-lunch slump and I began to practise his morning routines of huffing, yogic movement in the misty light of my painting room, I sank deeper into the solace his presence and practice provided. Soon, I was looking up his ashram in Tamil Nadu and the programmes of self-exploration they offered there. A door had been gently opened and I was pulled towards the potential for an escape.

There was something cocooning about the leafy humidity of Coimbatore, where the ashram complex was housed among tangled mangroves and sweeping palms. Everything there was enclosed, tessellated – branches locking into the curvature of wooden porch supports, tamarind water pooling in rutted hollows, hands in hands of the children skipping by the ashram's community school. As I walked, I felt the earth rising up to meet me, the soil cushioning the soles of my feet. There was a thick noise about the place, a buzzing of insects, clapping leaves and chattering voices, and it served as the perfect condition for an inner silence.

Sunil had bought me a stay in the ashram as a birthday gift – a welcome reason to get me out the house – and I had chosen to sign up to the silent retreat they offered before I arrived. As soon as I landed, I found I had nothing to say. The quiet of our early morning meditations laid upon me like fine silt throughout my first day, the shanti ringing through my ears as I made no eye contact, no attempts at small talk – I wanted to be left alone, left to the warmth of myself. On the second morning, a long-necked, English-speaking white lady who volunteered found me and enrolled me in the two-week silence program. She smiled and made me sign a commitment to no eye contact, to no note-making or passing, to relinquish my phone and to just be quiet for two weeks. Breakfast at 5.30am, lunch at noon, dinner at 5pm, bed by 7.30pm and silence and breathing in between. I could stop at any time.

I had never known that my mind could shout but in that first day of quiet, it screamed. Not in pain or anguish, it was just shouting over itself as my inner dialogue took the form of responses to hypothetical questions, each reply trying to make itself heard as another interrupted faster than I could think-speak them all inside.

What are you thinking? I would ask myself.

who will know me when I cannot tell them? – is this a good idea? – interesting that I'm here, wanting to try this and to push myself – there's an awkwardness I hope I'm not showing – I wonder what they think of me – if they think I'm white or Indian, or something else – here? – I wonder where that English lady came from, if she's even English – how do people end up here? – when will I release? – how long can you stay? – how long would I stay? – what if I stayed forever? – I wouldn't do that, no – I hope everything's ok at home, that the kids are looking after themselves and Sunil isn't too worried without me – is this just self-indulgent nonsense? – what would Mum think? – am I living, or am I feeding time? – Dad would hate it here – he wouldn't understand it but maybe he would need it – roughshod is a good word, you can see it coming together – I never understood him – and how does that make you feel? – it's mostly Indians though, or people I think are Indian, what are they escaping from? – is this all news to them too? – who would speak of me? – am I being selfish? self-centred? – who would tell me? – what will they make for lunch? – what are you waiting for?

Yet, as I fell into the comforting routine of the days, the stickiness of that internal chaos slackened. The hardness of each moment became tender. A placidness came over me and a single, clear voice would make itself heard through the day before retreating back into its resting place. *See this, be here, take your time, no one is watching.* In fact, it was the silence itself that became eloquent, it opened itself up to everything that was held within it – the humming of the ceiling fans, the shuffling of cramping feet, the weight of air batted between trees and bodies, the open palms of this atmosphere sinking down to scoop me up, whole and unadorned. My mind had nothing important to say at all. There were moments where I would lose the thread of time entirely, I would be the pencil drawing a circle, only knowing itself at that moment as the progression of a line. I would not see things as a whole, only as the brief instances of themselves. This was a history made in the gaps.

A breath in/out.

Here.

There.

Once the two weeks were up, I barely spoke to anyone until I got home. I carried a restfulness within me like a body of water. But as soon as I set foot in the house and hugged my boys, it all came rushing back. The questions, the answers, the silliness, the noise. I realised that I had missed the mundanity of it all, the way we fill our lives with talk and thought merely to pass the time, worrying about things that often have no consequence at all. All these comforts of so many unknown lives. Because that silent eloquence brings its own heaviness;

there is a responsibility to being known – sometimes you just need to be light, to sing and to shout.

'It was quieter before,' I answered John, smiling. 'But it's nice to be together now, in the mess and the noise.'

We paused, listening to the polyrhythms of passing mopeds and grunted conversation, taking in the ambient weight of the smoggy sky. John hiccuped and laughed in surprise at himself.

9

I had been dreaming of rivers for a long time. Swirling blacks and blues that wound their way into my sleeping visions – a contained wildness that thrashed and threatened to burst at any moment.

It isn't that I would drown in the dreams but rather I would feel the water's certainty, welling up in defiance of gravity between the scratched floorboards of our hallway and coldly enveloping feet that were cemented in stasis, or I would look through the windows at the other end of our bedroom and see a violent rut being carved through the garden by the force of a torrent, battering itself against our doors until its icy fingers gripped me and I woke up in a panicked sweat.

I would sometimes try to paint out these aquatic scenes but I could never finish – I only put down gestures of thin paint and trailing brush marks, not the feeling itself. Something was missing that would pull it all together and give it movement, its own presence in the room. Richard had said that floods could mean the emergence of repressed emotions in my dreams, that if we took every part of the dream to be a part of me, the water was something indefinable trying to get in – or be let out. A Google search, meanwhile, told me that rivers symbolised the flow of my life, the potential for new opportunities or pleasures. But all I could be sure of was fear, the understanding that water would adapt to any form it found itself in, that it would take the path of least resistance, even if that meant charging straight through me. The river was like my life – something that was entirely out of my control.

I had developed a fear of water ever since my primary school teacher literally threw me in at the deep end, thinking my instinct to swim would kick in and lead me to the surface. Instead, my instinct was to thrash and somehow sink, leaving me to be fished out of the water, my ears thick with the sting of its chlorine. I eventually learned to float, but I still always kept my head dry, paddling in a senile, rippling breaststroke. And when we took a holiday by the sea, I would spend my time looking out at its shimmering mass, hearing the surf break on the shore like rounds of applause and then I would wait for a current to wordlessly pull its swimmers deep into itself. I would call out to Amman not to swim too far – he always wanted to reach the horizon – and I would inwardly count as his bobbing head drifted and eventually came closer again, digging my toes into the sharp, warm sand.

The thought of Rohan being subjected to the dunking humiliation our dad had encountered when he came here was enough to make my chest begin palpating. And why hadn't I gone with him then? Why hadn't any of us? I knew we had our excuses – I had just given birth, I felt emptied, raw – but I should've been there to say goodbye properly. Sunil had been when his dad died and he was just a teenager. Ever since I had known him, he had hardly talked about his father or his experience, but my mum still haunted me, appearing in my dreams when I wasn't almost drowning, her voice cutting through my head's meandering noise.

Had I kept her here without me taking part in the ritual

goodbye? Was she now stuck in some afterlife waiting room, eternally leafing through old copies of *OK*?

Perhaps now we could make things right.

Here?

And now the sun had begun to trail down its westerly path, sinking as if tired from the day's efforts, and we were following it, walking down the main road towards the river. Sunil, Rohan and Sel had found a pandit who would step in and do the job and they were relieved, setting down with a deep sigh at the streetside cafe when they eventually returned to tell us. They often looked like brothers when they were together, Rohan and Sunil, conspiratorially bargaining as Sunil would place his hand reassuringly on Rohan's shoulder, urging him out of his comfort zone. It was good he was here to help and it was good that he would be there still once I am gone.

And now I can hear the water slapping the stone steps down to its surface, as if marking out a rhythm for our approach. And Rohan telling us that he won't have to go in, that we just need to stand together as the pandit recites his prayers and we tip in the remains, so I pull my paisley headscarf over my warm hair and link arms with Sel as we ease down the three steps to the water's surface. I can hear the *Hanuman Chalisa* playing from somewhere and my cheeks tickle as I realise I have begun to cry, remembering how Mum would ask me to put it on when she lay in the front room and couldn't breathe. I still don't know what the words mean. I want someone to hold me and to forget all this time, if only for a moment.

And now he begins to speak as if just to himself and we place the petals in with Dad and I take a handful of them both and let it drop into the water, watching the cold, unmanageable grains of him sit on the surface, almost fizzing. I feel the inside of me kick and heave with each fist we empty out, as if I am pouring myself into the water, as if it is as simple as that. But I know there is something wrong in me, something that cannot be exorcised so easily, a snow flurry irreproachable in its blanketing whiteness, a steady force coating and killing everything it touches.

And now all of Dad is in the water and Sel and Rohan bow their heads for a moment of silence amid the strange harmonies of splashing, calling and praying. And I see myself, as if in a painting, unhook from their chain and step into the water, as if in my dreams, and I can feel its cold needles between my toes.

And now I am still going, now my knees and thighs and hips are melting into this mass, like so much sugar swirling in warm water, and I feel like blue mixed with too much red, like a fizzing violet, like I am the grieving emptiness of an open hand, like an unreachable memory.

And I am going under.

And I feel a palm on my head, pushing and grasping and pulling.

And I breathe hard.

Coda

19 March 1955

Longing

Sushma waited. She had lined her eyes with kohl, just as her mother had told her to. She had pinned her hair into a neat bun and cleared away the stray baby hairs from her face. She had practised her smile to herself, to make sure that she looked like a real woman, and now she sat gingerly on the edge of her bed, trying not to crease the lines of her sari.

She hated waiting, feeling the minutes trickle through her while she was held in their silence, forced to remain in a state of suspense. She picked at the dry skin at the edge of her nails so she wouldn't resort to biting them. Her life so far had felt like an endless waiting – hoping for someone to allow her to act rather than to merely anticipate. This was meant to be it, the start of the rest of her life, her way out of its long pause.

She had woken early and paced downstairs as her mother began readying the lunch, stirring, smelling and tasting, while she hummed softly to herself; she had seen her father through the doorway of his study, poring over a book and making notes – perhaps questions for the man – on his yellow pad of paper; she heard her brothers playing in the garden. She tried to make herself as small as possible among her family, since she knew they were creating today for her. Her time would soon come to make herself known. She had written it already.

Hours passed and the hum of activity in the house had shifted into a soft silence. The sun was rising in the sky, casting a golden glow through the interlacing branches of their garden's trees. Her father had briefly emerged, noted the time and told her 'not to worry' and was back in his study, reading again, while her brothers had been sent off – one to the neighbour and the other to play cricket with his friends. She had nothing else to do but to wait for him to arrive, so she came back up to her room and sat on her bed, trying not to think.

She followed the line of a crack along the ceiling as she heard familiar footsteps on the staircase, shuffling towards her door. She smelled a sweet prickle of sandalwood in the air. It was her mother, Asha. She stopped in the doorway and gave her a warm, entreating look, before coming to sit on the bed next to her, sagging the mattress. Asha took Sushma's hand and she noticed the skin between her mother's thumb and index finger was cracking with dryness.

'You should put some oil on that,' Sushma said, looking down at their fingers locked together.

'Yes, beti, I will. Nothing for you to worry about.' She reached around with her free hand and placed it on Sushma's cheek, guiding her head to her waiting shoulder. She let her head rest there and felt her mother's hair tickle her nose. It smelled like the cumin and ghee from the dal she had been making. She felt her eyes sting and she swallowed as tears began to prick her cheeks, wetting her mum's blouse.

Her mother placed her arm around Sushma's back, holding her.

'I know,' she said. 'I know.' They waited, listening to the rustle of the leaves outside.

'It's ok to be scared. These meetings can be scary,' she said.

'But I'm not scared, amma,' Sushma scoffed.

'Then why are you crying?'

She tucked her head further into her mother's shoulder. 'I don't know.'

They waited and heard Pintu crash through the front door with his cricketing gear.

'You know, I never told you what it was like for me meeting your father,' her mother finally said. 'I was so frightened, I spent the whole week leading up to the wedding shaking. I just wanted things to stay the same as they were. I didn't know why I had to leave my parents who loved me for a stranger who didn't know anything about me. When the day of the wedding came, I felt sick – I just wanted it to be over and to wake up and realise it was all a dream. But, of course, it wasn't. I had to go through with it and to be truthful with you, I don't remember much. All I remember was not liking your father at all.'

Sushma adjusted her head and Asha gave the small of her back a rub. She had stopped crying now.

'He was this arrogant man – so sure of himself and what he wanted, and he made me feel so small, like I was something he had simply picked up on his way through life. I was so angry at my parents for making me do this, for letting me leave. I was so far from home and I kept picturing spending the rest of my life as this man's afterthought.'

'Why are you telling me this, amma?' Sushma interrupted.

'Well, if you wait a minute, I just wanted to say that things change. They don't always seem like a good or happy change, but if you live with it – they usually turn out just fine. I mean, look at me and your father.' She paused and Sushma blinked. 'What I was going to say was how our marriage started off so poorly but then I learned to love him –'

'Yes, but I don't even have anyone who loves me yet,' Sushma said, as a lump rose in her throat again. Her mother let out a sympathetic chuckle.

'Don't be silly, darling, you are loved, of course! What I am trying to say is that I didn't want to be married but then I was and it has led me to you beautiful children and such a happy life. You do want to be married and maybe this man might not be right for you. When you meet him, make sure to ask all the questions you want, so you can see if he is a good fit.' She paused for breath, rushing through her words. 'Maybe there is a change coming for you also, one you didn't expect, and it will be in your best interests too? You don't need to rush to leave us just yet, you just have to trust that it will happen in its own time. Trust that God knows what is right.'

Sushma wasn't sure that she was rushing, nor that she trusted in God – or wanted a change that was out of her control. But she liked her mother letting her in on her life. It made her feel less like a child, even if she still ended up crying on her shoulder.

'You have so much life to live, beti,' Asha continued. 'And it is yours, don't you forget that. You know you can do anything you want to – we will support you – and someone will love you for exactly who you are.'

'Can't I just live it on my own? I'm so tired of having to wait.'

Her mother turned to look Sushma in the eye. The bed creaked as she placed her hands on her shoulders.

'You might not want to hear this, but you are old enough now.' She took a breath. 'You always will be alone. Even when you are married, at your most important moments – when you need someone else the most – deep down you will realise it is only you in charge of yourself. No one else can do that for you.' She detected a quiver in Sushma's lip. 'It takes time to be at peace with that. Patience too. But in the meantime, we can help, your family. You might be alone sometimes but you don't have to be lonely. I don't want that for you, for any of you.' Asha felt her own emotions rise in her chest, but she was practised at keeping them at bay.

Sushma looked confused. 'I thought you might say that things would get easier, amma, that they will get better.' She wanted to be left alone if she couldn't be comforted. She didn't know what to do if she wasn't wanted.

Perhaps she wasn't old enough yet, her mother thought. Deep down, she knew she wanted her to stay, to be given the chance she was never afforded. The world was frightening and unpredictable; her daughter needed her still.

'What I am trying to say is that this is your life. You can do with it whatever you please and we will be here, always. Just try to remember that if this man is disappointing, that isn't a failure. Because when you get to my age, you realise that everything has happened for a reason and that none of us is really in control of the world. All we can do is to be in the flow of it, patiently, and to hope that the outcome is in our favour.'

She drew Sushma close, wrapping her arms around her and feeling her light head rest on her chest. She felt just as she used to when she was a baby, sleeping on top of her.

'You are at the beginning of so much that is to come. You will be happy and you will be sad and disappointed and angry and everything that it means to be alive. And it will be alright. Just promise me that you will try. That you will hope too?'

Acknowledgements

Thank you to Seren for believing in this book, and me, from the very beginning. Here's to just getting started. Thank you to Sinead, Will, Ion, Ellie, Lisa and everyone at Practise Music and Oldcastle Books who turned these words into something you can hold and hopefully cherish. Your care and commitment to the entire publishing process has been such a joy to be a part of and to learn from. Special thanks to my family for journeying across uncertain waters in hope of a better life and for giving me mine. To my mum and dad, thank you for instilling your unwavering belief in me and for understanding that not every Indian son has to be a doctor. Thank you to my big brother Amun for also becoming a doctor and taking the heat off. And to Sophia, thank you for your love, kindness, patient note-giving and eternal support. None of this would have been possible without you.

Author's Note

In October 2019, I was in India spreading my grandmother's ashes in the Ganges. She hadn't lived in the country for the last 50 years and hadn't even set foot in it for a decade at least. My parents had never lived there and neither had my brother and I.

This wasn't a homecoming. It was a ritual; a performance of last rites in the place she had barely clung on to. It was a strange holiday.

In August 2023, it will be ten years since my mother died. When she passed, we spread her ashes around her favourite tree in a local park in West London. Home, or a familiar resting place.

Grief, when it inevitably happens, explodes outwards to touch everyone who knew the person who died. It is sticky stuff – coating the bereaved to glue us uncomfortably close together or getting gummy and fixed so that we become singularly consumed with trying to wash it off as fast as we can. It can prize us apart.

In my experience, the more time that passes after a death, the smaller and more personal this grief becomes, until we carry it with us as such unique fragments: memories, mementoes, versions of a history. If we were stuck, we now peel away from each other, and if we have always been trying to grieve alone, that effort lessens.

You feel like you will never forget, until you begin to.

A Person is a Prayer is largely set in Haridwar, in the same place I found myself while spreading my grandmother's ashes. It began life as I stood in the dust, traipsed towards the Ganges, and started to forget – where did my grandparents grow up? How did they meet? Why did they move multiple continents in a lifetime (from Asia to Africa to Europe)? What were their dreams? Why did I never ask them anything important?

There was no one left to ask – no answers I could seek. Those migrations had left barely any paper trail and with English as a second or even third language, questions were usually met with warped recollections or broken responses when I might have had the chance to speak. What did the past matter, my grandad would have said, we're here to keep moving forward, for the future.

But what is the future without somewhere to come from? This novel became a way to collect the strands of the past, to pull these disparate lives together and to give me an imagined place to stand upon.

I like to call it an act of remembrance, but it's all fiction. It's bringing people back to life – a connection with those we can no longer reach. This is a story of a family like mine, but that isn't mine; it is a novel about people hoping for a better future, longing for an idealised past and striving to survive in the present. It is about so many families.

Since there was no one to ask, I made up my own reasons for why we thought we had to keep moving forward. I wrote why even though none of us chooses where we are born or who we are born to, we still long for somewhere we can call home. Something to belong to.

Author's Note

The book is dedicated to my grandfather, who always thought I was writing a memoir about him. But he died in 2021, before I had the chance –

– Ammar Kalia, June 2023

Book Club Questions

1. Was there one character you sympathised with in particular? Why?
2. Why do you think the author chose to divide the narrative between three single days? What did the time jumps add, or take away, from your reading experience?
3. Why do you think the author split Part Three into three individual first-person narratives? How did each character's account of the day differ?
4. The novel is concerned with themes of belonging and identity – did it make you reflect on your own ideas and ideals of what constitutes 'home'? What did you learn?
5. Did Bedi and Sushma's initial meeting challenge your preconception of arranged marriages? What did you think of her relationship with her family?
6. In Part Three, what does the inclusion of the characters' online identities reveal about themselves?
7. What did you think of the questions Tara asks herself throughout her section? Why do you think the author included them?
8. How did the novel challenge your ideas about immigration and displacement? Do you feel any differently about minority communities now?
9. What did you make of the final line of the novel and the entreaty for Sushma to have hope? How did it make you feel, knowing what happens to her character in the future?
10. What does the title of the novel mean to you?

About the Author

(Author Photo: Richard Dowker)

AMMAR KALIA is a writer, musician and journalist living
in London. Since 2019, he has been the *Guardian*'s Global
Music Critic and he has written for publications including
the *Observer*, BBC, *Dazed, Mixmag, Economist, Downbeat*
and *Crack Magazine*. In 2020 he published a collection of
poetry and an accompanying album, *Kintsugi: Jazz Poems for
Musicians Alive and Dead*, and in 2022 his essay on music
and identity was included in the collection *Haramacy*. *A
Person is a Prayer* is Kalia's debut novel and was shortlisted for
the Unbound Firsts Prize in 2022.

ammarkalia.com

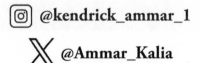 **@kendrick_ammar_1**

𝕏 @Ammar_Kalia

●LDCASTLE BOOKS

POSSIBLY THE UK'S SMALLEST
INDEPENDENT PUBLISHING GROUP

Oldcastle Books is an independent publishing company formed in 1985 dedicated to providing an eclectic range of titles with a nod to the popular culture of the day.

Imprints include our lists about the film industry, KAMERA BOOKS & CREATIVE ESSENTIALS. We have dabbled in the classics, with PULP! THE CLASSICS, taken a punt on gambling books with HIGH STAKES, provided in-depth overviews with POCKET ESSENTIALS and covered a wide range in the eponymous OLDCASTLE BOOKS list. Most recently we have welcomed two new sister imprints with THE CRIME & MYSTERY CLUB and VERVE, home to great, original, page-turning fiction.

oldcastlebooks.com

  kamera BOOKS   HIGH STAKES

OLDCASTLE BOOKS		CREATIVE ESSENTIALS		THE CRIME & MYSTERY CLUB
POCKET ESSENTIALS		PULP! THE CLASSICS		VERVE BOOKS
KAMERA BOOKS		HIGHSTAKES PUBLISHING		